Multi Level Murder

The Wronged Women's Co-operative: Book 8

T E SCOTT

Copyright © 2024 T E Scott

All rights reserved.

ISBN: 9798323641833

Chapter 1: Bernie

It was ten minutes before the start of the Scotland versus England rugby match and Bernie Paterson had decided it was the perfect time to hoover the living room.

"Are you kidding me?" her husband Finn said, lifting his feet as she jabbed the hoover underneath them. Her son, Ewan, grunted in displeasure as she did the same to him.

"It needs done," Bernie snapped.

Finn reached over to turn up the volume, but it was already on full blast. "Look, just leave it and I'll hoover after the game."

"Promise? And under the sofa as well?"

"Sure."

Bernie left the hoover behind and exited the room without letting Finn see the smile that tugged at her lips. He fell for it every time, she thought happily as she went to put the kettle on.

Now that the chores were taken care of, she put her laptop on the kitchen table and opened up the folder for her private investigation business.

It was the start of April which meant that the last couple of weeks had been a miserable slog getting their tax records sorted. Liz Okoro, one of Bernie's partners and the team's financial expert, had insisted that every spreadsheet needed to be perfectly in order. Although Bernie had initially found this chore tedious, she had enjoyed learning exactly where and how the Wronged Women's Co-operative had made their money. Last year had been a profitable one, with each member taking home a decent wage as well as leaving some money in the business to tide them over for leaner times.

There had, however, been some anomalies. Despite her claims of frugality, Mary Plunkett's expenses had trended upward. Bernie still didn't understand why she needed to consume quite so much cake when on stake-outs, but she was willing to let it slide. Especially when the spreadsheet had revealed that Mary brought in considerably more money than she cost.

Bernie knew this because she had forced Liz to write her a formula. A productivity equation, where 'cheeky blooming expenses' were put in a ratio with 'new cases brought in' and 'actual useful leads'.

When they did the maths, Mary's multiple came out at 7.2. Despite all appearances to the contrary, Mary's flaky attitude to work and life seemed to bring in results. Liz Okoro, even though she was responsible for a lot of the behind-the-scenes work, still scored a respectable 5.8.

Bernie had only scored 2.5. She had made Liz check the results three times, but it was still the same. She hadn't told Mary about it and Liz had been sworn to secrecy. Bernie wasn't normally one for introspection, but it didn't please her that according to the maths, she was the least effective member of the Wronged Women's Co-operative.

Ever since those results she had re-doubled her efforts in the business. She had left flyers for their services everywhere she could think of and had made sure to personalise them to each particular clientele. At the women's gym she had left a load of cards stating their ability to chase down errant husbands and child support. She had persuaded Liz to email around a bunch of her business contacts offering their services in corporate investigations and fraud, an avenue that was proving to be particularly lucrative. And at the care home where she used to work Bernie had put up a poster offering a service for contesting wills, something that was always popular with disgruntled relatives.

The thing that her equation for 'who's the best worker' failed to notice was that Bernie's main role was leadership. Without her, she was sure that Liz and Mary would be utterly lost. She just had to make sure they realised that.

Bernie was adding some posts to the local social media sites when the doorbell rang. Knowing that there was no way Finn would be moving from the screen, she closed her laptop and made her way over to open the front door.

A woman in her seventies with blond hair and bright pink lipstick stood on the step.

For a second, Bernie couldn't say anything.

"Aren't you going to invite me in?"

Her mouth wouldn't work and just as her lips were forming the word 'no', the woman sailed past her on a cloud of expensive floral perfume.

"Granny!" Ewan leapt up and gave the woman a hug. Finn gave Bernie a sharp look as he clicked off the television, but Bernie pressed her mouth shut.

"I didn't know you were coming over, Deborah," Finn said, as he allowed the woman to hug him.

"Neither did I until this morning. I thought I would surprise you all."

Bernie still hadn't found a way to speak. It wasn't that she was afraid of offending the woman. Her mother knew exactly what she thought of her. But even Bernie wasn't the sort of person to rip her apart in front of her grandson.

"Can I speak to you in the kitchen," Bernie said finally just as the woman looked like she was going to settle down on the sofa.

Deborah gave Ewan a little wink that made Bernie's blood pressure rise.

"Whoops, looks like I'm in trouble. I'll see you in a minute, Ew-bear."

Bernie was pleased to see her son flinch at the babyish nickname and followed her mother into the kitchen where the woman had already clicked the kettle on.

"Don't get comfortable," Bernie said. "You're not staying."

"Well, that's nice isn't it," Deborah replied, the lines appearing around her lips when she pursed them. She was the sort of woman that people said was 'well-preserved' for her age, although that preservation had a little help from a bucket load of face powder.

The kettle hissed in a crescendo. Reluctantly, Bernie placed two mugs on the counter. "A quick cup of tea and you're off. You remember our agreement."

"Oh, I remember." Deborah pouted. "I'm not about to forget the discussion where my daughter wouldn't allow me in her house without an appointment."

"It's not just me," Bernie said, unable to resist the urge to correct her. "Every one of your daughters feels the same. Doesn't that tell you something?"

"That you've poisoned them against me," Deborah replied, with a theatrical wobble of her bottom lip.

Bernie gulped down her tea even though it was still scalding hot. "Did you just come here to have the same argument again?"

"Well, actually I –" Deborah broke off as a streak of fur bolted into the room past her and jumped up on top of the fridge, hissing as she did so.

"What in God's name was that?" Deborah said, smoothing down her hair.

"That's Witch," Bernie said, picking her up and giving the cat a scratch between the ears. "She's an excellent judge of character."

"What do you want with a cat? You always hated animals."

"You always told me I did." When Bernie put her down, Witch sensibly decided she had had enough and made her way out of the cat-flap in the back door.

"How is Ewan doing at school?"

"Brilliantly," Bernie snapped. "Anything else?"

Deborah pouted again. "Come on, Bernadette, I'm allowed to ask about my grandson."

"You're allowed to see him too. I never tried to stop you from doing that. But you haven't shown much interest there, have you?"

"I'm here now."

"Because you're in trouble."

Deborah huffed. "Why would think that?"

"Come on, you're only here because you want something," Bernie said. "I'm not an idiot."

For a moment, Bernie thought that her mother was going to deny it and then the other woman laughed.

"All right, you just have to show you've won, don't you Bernadette? There you are then, you did it. You worked it out. I'm here because I'm in a tiny little bit of trouble."

"What sort of trouble?"

Deborah leaned forward so that Bernie could see where the makeup had clumped on her cheeks. "I'm being framed for murder."

Chapter 2: Walker

A dog barked in a nearby garden when Sergeant Owen Walker arrived at the home of Holly Moore, recently deceased.

"Forensics are just finishing up," Detective Inspector Macleod said when Walker arrived at the front door. They had set up the conspicuous white tent outside where men dressed in white paper suits were collecting evidence.

"There's no doubt it's a suspicious death, then?" Walker asked.

"No. We'll wait for the post-mortem, of course, but judging by the blood and the state of the body, we're looking at blunt force trauma to the back of the head."

"Any suspects?"

"No one obvious. The neighbour reckons she was separated from her husband."

"A bad split?"

Macleod shrugged. "Could be, we don't know yet. But if you're thinking he's going to be our top suspect, then it's not going to be that easy. He was at work until an hour ago and the Doctor reckons she's only been dead for three or four hours max. We'll question him of course, but we know there are at least a dozen people that saw him at his desk during the entire night-shift. He's on his way over."

Sergeant Neil Michelson walked out of the front door.

"They've got the rooms ready for you now, sir," he told Macleod.

"Do you want me inside?" Walker asked hopefully as Macleod turned towards the door. It wasn't a given that he would be allowed to enter the crime scene. Once the officers from the Major Investigation Team turned up – which they would as soon as it was confirmed as an unlawful death – he would be fighting to be allowed on the team.

"Aye, but check out the garage first. The forensics lads have been in and they reckoned someone has been at the car."

Intrigued, Walker made his way over to the garage which was attached to the left-hand side of the house. He couldn't miss Holly Moore's car, that was for sure.

A bright pink SUV was parked in the garage and it was so clean that it shone. But there was something a little odd about it. Walker walked closer to see what had caught his eye, then he worked it out. Down one entire side of the car was a series of jagged lines, scraped into the paintwork.

"Someone didn't like the colour," Neil Mickelson said, appearing at Walker's side.

"You're not kidding," Walker said, running a gloved finger along the scratch. "It's gone into the bodywork, not just the paint."

"Could have been kids. Or those weird Extinction Rebellion people. I mean, that car offends me and I vote Tory."

"Maybe. Have forensic taken a look?"

Neil nodded. "Yeah, they've taken samples and prints. If there's anything relevant, they'll get it."

The two police officers walked back outside to the front of the house.

"Bit posher than our usual neck of the woods," Mickelson remarked, looking up at the crisply rendered building.

"Aye, it is that," Walker replied. The last time they were at a similar scene it was for a homeless guy who had passed away under a bridge, nothing to show he had been there except for some cardboard boxes. This new build with its anthracite windows and gravel driveway was definitely a step up.

A white Range Rover pulled into the drive and an agitated civilian male got out. At least Holly Moore had someone to miss her, Walker thought. It had taken them two weeks to find anyone who could identify the homeless guy and there had been more social workers than family at his funeral, the poor soul.

Walker shook his head to clear it from such maudlin thoughts and went over to meet the man getting out of the car.

"It's true then," the man said, running a trembling hand through his hair. He was mid-thirties with dark brown hair that was just starting to recede from his temples. Tanned, tall and with expensive-looking clothes, he seemed to match the upmarket house quite nicely.

"Are you Mr James Moore?"

"That's me," the man said. "Is it true that she's… that Holly is inside?"

"I'm afraid so."

The other man hissed in a breath. "I never thought she'd actually do it, the poor cow."

Walker frowned. "Do what?"

"Well... kill herself. I mean, she'd threatened before, but I always thought she was just trying to piss me off, you know? I would say I was leaving, then she would scream and shout and say she would slit her wrists, that sort of thing."

Walker wasn't sure what to say. He didn't want to let the husband know any information that might jeopardise the case. After all, until they discovered otherwise the partner of a murder victim was always the most likely suspect. But he didn't want the man telling everyone it was a suicide either.

He settled for being noncommittal. "We have yet to determine a cause of death," he said.

"But..."

Walker touched his arm. "I'm afraid I'm going to have to get you to come to the station with me. We'll have to take a statement, that sort of thing. Is there anyone you would like to come with you? Any family members?"

"No. I don't... I'll be fine by myself. But someone will have to tell the wife's sister. Oh god, her parents as well, they're going to be devastated."

Walker nodded. "We'll take care of that," he said, glad that it would be a more junior officer that would have to do that particular task.

The man was starting to look a bit unsteady on his feet, so Walker called over one of his Constables.

"PC Flint here will take you to the station."

"Can't I… I can't go inside?"

Walker shook his head. "Sorry, no."

"All right." Shock was making the man compliant and he got into the car with a glassy expression on his face.

"Keep an eye on him," Walker said to Flint as he got into the car.

Flint nodded. He understood that the instruction was two-fold: they needed to look after the man and make sure that the effects of shock weren't too severe, but they also had a duty to consider James Moore a suspect, at least until his alibi had been proven unbreakable. And there was always the chance that he had been involved in his wife's death even if he hadn't struck the final blow himself.

Walker stared up at the house. There was money there, that was for sure, and money was always a motive for murder. He stopped at the forensics tent to pull on the scratchy paper suit that was required in these situations then went inside to find Macleod.

He discovered the DI chatting with one of the forensics team in the front room. Judging by the patch of dried blood on the grey carpet, this was where the late Mrs Moore had been discovered.

"Who found the body?" Walker asked, realising he hadn't heard.

"We got an anonymous call this morning. A woman's voice. Said that they thought someone was 'hurt' at this address. Constable Flint went to check it out and saw the victim through the window. He broke in, but rigour had already set in so he called the station."

"He did well not to disturb the scene," the forensics technician said. "Not all cops are quite so neat."

Walker and Macleod shared a knowing look. Forensics seemed to think that you could enter an active crime scene without touching anything. Walker guessed they wanted you to levitate.

"When can I have a report?" Macleod asked the technician.

"I'll give you a very basic interim report tomorrow morning, but you're looking at a few days before we can get through all this stuff. By the looks of things, she liked to entertain. There are plenty of empty bottles in the bins and fancy food in the fridge. And there are hundreds of prints to go through, probably from a dozen people or more."

Macleod groaned. "Bloody typical. I'll get you the ex-husband's prints as soon as I can and I want you to check for them. They were meant to be separated, so his prints shouldn't be anywhere near the place. If you find evidence he was here then we might just have something."

The technician nodded and hurried away.

While Macleod took out his phone and relayed some messages to the station, Walker took a proper look around the room. It was very clean – apart from the stain on the floor – and the white leather couches looked brand new. The bay window at the front had two armchairs in it and a table with a laptop on it. That would be bagged up and brought back to the station, Walker knew, and he was looking forward to seeing if there was anything on it that might give them a clue to her murder.

Apart from the plush sofas and the thick carpet, the rest of the room was metal and hard edges. There was too much reflective material for his liking. A mirrored TV unit and a glass light fitting sent rays of light around the room and dazzled his eyes. It reminded Walker of those show-homes that they built on new estates where everything was designed to suggest the people living there were wealthy, with great taste and the sort of lifestyle to be envied.

Holly Moore was someone who wasn't afraid to flash her expensive tastes, this room showed that, just as the pink car had.

"What was her job?" Walker asked once the Inspector was off the phone.

"Self-employed," Macleod said. "The ex-husband said she owned her own business. He was a bit vague about what it was, so I'd like to find out more. Add it to our list of actions, will you?"

Walker made a note.

Macleod grabbed one of the forensics guys. "Did we get her phone?"

"Not yet, sir. Not on the body or nearby. We'll keep looking."

The DI frowned. "You would reckon she'd have a phone on her, wouldn't you?"

"Do you think the killer took it?" Walker asked.

"Might have done." Macleod looked around the room as if expecting the object to leap out at him. "We'll make sure they fast-track that laptop over to the technicians at the station."

Macleod rested his hand on his chin, a curious sight when he was still wearing the paper suit. "I've a feeling this is going to be a twisty one."

Walker nodded. The sad truth was that in ninety per cent of violent deaths, it was patently obvious who the killer was. Often it was the husband or wife, standing nearby with bloody clothes saying: 'I never meant to do it'. Crime was generally a lot less complicated than the general public believed. But with a husband with an alibi and no other obvious motive, this was indeed going to be twisty. And that was just the sort of case that Walker enjoyed.

Chapter 3: Liz

As soon as Liz Okoro answered the phone, she knew that something was seriously wrong. Bernie, her good friend and colleague, was never someone to get in a flap. In fact, the more desperate the situation, the more Bernie's personality turned in on itself. She would get more and more ruthless and efficient until she was as effective as a bullet. And as subtle as one.

So when Bernie began to talk, with short, clipped sentences and one syllable vocabulary, Liz knew something awful had happened. But she still wasn't prepared for what came next.

"Mum is here," Bernie said.

"What… you don't mean *your* mum, do you?"

"Yes. She's got herself in trouble. Talking about murder."

"Murder?" Bernie might have been as cold as ice, but Liz could feel her throat tighten. "What do you mean murder?"

"Says she's being framed. Can you look up Holly Moore? Death might not be announced yet."

"Okay."

"Won't make the meeting. Make sure Mary doesn't try and put cake on her expenses again."

"All right. But Bernie, do you think it's a good idea to –"

"Got to go." Bernie ended the call.

"Wow." Liz stared at the phone while she tried to gather her thoughts. So Deborah was back on the scene. That was... interesting information. Liz had known Bernie for long enough that even though Deborah was barely mentioned, she had managed to glean enough information to understand that the woman was a complete nightmare. And now she was involved in a murder case. Which meant so was Bernie and the Wronged Women's Co-operative.

But there was no point in doing anything other than working the problem. Liz shrugged off her worry and opened up her laptop. She typed 'Holly Moore' into her search engine and began scrolling through the entries.

It didn't take her long to discover that there was only one Holly Moore in Invergryff and that she was all over the internet. If this was the woman who had been murdered, there was no sign of that unfortunate event online. All of her social media was still active and there were pictures of her uploaded as recently as the last week.

From her photos, Holly Moore seemed to be in her thirties, pretty with tanned skin and blond hair which was often curled and down to her shoulders. Liz was no stranger to hair extensions herself, and she reckoned that the ones Holly used were expensive. All her photos seemed very carefully posed and Insta-worthy.

But her appearance wasn't the most interesting thing about Holly's socials. What struck Liz the most was how many references she made to her business. Even on her personal accounts, she was always hashtagging herself as a 'boss babe' and saying things about 'working smarter' and 'living your best life'.

Liz found it all a little bit cringe, but the weirdest thing was that she couldn't work out exactly what the business was, not at first glance anyway.

She was just about to look at Holly's website when the alarm on her phone went off, reminding her that she had a job to do in the kitchen. Putting down the laptop she went through to the back of the house to the kitchen diner.

Liz checked her rice which was just starting to stick to the pan. A little browning on the rice was no bad thing when making Jollof, but this was for her mother, Grace, and the woman could smell a burnt grain of rice at a hundred paces.

She turned the heat off the rice and checked the time. Not long until her mother would arrive to collect the food. It was for some church occasion or other, and Grace Okoro was never one to skimp at these things. She was making meat stew and various side dishes at her own home, but had delegated the rice to Liz. Liz had dared to suggest at the time that she could just buy something in, which had earned her the silent treatment for over an hour. Grace Okoro took being the hostess very seriously.

At that moment Liz heard a tapping on the kitchen window and jumped as she saw her mother's face staring in at her.

"Talk of the devil," Liz said, opening the back door and giving her mum a hug.

"What?"

"Never mind. You're early. The rice is still hot."

"Wrap the pot up in some tea towels, it'll be fine," Grace said. She walked over and took a spoon out of the cutlery drawer to taste it. Liz held her breath.

A tiny nod. "Pack it up for me and I'll get it in the car. I've got to pick up some cakes from that Trisha girl and I said I would be there by six. She always puts far too much icing on, but what can you do? I've told her a dozen times already."

Liz was impressed that Trisha was willing to risk her mother's ire over some frosting. In the church community, Grace Okoro ruled like a tiny, angry Queen.

"Is the baby asleep?"

"Yes. Please don't wake her," Liz said. "I've just got her down."

"Where's my boy, then," Grace said as she started rooting around for tea towels.

"Sean is at football tonight. They're playing a match over in the East End. Dave's with him."

"Good," Grace said, "boys should be out getting exercise. Otherwise they get into trouble."

"Sean doesn't get into trouble."

"Not yet," Grace said darkly. "You need to look after that boy. Men are too easily led. They don't have the strength that women have."

Liz wasn't sure if that was true, but she knew better than to argue. "Speaking of men, how's dad getting on?"

"I hardly see the man. Your father spends all his time on that computer." She tutted. "Like I said, men need looked after. I think he needs a new car or something. Get him out of the house."

The doorbell rang, saving Liz from having to reply.

"That's Mary," Liz said, leaving her mother to the tea towels.

"Don't worry, I'll get out of your hair," Grace said, picking up the pot. "I don't want to interrupt any important business. How many creepy husbands have you caught this week?"

"A few." Liz felt it better not to mention Bernie's mother and the possible murder case. She didn't want it getting around the church community and therefore half of Invergryff in about five minutes.

At the front door, Mary was already making small talk with Grace.

"Lovely to see you," Grace managed to hug Mary around the rice pot. "How are the children?"

"Oh fine. Causing mischief as usual." Mary continued to chat away for several minutes about her brood and the current scraps they were in.

Liz stood to one side, feeling like a third wheel in her own house. The thing was, everyone liked Mary. She had that friendly puppy quality that it was impossible not to like. Bernie always said that was worth her wage by itself, and Liz tended to agree. And of course even tough-talking Grace Okoro would soften up around her.

"I'd better get going, lots of hungry mouths to feed."

Liz closed the door with relief.

"Your mum is so lovely," Mary said, pulling off her boots.

"Other people's mums always are," Liz said, a little more bluntly than she meant to. She had just realised that her mother hadn't once said thank you for the rice.

"Fancy a wine?"

"Can't," Mary said, flopping down on the sofa. "I've brought the car."

"Well I'm going to have one," Liz said as she grabbed a bottle of red out of the cupboard.

"I always need a glass or two after my own mum's been over," Mary said. "Last time she was babysitting the kids I found her ironing their pants. Who the hell irons pants?"

Liz said nothing. She was secretly partial to a pair of freshly ironed pants herself.

"It's the silent judgement," Mary continued. "You know, what sort of mother am I that I haven't spent the whole weekend ironing?"

"I'm always getting in trouble for Sean's terrible Igbo," Liz said. "I get where she's coming from: she doesn't want him to lose that connection to Nigerian culture. But I was the same when I was thirteen. He'll come back to it eventually."

"Mothers," Mary muttered, "I'm glad we're so much more reasonable and our kids will never have to complain about us."

"Exactly. Mind you, we're lucky we've not got a mother like poor Bernie. She turned up at her house today."

"Bernie's mum turned up? I thought her mother was dead," Mary said, stuffing a crisp into her mouth. "I mean, she's always talking about her sisters, but she never mentions her mum."

"There's a good reason for that. If you think Bernie's a nightmare... well, let's just say she's got her reasons, all right?"

"That bad?"

Liz swallowed. She wasn't sure how much Bernie would want her to say. The only reason she knew anything about Bernie's childhood was because Bernie had been drunk on pre-mixed cocktails at her sister Laura's wedding. Someone had asked why their mother wasn't there, and that had set Bernie off.

"Deborah is a total nutter," Liz said, deciding that if it fell within the interests of the WWC, she had a duty to tell Mary at least some of what she knew. "None of the girls still speak to her. She walked out on them when Bernie was just sixteen, leaving her to look after the younger ones. But she caused a whole lot of damage before then. And now she's turned up saying that she's wanted for murder?"

Mary spat out a crisp. "What?"

"Ah, I forgot you hadn't heard." Liz quickly filled her in on the conversation with Bernie, which didn't take long.

"So Bernie hasn't seen her mother for ages and now she's asking for help. And she's somehow mixed up in this murder case?"

"Looks like it," Liz felt her forehead crease into a frown. "And I don't think it is good news, for any of us. Bernie won't be able to keep her emotions out of this one. The best solution would be for you and me to take over the case. Keep Bernie and her family at arm's length. But you can imagine how that suggestion is going to go down."

Mary bit her lip. "Well, it seems to me like we could outvote her. I mean, she did make me a partner in the business after all. Between the two of us, we're sixty-six per cent of the WWC. So she's got to listen to us, right?"

Liz snorted. "I'm not sure that sort of maths is going to hold much sway when Bernie is on the warpath." She tapped a long fingernail on the table. "But I guess we could give it a try."

"Let's give it a little time," Mary said. "I mean, we don't even know what's happened yet. Maybe it will turn out to be nothing, just Bernie's mum looking for a bit of drama."

"Let's hope so."

Chapter 4: Mary

Mary made it home in time to relieve the babysitter and start the children's baths, her least favourite part of the day. The two bigger kids would tolerate the shower now, at least, but Mary still had to wrestle her two youngest in and out of the bath. Soapy suds seemed to cover every part of the small bathroom by the time she was finished and there was more water on the floor than in the bath. She only fell over once, and none of the water came through the kitchen ceiling, so she notched that one up as a win.

When the children were finally dried and tucked into bed, Mary went into the kitchen in search of sustenance. Unfortunately, the Mary that had done the shopping yesterday was Healthy Mary and had decided not to buy any treats. Today's Mary – stressed out, Unhealthy Mary – hated that earlier version of herself who hadn't even replenished the chocolate biscuit drawer.

By the time Walker arrived after he finished his shift, Mary had managed to find a bag of chocolate coins from Christmas hidden at the back of the cupboard and was curled up on the couch watching telly.

"Don't those belong to the kids?" Walker said as she peeled the foil off another chocolate coin.

"I need it today. Do you want a cuppa?"

"Yes please."

She followed him into the kitchen where he was taking off his coat.

"Bad day?" Walker asked.

"Busy. You?"

"Very busy."

Mary couldn't resist. "That would be because of that murder, right?"

"How the bloody hell did you know about that?" She was pleased to see that his handsome face was turning pink. "We haven't even put out a statement yet. Don't tell me Bernie's been following the squad cars again."

"She didn't have to this time. Her mum is involved."

"What? I didn't even know she had a mother." Walker shook a bouncy ball out of a nearby mug and poured himself a tea. "I thought she popped out fully-formed from whatever alien spaceship she arrived on."

"Harsh," Mary said, who had been thinking the same thing a few hours earlier. "They don't speak, apparently. Until this morning when her mum turned up and told her she was a suspect in the Holly Moore murder."

"She is? I didn't know we had any suspects yet."

Mary checked her watch. "You will do by now. Bernie told her to go to the police station and hand herself in."

Walker put down his cup. "You better start from the

beginning. And I'm going to swap this for a beer."

Once he had been suitably refreshed, Mary told Walker everything that she knew about Bernie's mother and her involvement in the murder case.

"I guess I should warn Macleod," Walker said, taking out his phone. "If she's anything like Bernie then he'll be in for a hard time."

"Liz said she was the exact opposite of Bernie."

"That's good then."

"I know you have your issues with Bernie," Mary said, feeling the need to defend her friend. "But I don't think her mum is going to be any better. Liz seemed to think she was much worse. She's got a reputation for being a liar and whatever you think of Bernie, she never lies."

"Honest as a sledgehammer," Walker nodded. "I've sent Macleod a text anyway. I don't think it's going to make his day. No doubt Bernie will be thrusting herself into the investigation."

Mary chewed her lip. "I don't know about that. We're going to have a WWC meeting tomorrow to discuss it. But like I told you, they don't get on. This might be one murder that Bernie doesn't take an interest in."

Walker snorted. "I'll believe that when I see it."

"I guess it's a bit like your parents," Mary said, not able to stop herself. "I mean, Bernie doesn't speak to her mum, and you don't speak to yours either, right?"

Walker stiffened and Mary mentally cursed herself. His family was a painful topic for Walker, and she had always tried her best to avoid the subject. The last thing she wanted was to cause him any additional injury, but she couldn't help her curiosity.

"I bet Bernie's mother is a teddy bear compared to mine," Walker grunted, finishing the rest of his beer in one swallow. He got up and went to the kitchen for another, turning his back on the conversation.

Mary stared after him. She was getting a churning feeling in her stomach. She'd been seeing Walker for almost two years now, was it okay that there was this whole part of his life that he didn't talk about? When she had been married to Matt his family had been entwined with hers, one of the things that had made divorce such a nightmare. Was it a red flag that Walker didn't feel the same way? He knew everything about her life, Mary realised, but she didn't really know much about his.

"You looked a million miles away," Walker said, kissing her as he sat back down. "What were you thinking about?"

"Oh, just the usual," she said, not having time to think of a lie.

"Whether the Borg or the Xenomorph from Alien would win in a fight?"

"Exactly."

Chapter 5: Bernie

Not many people realise that there are more calories in an avocado than in a doughnut. Bernie Paterson did. And she could tell you how much fat you burned in one gym session – never as much as you think – or how much sleep a forty-year-old needed to keep their metabolism working. The reason she knew all these things was the woman that Finn had just dropped off at the police station.

It was good that she knew about calories and macros and deficits and all those things. Of course it was. She wouldn't have been Renfrewshire's best slimmer three months in a row otherwise. But even Bernie had to admit that her life would be simpler if she could watch her son eat an Easter egg without flinching or watch a mother give her baby a rusk without staging an intervention.

And that was just the obvious effect of growing up with Deborah O'Flannery as a mother. Bernie considered herself pretty lucky. Many of her sisters hadn't got off quite so lightly. It had been the happiest day of Bernie's life when her mother had left them to look after themselves. Bernie had been just barely sixteen, but she was already running the household. She had started work in the care home soon after, bringing an income home that was sorely needed. And that might have been her whole life, if she hadn't started the WWC. Funny how things turned out.

"You all right?" Finn said, poking his head around the kitchen door.

"Fine, now that she's gone," Bernie replied.

Finn came over to her and wrapped his arms around her. Bernie let him hug her for a long moment before pulling away.

"Was it true what she was saying?" Finn asked. "About being involved in a murder?"

"No idea," Bernie said, taking a cloth and wiping down the kitchen counters. "I didn't want to ask too many questions, but it's something to do with this job she's been doing. Selling makeup or whatever. The woman that's been killed was her boss, but I don't know why she thinks that will make her a suspect."

"But you think you were right to tell her to go to the police?"

A stubborn tea ring was no match for Bernie brandishing the scourer and she smiled as it disappeared. "Of course."

"And you're not getting involved."

"Nope."

Finn sighed. "That's good. I was worried that Deborah would use the WWC to suck you into her crap again."

Bernie smiled. It was good that Finn would always be on her side. But he didn't realise that anything where her mother was concerned would not be simple.

"The problem is she never tells you the full story," she explained to her husband. "Like this woman who was killed. I asked her how she knew she was dead and Deborah said she'd seen the police cars outside her house. And then when I asked why she was at the house, she said it was to apologise."

"Apologise for what?"

"That's what I asked. And then Deborah told me that they had had a row the night before. That's why she thinks the police will suspect her in this Holly person's murder."

"How did she even know her? I thought she had nothing to do with Invergryff anymore. The whole town hates her, right?"

"Aye, but Holly had only been here a couple of years. She probably hadn't heard Deborah's reputation for being a total nightmare. They knew each other through this beauty business, and Deborah said it was just a coincidence she lived in Invergryff."

"I guess that could be true," Finn said.

"Maybe at first. But you can bet half the reason Deborah was involved with this woman was that it was a way back in here. Can you imagine if I'd bumped into her somewhere?"

The sink was gleaming and Bernie finally stood up from her cleaning. "What really irritates me is that I'm going to have to call all my sisters and warn them that Deborah is on the loose again. They don't deserve to have to deal with all that rubbish again."

"Neither do you."

Bernie shrugged. She had been protecting her sisters from their mother for more years than she could remember. It was her job.

"You don't think… I mean, she couldn't really have killed anyone, could she?"

Bernie burst out laughing. "God no. Deborah prefers to leave her victims alive."

Chapter 6: Walker

DI Macleod was leading the briefing at the station first thing on Monday morning but he had delayed it for five minutes so that he could eat a sad-looking strawberry yoghurt.

"Doctor said I was pre-diabetic," Macleod said when he caught Walker's gaze. "So I'm off the chocolate."

Walker, who had witnessed the man's attitude change when his blood sugar dropped, could only see this as a good thing, even though Macleod's face suggested he thought otherwise. He decided solidarity was a good idea, so he kept his own bar of fruit and nut in his pocket.

"How did it go with Bernie Paterson's mother?"

Macleod grimaced. "She had an answer for everything. I'll give you the details at the briefing, but she was presenting herself as a witness rather than a suspect. I've released her for the moment. At least she's a bit more polite than her daughter."

"She has a reputation for being a liar," Walker warned.

"Is that right? I'll make a note to interview her again soon. You coming to the briefing?"

"Sure."

Walker tried not to mind when the SCD officers in plain clothes walked to the front of the meeting room and he was left at the back. The whole world knew that he was dying for a move over to the detectives, but it had been months since he had talked to the Superintendent and there didn't seem to be any sign that he was going to get his chance. As Macleod turned on the smartboard and started to go through the case, Walker comforted himself that the DI at least seemed to think he was good enough to be in the room.

"Thanks for coming everyone. We're here to look at this violent death. Now, we've had officers all over the neighbourhood since the body was discovered, but we're still short on suspects. So let's start from the beginning again."

There were a few whispers around the room at that. Normally in these sorts of cases there would be at least some sort of evidence in the first few hours. It was not a good sign that the police hadn't found anything so far.

"All right," Macleod's soft Shetland accent managed to quiet the chatter, "let's take a look at our victim. Full name: Holly Mackay Moore, residing where she was found on South Park Avenue. Recently separated from her husband, James Moore, and we'll get to him in a minute. Is Constable Flint here?"

Flint stood up. "Yes sir."

"You were first on the scene, is that right? Can you give us a quick report?"

The young man swallowed, his Adam's apple bobbing in his throat. "I took the call at ten forty-five on Sunday morning. Dispatch told me that they had had a welfare concern call for a woman at South Park Avenue. I got to the address just after eleven. When I arrived at the house the front door was open.

I called out but there was no answer. Then I saw what might be a person on the floor from the window. Once inside I discovered the deceased in the front room. I checked for signs of life, then called it into the station."

Flint sat down again, his chair squeaking as he did so.

Macleod folded his arms. "All right, so I want to get a tape of this anonymous call. Sergeant Michelson, can you look that up for me? Apart from that, I want background on the victim. We've already had an initial interview with the husband. They were separated, but not divorced. His name is James Moore, runs a security firm based in Glasgow. Which means he works nights and he appears to have been in the office on Saturday until Sunday morning. Now at the moment, this husband has an alibi, but I want to triple check that. If it turns out he's not involved, then we've got to dig a bit deeper."

Walker could feel his interest growing. Standard domestic murders were a sad but not uncommon part of life. But the killing of the unfortunate Holly Moore seemed to be something different.

"What about the woman that came in last night?" Michelson asked, and Walker's ears pricked up. This had to be Bernie Paterson's mother.

"That would be Deborah O'Flannery. We took a witness statement. She had an argument with the victim not long before her death. Now, O'Flannery is claiming that she was long gone before the time-of-death, but we'll need to check that out too. The fact that she came in willingly makes me think she might be telling the truth, but I want to make sure."

"How did she know Moore was dead?" Walker asked.

"She says that she went by the house to apologise and saw the ambulance and forensics outside. But again, we're going to check that."

Macleod didn't mention Deborah's connection to the WWC and Walker didn't feel like bringing it up either. He just had to hope that it wouldn't be relevant.

"Now, we're waiting for reports from forensics and pathology, but I've got them to give us a few ballpark estimates. The victim died due to a massive head trauma, but there was no sign of the weapon at her home. That means our killer took it with them. I've got some constables out checking the bins and waste ground around the area just in case they chucked it somewhere. We'll have a better description of the weapon when the pathologist has taken a detailed look at the wound."

"In terms of time of death, again this is approximate at the moment. But it looks like she was killed late on Saturday night or early Sunday morning. We're checking CCTV and we're going door to door asking for doorbell camera footage."

Macleod barked several more orders at his sergeants until all the listed actions were taken. Walker just had to hope that someone would allow him to be part of the investigation. When the briefing finished Macleod left the room with Superintendent MacKinnon who had been standing at the back. In the main office, the SCD officers had taken position next to the windows. Walker wasn't sure if he should invite himself over when Detective Sergeant Suzie O'Connor waved at him.

He hurried over. He had worked with Suzie several times, both when she had been at the station as a uniformed officer and after her move to the detectives. Suzie was ambitious and clever, just the sort of plain clothes officer that Walker hoped to be one day.

"Macleod just told me that Deborah O'Flannery is the mother of that Paterson woman from the private investigators. Know much about her?"

Walker's relationship with the WWC, and one of its members in particular was viewed with some suspicion by most of the officers, so he answered carefully.

"I hadn't heard of her until this case. Mary told me that she was estranged from her daughter. From all her children in fact. She has a reputation for being a liar."

Suzie raised her eyebrows. "That's interesting. Especially as she's the only person we know who went anywhere near the house on the day that Moore was killed. We'll make her the number one priority. Macleod is going to speak to her himself later today, but for the moment I'm looking into the ex-husband. He used to be in the army so I thought you might have some insight."

"Sure, let me see the file."

She pulled the monitor towards him so that they could both have a look.

"The only reason he's on the system is from a couple of speeding tickets in the last few years. But we got through to the MoD an hour ago and they've sent over his army record. Is there anything interesting there?"

Walker looked through the document, but it was densely written and the photocopying had made the handwriting even harder to scan. He swallowed.

"Would you mind reading aloud for me? Especially the section where it describes his discharge. Sometimes I read words wrongly you see so… I want to make sure I'm taking it in."

If Suzie thought he was being particularly stupid, she didn't say anything.

"Sure. It lists his enlistment as being through the OTC through university."

"He joined as an officer, then," Walker explained. "If he had a degree it's the usual way in. The army might even have paid towards some of his tuition, depending on what the scheme was at the time."

"You're right, it says here he had a Uni degree in Business Management from Strathclyde University."

"Probably explains why he's running his own business now," Walker pointed out.

"The next section lists his deployments, but they seem to all be around Europe. No war zones or anything."

"He's only thirty-two," Walker said checking his date of birth. "Probably just missed the big push in Afghanistan. I was on one of the last tours over there, and I'm a bit older than him.

Quiet time to be in the forces."

"Okay, let's take a look at his discharge. There's a note here and I'll read it all out. 'Second Lieutenant Moore leaves with full honours and intends to start a civilian role in the security industry. He has been provided with resources to enable this.' Not much there, is there?"

Walker shook his head. "Nope, but then these things tend to be pretty brief. See here, that's the name of his commanding officer when he left, Lieutenant Colonel Philips. We could track him down, see if there was anything that he wouldn't mention in an official document."

"Anything else?"

Walker rubbed his hand over his stubble. "How long was he in for?"

"Six years."

"There could be something there. You would probably expect him to be a Captain by then. Second Lieutenant is the starting rank for an officer, you'd think he'd have been promoted at least once by then."

"Then we should see if we can get hold of this Lieutenant Colonel Philips and find out if there's anything more to the story. I'm going to track down his current associates. He owns the security firm and when I called his secretary this morning she just gave me the 'best boss ever' speech. Maybe someone else that works for him knows something about his marriage."

Suzie offered him a smile. "Thanks for the help."

"No problem," Walker said, although when she turned back to her computer he realised he had been dismissed. As he walked back to his desk where the other uniformed officers were, Walker tried his best not to be downhearted. But as he sat down he couldn't help but envy the detectives at the other end of the room. Any chance of ever joining them seemed to be slipping away.

Chapter 7: Liz

Liz Okoro was worried. Baby Issy had been dropped off at nursery, Dave was at work and Sean was in school so the house was lovely and quiet. But Bernie wasn't answering her phone and that was making Liz chew her very expensive acrylic nails.

Not that Bernie was one of those people who always picked up a call straight away. Wednesdays were aerobics, Thursdays were park run and the rest of the week was filled with gym sessions and outdoor training for whatever excruciating fitness test the woman was currently putting herself through. But it was Monday, and that was normally reserved for WWC business. Sometimes they would meet in a café where Bernie would have a skimmed milk latte while Mary ate her way through the bakery section.

But today Mary was busy with some PTA thing at the school and Bernie was AWOL. Liz had a horrible feeling that her friend was poking around the Holly Moore case. She could hardly blame her, but Liz knew that where Deborah was concerned, Bernie would find it impossible to avoid being biased. She sighed and opened up her laptop.

Holly Moore's professional website was called dare2dream.org. Liz had found it when searching through the woman's social media the previous day, but now she wanted to take a closer look. It still wasn't entirely clear what it was that Ms Moore's business was selling. On the website, dare2dream was described as a 'lifestyle brand' and there were multiple mentions of 'coaching opportunities'. This didn't seem to tally with what Bernie had told her about Deborah selling makeup. Was makeup by itself considered a lifestyle? Liz was partial to some reasonably expensive skin care herself on occasion, but she hadn't considered it to be a whole identity. Mind you, she was vaguely aware that the younger generation seemed to spend a lot more time and money on products than people her age did. She clicked through the website, hoping for something more substantial.

There was a page called 'Our Story' which Liz found interesting. It had Holly Moore's picture at the top, taken on holiday somewhere. Holly was blond, pretty and wearing a lot of makeup and stood next to someone else. The woman who had her arm around her could only have been her sister. Unlike Holly she had dyed red hair, but apart from that the full, pink lipsticked lips and the rest of their features matched perfectly. Liz looked at them closely. She didn't have any sisters herself, and she could never decide if she had missed out or not. Bernie seemed to equally love and hate her siblings, so maybe it was better that Liz had been an only child. Holly Moore, on the other hand, clearly got on well enough with her sister that they had started dare2dream together.

In March 2021 Holly and Bella were in Holly's kitchen wondering why they were working so hard in their 9 to 5 jobs with so little to show for it. That's when Holly had an idea. Why couldn't they work less, be happier, empower women and build their business empire!

With Holly's networking skills and Bella's head for business, they set up dare2dream! Within six months they had recruited a team of wonderful women to work alongside them and set about changing the lives of others!

Liz couldn't help making a puke face at her laptop. For one thing, there were far too many exclamation marks. For another, she found she was getting increasingly irritated at how vague the women were where their business was concerned. She decided to dig a little deeper. Liz brought up the website for Companies House and searched for dare2dream. It only took a few moments to realise that there was no listing for the business. Huh. Liz tapped the keyboard some more, but it was no good. No sign of dare2dream on the official register.

Were they tax evaders? It was possible, but if they were, having an extensive website to advertise their business seemed a bit silly. They could be operating as sole traders, but that didn't seem right if they were a business that employed others, just as they claimed.

Feeling stumped, Liz went back to Holly Moore's website. It took several minutes of scrolling through 'life-changing' testimonials from white middle-aged women with spray tans before she found something surprising. Underneath a big spiel from Bella about how dare2dream had changed so many people's lives, there was a single sentence that got Liz's attention.

Dare2dream is proud to be part of the Better Life Now family since 2022.

What the hell was 'Better Life Now'? Liz typed the name into her search engine and whistled through her teeth as the results came back.

Where dare2dream seemed to only exist in the world of Holly Moore's social media, Better Life Now was all over the internet. They were on every social media network with thousands of followers, as well as video channels and their extensive website. The words 'lifestyle brand' appeared again, giving Liz the same shudder she got when she first read them.

The home page of the Better Life Now website directed the user to a variety of coaching options. The most popular one seemed to be in property rentals. This was something Liz didn't know too much about – being a landlord had always seemed like a hard way to make money as far as she was concerned – but she started making notes anyway. It didn't seem like members of Better Life Now were acting as landlords, more as some sort of agents to connect landlords with new properties. Not seeing the connection to Holly Moore, Liz clicked around the other pages until she found some more information on 'lifestyle branding'. Here the site mentioned their 'favoured partners' and that they could set people up with all sorts of businesses from high fashion to nutrition.

Liz rubbed her eyes which were getting tired from the cheerful colours on the website. She still wasn't clear on the exact nature of Holly Moore's business. The dare2dream website had suggested that the two sisters had set up the business on their own, but from what she could gather they seemed to be a subsidiary of Better Life Now.

Back to the Companies House website and Liz printed off the details of Better Life Now. Unlike the Moore family business, this one did have a full listing. There were two Directors named and Liz was pleased to see that they were based in Glasgow. She entered it all into the case file which Mary had already set up on the WWC server. Then she checked her phone. Still no reply from Bernie.

Time for some more deep dives online. Mary once described the main purpose of the WWC as 'uber stalkers'. That made Liz feel more than a little uncomfortable, but as she pulled up the social media profiles for Bella Terrance, Holly's sister, she had to admit she felt a bit stalkerish.

Luckily for Liz, Bella had plenty of posts on her social media pages set to public. For Liz, who guarded her privacy like an angry bear, it was bewildering. Until she realised that most of these public posts were actually adverts for the business. Liz checked out the most recent one.

So blessed today to be working from home on our new product line and some great surprises coming soon #zerocommute #girlboss #crueltyfreebeauty

There was a photo of some tubes and bottles with white packaging and the brand name 'Solaverse'. After another few minutes of internet searching, Solaverse turned out to be a small makeup brand that was mainly touted by influencers online. There was a website, but you didn't seem to be able to buy it direct. Liz thought it was a bit weird that Bella seemed to be claiming they were 'working on the product line' when they were just distributing someone else's product, but she didn't have time to look into it. That was because she had just read one of the comments on the post.

Loving it, you go girl!

The poster was named Didi O'Flannery. That couldn't be Deborah O'Flannery could it? Liz clicked on the link and hissed in a breath as a profile came up with Bernie's mother's picture on it. Like Liz, Bernie was fierce about avoiding social media, so it was likely that her friend didn't know about her mother's page. And that became even clearer when Liz scrolled down through the posts. Many of them were similar to Bella Terrance's, noting how wonderful the Solaverse products were. But alongside those posts were comments about the importance of family, cute little memes about a mother's love along with pictures of the girls from when they were small children. To look at Deborah's social media you would think she was a doting mother and grandmother.

"Bernie's going to go mental," Liz said out loud. Should she tell her friend? Probably. But she would need to find a way of doing it that wouldn't make things worse. Diplomacy, that was the order of the day. The problem was, Bernie treated diplomacy like a country who has already decided that nuclear war is the only option. Better to put it off for the moment, Liz thought. At least until I've written the full report on dare2dream and these other companies.

Because she was certain of one thing. Whether there was a connection to her murder or not, Holly Moore's business seemed to rely more on persuading people that they needed to better their lives. The sort of business that attracted vulnerable people and used them. And that might just give someone a motive to kill her. Liz sighed. She just had to hope that that someone wasn't her best friend's mother.

Chapter 8: Mary

Mary Plunkett was hosting the emergency meeting of the Wronged Women's Co-operative and she was feeling rather nervous about it. Normally they would meet in the house left to them by Annie McGillivray, an old friend of Bernie's who had left it to them in her will. But Annie's house was undergoing some significant renovations ever since the roof had leaked into the living room last month, splattering dirty water all over Mary's Chelsea buns. Bernie's Finn was doing the repairs, but as it was a homer they had to wait until he could fit them in.

The next choice of host should be Liz who had by far the nicest house out of the group. But Liz's husband Dave had already arranged to have his golf friends around for drinks, so that was out. When it had been suggested to Bernie that they meet at her place, she had murmured darkly about the possibility of her mother barging in, so that was out.

It was up to Mary to host, therefore, but things had started badly. The kids were in their pyjamas, but like hyenas with the scent of blood, they had sensed that there was excitement to be had.

"What time is Scary Bernie coming?" Vikki asked, bouncing on her heels at the top of the stairs.

"In about fifteen minutes. And please don't call her that to her face."

"Oh don't worry, I'm not suicidal," Vikki replied, with a preteen eye roll.

"Where's Peter?"

"Playing his computer game. I told him that if he came downstairs you would murder him."

"That's an exaggeration," Mary said. "Probably. Just make sure everyone stays in bed, okay?" She hurried into the kitchen and checked that the wine was still cooling in the fridge. It was, but a trail of crumbs on the counter told her that the snacks she had purchased for the evening had not survived the after school hours unscathed.

"Who ate the posh snacks from Markies?" Mary yelled up the stairs. Her children were silent, for once. She went back into the kitchen and rummaged around in the back of the cupboards. Just as she finished putting the last of her salvaged snacks into some bowls, the doorbell rang.

"Come in," she said, trying to smooth the creases out of her 'Frankie Says Anxiety!' t-shirt.

"I'm bloody dying for a gin," Bernie said, shrugging off her coat.

"Don't worry, I've got the drinks ready," Mary replied, hanging the coat up and leading Bernie towards the living room.

One of her hilarious children had started playing the witch's theme from *The Wizard of Oz* through the smart speaker in their bedroom.

"That sounds familiar," Bernie said, tilting her head to the side. "Is it from a TV show?"

"No idea," Mary said, manoeuvring her into the living room. "They watch the weirdest stuff, don't they? Why don't I pour you that gin?"

"Make it a big one, I'm not driving tonight."

"Great," Mary said. She grabbed the bottle of diet tonic that only came out for WWC meetings.

"Where's Taggart?" Bernie asked as she settled down on the sofa.

"He hates it when you call him that," Mary said as she handed over a glass that contained more gin than mixer. "And he's at work. He's been mad busy for the past couple of days because… well, because of the murder."

"It's okay, you can mention it," Bernie said with a pinched face. "That's why we're here, isn't it?"

"Sure. Maybe we should wait for Liz though," Mary said, grabbing the bowls of snacks and putting them on the table. "I know she's been looking into Holly Moore's business."

"That's how Deborah knew Holly," Bernie said, her mouth turned down at the corners. "She phoned me this morning. They haven't arrested her yet, but she reckons they might do soon. I can't tell if she's just being dramatic or if she's really a suspect. I don't suppose Tagg… Walker has said anything?"

"Like I said, I haven't spoken to him. And you know that he's not allowed to tell us things like that."

Bernie let out a snort which told Mary what she thought of that idea. Thankfully Mary was saved from replying as the doorbell rang once more.

"That'll be Liz. You just grab a snack and I'll let her in."

Bernie looked dubiously at the bowls. "Is that the chocolate out of an advent calendar?"

"Don't think so," Mary said cheerfully as she went to the front door.

Liz was already inside the door, taking off her shoes. "Are the kids asleep?"

"Pretending to be, I reckon," Mary said with a quick glance up the stairs. "But as long as they're quiet that will do."

"Sorry I couldn't host tonight. I think Dave's having a midlife crisis a few years too late. What is the point of Poker anyway?"

"To lose money and get drunk?" Mary said, leading Liz into the living room where Bernie was checking her phone.

"That was one of my sisters," she said, running her hand through her short-cropped hair. "The whole lot of them are losing their minds. Deborah has been ringing them up and turning up at their houses. I keep telling them to ignore her, but one of them is bound to crack eventually."

Mary looked at Liz who grimaced. Neither of them seemed willing to question Bernie further on this insight into her fractured family.

"Ooh chocolates…" Liz said, reaching out her hand and then pausing. "Why do they have snowflakes on them?"

"They are spring stars I think," Mary said desperately. "Something to do with the Easter bunny."

Liz popped one into her mouth. "They taste like the boot of a Ford Fiesta," she moaned.

"The kids ate the posh snacks," Mary confessed. "Sorry."

"Let's just have some drinks," Bernie said and Mary scurried off to prepare them. By the time she came back the other two were hunched over Liz's laptop.

"Liz had done a grand job on our murder victim's business," Bernie said, grabbing her glass.

"It's definitely our murder then, is it?" Mary asked. There was a horrible moment of silence. "I mean, that's fine if it is. I just wasn't sure."

There was still no answer, and Liz didn't look like she was going to back her up any time soon.

"It's just that… well, weren't you the one that said we couldn't do any more free investigations? And if your mother's involved, then it might not be the best thing for us to interfere in the investigation. Isn't that right Liz?"

Bernie's eyes swivelled to rest on her friend.

"Well, Berns, I was a bit concerned about you getting involved with Deborah again. I mean, I would understand if you want to help her, but you know how upsetting she can be. We'll be behind you whatever you choose, of course."

Mary was so nervous she chucked a handful of advent calendar chocolate into her mouth. It tasted like feet.

"The sooner I get Deborah out of my life the better, and the best way to do that is to solve this murder and find whoever actually killed Holly Moore. It's my problem, though, and I would understand if neither of you wanted to help. I wouldn't like to be unprofessional, after all."

Mary, always afraid of social awkwardness, felt her shoulders cringe so hard they almost met her ears.

"Of course we'll help," she said quickly. "I just wanted to check that it was what you wanted."

"Exactly," Liz agreed. "We're a team, aren't we?"

The sharp edges of Bernie's expression smoothed a little. "All right, let's get on with it then. Tell me about this dare2dream business."

Liz gave them a rundown of Holly Moore's company. Mary found it hard to follow.

"So they sell makeup, but they also provide some sort of course, is that right?"

"Yeah, it's meant to be a whole life change," Liz explained. "You think you're signing up to sell some makeup, but really you're buying into this lifestyle coaching thing."

"Who the hell needs 'lifestyle coaching'," Bernie said. "I mean, surely your lifestyle is just what you do every day, right?"

"Maybe some people just lack direction," Mary said. As someone who had often been buffeted along by other people with stronger personalities, she could understand the appeal. "I mean, maybe they just need someone to steer them the right way."

"Sounds like they need therapy," Bernie said.

"Is there something wrong with that?" Mary asked.

"Not at all. But they should get it from a licensed therapist, not some crook with a fancy car who is going to tell them what they want to hear."

Mary was about to argue when she realised that Bernie was actually agreeing with her.

"Oh, yeah," Mary said. "I thought you were going to say therapy was a waste of time."

"A few of my sisters have found it helpful," Bernie said in a matter-of-fact tone. "You can imagine that living with Deborah means that you might need some extra help. Not me, of course. I don't need another person telling me what to do. I just do it myself."

Mary decided not to unpack that one.

Liz cleared her throat. "All right then, we're all clear that this company might be a bit airy-fairy. But that doesn't make them illegal. I'm going to do some digging into their finances and see if there's anything there that someone might want to kill Holly over."

"Do we have any idea how she was killed?" Mary asked.

"Not yet," Bernie said. "You could ask Morse for us and see if he knows anything."

Mary scowled at the nickname but said she would at least try.

"I'm sorry to say this Bernie," Liz looked down at the table-top as she continued, "but I think we need to talk to Deborah. We need to find out exactly how far into this company she was. If she was just one of many recruits, then she might be okay. But if she was further up in the scheme then it might look like she has a motive."

Bernie sucked her teeth. "I can see that. Do you think I should talk to her? Or one of you guys?"

"Are you... are you asking for my advice?" Liz looked shocked.

"Don't get used to it."

"All right, maybe we should all talk to her together. Strength in numbers and all that."

Bernie shrugged. "Backup might be a good idea. I think you should come, Liz, but there's no point in Mary wasting her time too. She can work on the background to the case."

Mary tried not to look hurt. Despite being made a partner in the business, it was moments like this that made it clear Bernie still thought of her as just the admin girl. After that the meeting broke up and Mary put the children to bed and not even another rendition of the Wicked Witch was enough to cheer her up.

Chapter 9: Bernie

It wasn't that Bernie didn't love her sisters. Of course she did. Unlike her mother, there was no doubt that there was a decent amount of love there. She just didn't always like them.

Martha was Bernie's oldest sister. She was just a year off her fiftieth birthday but she dressed like someone twenty years younger. Bernie got on best with her out of the sisters, even though Martha had lived with their dad for most of their childhood. Martha had provided Bernie with no less than seven nieces and nephews that she doted on, seeing as she had only one son herself. And the 'N's as Bernie called her nieces were always willing to help the WWC out with babysitting duties or when they needed extra bodies for stakeouts, so Martha had that in her favour. Even if she did have a terrible taste in interior décor.

"I can't believe you have a 'live, love, laugh' sign," Bernie said as she sipped her black coffee in Martha's kitchen diner. "I thought that was just something people made up."

"Just because you never laughed in your life, Bernadette," Martha said, but she said it with a smile. "Anything else you want to slag off?"

"I'm sure I'll find something." She was just about to start on the curtains when her younger sister, Eilidh burst in through the door.

"I let myself in," Eilidh said, showering the two of them with cheek-kisses. She was one of those women that never stopped talking. Bernie reckoned she would probably have been diagnosed with some sort of disorder had she been born ten years later. "It was peeing down outside so I wasn't about to wait for the doorbell. Lord, let's grab a seat. I'm just after spending a day at the shops and my feet are killing me."

"Spending Graeme's money again are you?" Bernie asked.

"Maybe," Eilidh said, giving her a wink. "He never complains. I've brought two bottles of red. If we're going to talk about that bloody woman I figured we would need it."

Drinks were poured and Bernie had to admit that with all her money, Eilidh wasn't afraid to share it out. The wine was exceptional even though she just had a taste as she would be driving later. Eilidh gave her a bottle to take home and Bernie had to admit it was seriously challenging her general disapproval of her younger sister's lifestyle.

"So what are we going to do about mum?" Eilidh asked once her glass was full.

"Is it all true?" Martha asked, turning to Bernie. "I thought maybe she was making up the whole thing."

Bernie shrugged. "A woman has been murdered and it does seem like Deborah knew her. Whether she's the chief suspect like she's making out, I'm not too sure. As you know, she loves being the centre of attention, so that's why I'm more worried this time. I wouldn't put it past her to confess to murder just to get some nice young coppers to chat to."

The others sipped their wine while this sunk in.

"I remember that time she went off, to Birmingham, wasn't it?" Eilidh said. "Chasing a man of course."

"Was that the airline pilot?" Martha asked.

Bernie laughed. "That's what he told Deborah he did. I reckon he'd never been on a plane in his life. Took her the best part of a week to realise he was full of crap and came back."

"She'd left twenty quid, do you remember Berns? Said she would only be gone for the night. It was only Bernie that stopped us blowing it all on a pizza. Thank god we didn't. By the time Mum turned up a week later, we were down to the last packet of noodles."

"I haven't eaten instant noodles since," Bernie said with a shudder.

Eilidh took a large gulp of wine. "And mum just strolls in the door like nothing happens and says to Bernie... well, she said something anyway."

"Don't worry, it's not like I've forgotten," Bernie said. "When I mentioned that we'd run out of food she said 'at least you'll have lost a bit of weight lass'."

"Right." Eilidh downed her drink. "She was a right cow to you."

"To all of us."

Martha shook her head. "Nah, Eilidh is right. She always

behaved worst to you. I think she felt threatened. Like you had taken her place or something."

"I never wanted to," Bernie snapped.

"I'm just saying I understand why she always gave you the hard time," Martha explained.

Eilidh bristled. "Mum gave Bernie a hard time because she can't bear anyone else to have a good time. Same as she did with all the rest of us."

Martha was starting to go pink in the cheeks. "What, you think because I wasn't in the house when you guys were growing up that I am some sort of spectator in all of this? I lived with her in the seventies, for Christ's sake. It wasn't all flares and glam rock. It was also the age where you could smack your kids about without anyone giving you a second glance. So let's not pretend I didn't know what it was like, okay?"

"Sorry Martha," Eilidh said.

"Aye, so you should be."

Bernie was finding the emotional outbursts tedious. "Look, I'm not interested in going over the past. What I want us to talk about is what we're going to do right now."

"Surely she can't actually be involved in all this," Martha said, with an inability to face the truth that Bernie was starting to find irritating. "I mean, if it was about fudging a benefit claim, or driving her car without insurance or something I could see it. She always thought that the rules applied to other people. But a murder? That doesn't seem like her."

"I agree," Bernie said. "I'm sure she'll be found innocent eventually. My problem is the havoc she's going to cause for the rest of us before then. Thank God that Amy is down in Sheffield. She was always a soft touch for Deborah."

"Yeah, although I'm sure she'll get around to Amy eventually. She's looking for sympathy wherever she can get it," Eilidh said.

"She even tried phoning my Clare over in New York," Martha said.

"She did not!" Clare was Martha's oldest kid, and Bernie had always liked her ever since she had taken a packet of crayons to her mother's wedding dress. She was now a fashion assistant at a fancy magazine, so it had all worked out in the end.

"Yep, only she got the time zones wrong and called her in the middle of the night. Apparently Clare provided some choice words when she answered half-asleep."

"Good for her," Bernie said. "She was always my favourite niece."

"Bernie, you can't say that."

"Can if it's true. Look, the main thing is that we need to provide a united front, right?"

"With you leading, I suppose," Eilidh said.

"Got a problem with that?"

"Not at all," Eilidh replied.

"It's not like I asked for this ridiculous situation," Bernie said, her temperature rising. "I don't want to be lumbered with sorting it all out."

"But you will, won't you?"

Bernie took a breath. "What do you mean by that?"

Her sister rolled her eyes. "Come on now, we all know how it's going to go. You're going to huff and puff and complain and then you're going to sort everything out. That's what you do, Bernie."

For a moment she was speechless. "But I... what if I don't want to?"

"You'll do it anyway," Martha chimed in. "Eilidh is right, it's part of who you are. You'll fix this problem with Mum and the rest of us can go about our lives. You've been doing it since you were born. And I guess..." her hand reached out and squeezed Bernie's own. "I guess that's not an easy person to be. But the rest of us need you to do it."

"That's it exactly," Eilidh said, nodding in agreement. "You've always taken care of us, protected us from Mum. You're not going to stop doing it now, are you?"

Bernie wished she could say yes, that she could abdicate this damn stupid responsibility that she had never asked for or wanted. But what other choice was there?

"I guess you're right. But I might need your help this time. This isn't the usual Deborah mess. It could be a lot, lot worse."

"You'll sort it," Martha said with more confidence than Bernie felt the situation deserved.

With nothing left to discuss, Bernie finished her coffee and left her sisters exchanging local gossip. Back in her car, she checked her phone before turning on the engine. Four missed calls from her mother. Bernie shuddered. It was as if the woman knew they had been talking about her. She took a deep breath, then clicked to return the call.

"Bernadette, those dreadful cops have stationed a car outside my house. Can't you do something about it?"

Bernie leaned her head against the steering wheel. "What do you expect me to do?"

"Well, tell them they're wasting their time, of course. You are going to sort this out, aren't you?"

"That's what I'm good at."

"Then do it quickly. It's putting quite the curb on my social life."

It took all of Bernie's inner strength not to fling the phone out of the window. But she made sure to drive home carefully, not exceed the speed limit and not be distracted by the storm going on inside her head.

Then when she got back to her own driveway she took out her phone and texted her mother: *I will sort this out. And then I never want to hear from you again. B.*

Yes, Bernie would fix everything, just like everyone expected her to. But she didn't have to be nice about it.

Chapter 10: Walker

It was time to visit the vending machine for some early morning chocolatey goodness. Walker had not slept well and when he unwrapped the sweet treat and popped it into his mouth, he could feel his energy returning. He had gone home in a foul mood on Monday night, fed up with being left out of the murder investigation. The problem was that he had got used to Macleod being able to get him into any investigation even though he was still in uniform. But Macleod had been too busy to notice his hopeful glances and by the end of the day he had been given something else to work on.

"Burglary statistics," Neil Michelson had said when he had come by Walker's desk only an hour before the end of his shift. "There's been another article in the paper about how theft is on the rise in Invergryff, so the Superintendent wants us to work the files. Double-check previous offenders, see if anyone's got out of prison recently, that sort of thing."

Walker didn't quite manage to stifle a groan.

"I know, mate, but I'm swamped at the moment," Neil managed to look genuinely sympathetic. "If I don't get these stats done then they're threatening to send me on school visits again. I've only just got the gum out of my hair from last time."

"Of course," Walker said, feeling bad for complaining, "just send me over the files."

So instead of the thought of a murder investigation to get his mind working, Walker had arrived at the station with nothing more to look forward to than the stolen property of Invergryff that nobody had managed to find for years. Hence the trip to the vending machines for some sugary solace.

He had just pulled up the spreadsheets on his computer when his work phone rang.

"Hello?"

"Hello yourself, how's life in the sticks treating you?"

"Dianna! How've you been?" Inspector Dianna Shearing had been one of his closest friends when he'd started out in Invergryff. After having a baby she had moved down south and it had been months since Walker had heard from her.

"Oh, I'm doing great. How about you? That wouldn't be a chocolate bar you're eating, would it now? I knew you would never keep up the protein shakes."

"Bloody hell Dianna, how did you know?" Walker said, hiding the wrapper as if she was in the room.

"It's ten o'clock on the second day of a murder investigation. An easy guess. How the hell are you anyway?"

"Good." They chatted for a while about their respective other halves. Dianna's partner Ricky was loving being a stay-at-home dad to their new baby and it sounded like Dianna had settled in well to life in London.

"Anyway, I've had a request for a background check on this

suspicious death of yours," Dianna said once they had finished the small talk. "I was going to just email it over but I thought I would ring you first to find out how the investigation is going."

Walker felt his shoulders cringe. "I'm not actually on the investigative team at the moment. I'm sure I can find out for you –"

"What? You've got the best brain of the bunch, why aren't you involved?"

"Well, obviously I'm still in uniform so –" Walker slumped down in his chair, hoping no one else in the office could hear Dianna's increasingly loud voice.

"Have you asked to be seconded to the SCD team?"

"No…"

"What are you waiting for? A gilded invitation? You need to push your way in there. No one's going to notice you at the back of the class, right?"

Walker lowered his voice almost to a whisper. "I haven't heard back about my transfer out of uniform. So I didn't want to seem pushy."

"Sulking, more like."

He didn't answer that one, which of course made it look even more like he was sulking.

"Look, I'm going to send this info on Holly Moore's business dealings over from the Met and then you can present it to the team. They'll be so impressed that they'll want to sign you up immediately."

"Um, okay. Thanks."

"You're welcome. Now give yourself a kick up the arse and get over there. No one's going to make you a detective if they can't remember your name."

After a few more minutes of talking shop, Walker ended the call with Dianna feeling more than a little bruised. She had always been supportive, but the thing was Dianna was one of those people that life seemed to come easily to. For Walker, it was a little more complicated. Yes, he was ambitious and yes, he would give his right arm to be a detective. But he was also terrified of making a fool of himself.

A pinging sound let him know that the email from Dianna had come through. He opened it and read it through twice to make sure he understood the contents. Then he went to find Macleod.

The DI was in the conference room they used when there was a major incident. He was sitting in front of his computer with his head in his hands.

"Everything all right?" Walker asked.

"She just had to be Bernie Paterson's mother, didn't she?" Macleod groaned. "I was hoping we could clear Deborah O'Flannery straight away. God knows, Bernie is sharp as a tack. I've used her investigation team myself enough times to know it. But the last thing I want is a case where she's got a personal involvement."

"So you didn't manage to clear O'Flannery?"

"Nope. If anything I've found a motive for her. We've got the first lot of emails off Moore's laptop. Take a look at this."

Macleod turned the monitor screen around to show an email exchange between Holly Moore and Deborah O'Flannery. A very heated exchange.

"Woah, does Bernie's mother tell the victim she's going to 'get what's coming to her'?"

"Yep. But Holly Moore gives just as good back to her. She says that Ms O'Flannery is to stop libelling her business and if she doesn't then she will get lawyers involved. Then there are some rather unflattering but probably accurate descriptions of O'Flannery's attitude towards men and her physical appearance."

"And this makes her a definite suspect?"

"It doesn't help her case, that's for sure. She already told us that she had had an argument with the victim on the Saturday night, but she didn't mention the emails."

"What did she say the argument was about?"

"A minor business matter."

"Doesn't sound very minor from these emails."

"No. I'm going to get Suzie to interview the sister and find out exactly what the issue was between O'Flannery and our victim.

But if we don't get another tangible lead then I'm going to have to bring Bernie's mother in under caution."

"Apparently they hate each other," Walker reminded him.

"You think that'll stop Bernie Paterson from making a nuisance of herself?"

"No. But I've got something to distract you." Walker pulled up the fresh files he had just added to the system. "Dianna Shearing called from London. They got a hit on a previous case when we entered Holly Moore's business details into the system. Possible connection with a company accused of fraud down south."

"Fraud? What sort of fraud?"

"It seems to be a business that she used to work for. Lux Holdings, based in Watford. About ten years ago there was a big tax fraud case and the directors faced criminal charges. Holly wasn't charged with anything, but look at this name that was flagged up."

"James Moore? The husband?"

"Right. He was one of the Directors when Lux Holdings was investigated. According to the dates he joined right after he left the army and then the company got in deep trouble less than a year later."

"If he was charged for fraud, why didn't it show up on his file?" Macleod asked.

"Because the company made a deal with HMRC. Paid around

half of the debt back and the charges were dropped."

"Interesting, but I can't see the connection to the death of Holly Moore. Can you?"

"Not yet, but I'd like to go through the file more carefully."

Macleod checked his watch. "That will have to wait. I'm about to interview James Moore downstairs in five minutes. Want to observe?"

"Of course," Walker said. "I've found out some interesting things about his time in the army that we could ask about too."

"Come on then," Macleod said, striding along the corridor so that even Walker who was half a foot taller had to hurry to catch up. Walker felt almost embarrassed at how easy it had been to get back on the case. Dianna was right, he just had to put himself forward.

James Moore was waiting for them in the interview room. In the fluorescent lighting his tan faded to a sickly beige and he kept licking his dry lips. Walker knew better than to judge on appearances, however. A man with a guilty conscience and a man who was grieving over his murdered wife would both look agitated and stressed. Evidence, not guesswork, was what was required here.

Macleod started by getting him to go over his movements on Saturday night and Sunday morning. Moore explained that his security business required him to work the occasional nightshift: "With plenty of witnesses, as I'm sure you already know".

It was interesting to note how quickly he had gone from being helpful to an edge of belligerence. The DI changed the subject.

"We're looking into your wife's business practices. Do you think there might be someone connected with dare2dream who would have a reason to hurt her?"

Moore grimaced. "Could be. There's a lot of weirdos interested in that social media selling stuff, wouldn't surprise me if they were a bit unstable."

"You didn't approve of your wife's business?"

"I did at first. When she started selling the makeup and getting a few recruits the extra money was nice. We went on a couple of holidays, that sort of thing. But it started taking over her life. I'd come home from work and she'd spent the whole day on her phone, trying to drum up interest in her social media stuff. And then when her sister got involved it was even worse."

Macleod checked his notes. "This would be when they started 'dare2dream', is that correct?"

"Aye. They'd been to some seminar, some 'women in business' thing. I said: where's the men in business meetings, am I right?"

If James Moore was looking for a chuckle in response to his, then he was disappointed.

"Selling a wee bit of makeup was one thing, but all of a sudden they're into everything. They were doing coaching sessions, offering property management packs, Bella started hawking fitness courses, despite the fact she'd only been going to the gym for a couple of months herself. And I mean, she never wanted to do anything that wasn't pushing the business. The first year, we'd gone on holiday to have a break, but last year when we went to Tenerife she had to publish every single photo on her socials, pretending that her business had paid for the whole thing."

"It hadn't?"

"No it bloody well had not. I'd paid for the holiday. By this point she was barely making anything, and any money she did make Bella was demanding her fifty per cent."

"And you weren't involved in the running of the business at all?" Macleod prompted him.

"No. Like I told you, it was Holly's thing. I wanted nothing to do with it."

"The thing is, we've found evidence that when you came out of the army you were involved in a firm in London that had some problems with HMRC."

Moore crossed his arms. "That's ancient history. The tax man wanted his thirty pieces of silver so they started throwing around all this 'fraud' crap. It all got sorted in the end."

"And it didn't stop you from opening your security firm up here?"

"Why would it?"

Macleod looked at Walker and nodded, giving him permission to play his remaining card.

"I had a look at your army record," Walker said. "I was wondering why you left."

"Did my time, had enough."

"I understand. I was a soldier myself a long time ago. And I still have some friends in the forces. I had a word with Lieutenant Colonel Philips. He was your commanding officer for a couple of years in the army, I'm sure you remember him."

"What the hell are you dragging this up for?"

"We like to be thorough," Walker replied. "I was wondering why your army career didn't seem to feature many promotions, especially for a guy smart enough to end up running his own business."

Moore said nothing, his eyes narrowed.

"Anyway, Philips told me the reason you hadn't progressed. You got yourself a wee bit of a reputation for shagging the other lad's wives, didn't you?"

"What the hell has that got to do with anything?"

Macleod took up the thread. "It suggests that you might be the sort of person that grows tired of being married. And that perhaps you had a reason to want to get rid of your wife."

"Look, I just like women, that's all. That's not a crime, yet, is it? To be a heterosexual man?"

Walker was inwardly rolling his eyes. "It's not a crime. But it might be motivation to get your wife out of the way. If she discovered you were having an affair."

"Look, while I was with Holly I was good as gold. After I left, well, it wasn't her business anymore, was it?"

After that, Moore clammed up completely. Macleod let him go in the end, but Walker got the feeling he was disappointed that they hadn't got more out of the interview. Was Moore just a guy who couldn't resist screwing around? Or was there something nastier at work. Was he a wife killer? If he was then Walker couldn't see how he had managed it. Evidence, that was what they needed, not vague stories about what he'd been up to in the past. And Moore knew that too.

"Reckon a man that owned a security firm would be able to find someone willing to kill his wife?" Walker suggested to Macleod as they watched the man walk out of the station.

"My thoughts exactly," Macleod replied. "But if that's the case it'll be the devil to prove."

Walker couldn't help but agree.

Chapter 11: Liz

Liz would rather have spent an entire hour listening to one of Dave's golf anecdotes than attend this meeting. The only thing keeping her going was that her best friend needed her there.

In the passenger seat of Liz's car, Bernie was sitting up ramrod straight. She had barely spoken a word since they left Invergryff and only now that they were pulling into a parking space on the Southside of Glasgow did she begin to speak.

"She's staying with some old pal," Bernie said, as if answering a question that Liz hadn't asked. "I don't even know her name. But if she's putting Deborah up then she must be a damn fool."

"How do you want to do the interview?" Liz asked, trying to focus on the case.

"You lead. I'll butt in when she starts with her most outrageous lies."

Bernie got out of the car and started walking up the stairs. Liz followed her a few steps behind. She wished that Mary was here. She would have said something silly to break the tension. As it was, Liz felt like there was a dark cloud hanging over them and they hadn't even asked any questions yet.

In a few moments, they were up the stairs and into the flat. Deborah showed them in, acting like it was her own place rather than somewhere she was staying in while under investigation for murder.

"Isn't it a lovely view, you can see the crane over by the river if you look hard enough."

Deborah directed her chatter to Liz, knowing that she at least had to be polite.

"Where's your flatmate?" Bernie asked.

"Oh, Paula's having her roots done. Not before time, I have to say. Grey is so draining, don't you think?"

Bernie sat down on the leather sofa that was partially covered by a rather horrible lacy throw. Most of the room was a bit too frilly for Liz's taste, but then she had to assume that was Paula's style, not Deborah's.

"Let's get started," Bernie said, taking out her phone and setting it to record.

"You won't have a tea first?" Deborah twittered. "Or something stronger?"

"No."

A tea would have been quite welcome, Liz thought, but there was no way she was going to contradict Bernie. Not today.

"So stubborn," Bernie's mother said with another little laugh. "All right, we'll do it your way as usual. What a dreadful week it has been for me, you would think you could cut me some slack."

Liz had to force herself to stop staring at Deborah. It was that weird moment that happened every so often when she could see the ghost of Bernie in the older woman's features. But the voice, and simpering to get attention, that was nothing to do with Bernie.

"I can't believe you talked me into going to that dreadful police station," Deborah was saying once Liz tuned back in. "Do you know that they kept me waiting for nearly an hour? And then they sent some baby constable who looked younger than Ewan to take my statement. They only sent the Inspector in after I kicked up a fuss, but I ask you, who pays for them, eh? Us taxpayers, that's who."

Bernie was examining the wood grain on the table and said nothing.

"Anyway, this whole thing is a big mess," Deborah did another little twittering laugh. "And I suppose I'll have to look for a new job as well. At my age!"

"At least you've not been murdered," Bernie reminded her.

"Murdered! That's what they were saying at the police station. But I'm sure it's all a misunderstanding. Holly wasn't the sort of girl to go and get herself murdered."

"I'm not sure anyone plans for it," Liz said. "Was there anything about Holly Moore that made you think she was worried about being attacked?"

"Of course not. Everyone loved her. She was such an inspiration."

"Inspiration?" Bernie narrowed her eyes. "In what way?"

"Well, because of her business, of course. That was what drew me to her in the first place. She said she could tell I was an entrepreneur just by looking at me."

Bernie snorted a laugh. "Really?"

"Yes, Bernadette. It may be hard for you to believe, but I have always wanted to be a career woman. I had to sacrifice all that to have you girls. Being the mother is truly the hardest job, I would have hoped you would understand that now that you are one too. And now I've got the chance to find the real me again."

Liz knew she had to say something from the look on Bernie's face. "Why don't you tell us everything from the start, Deborah? How did you meet Holly?"

"It was an advert on one of my friend's pages online. I can't even remember who now. But she said she was selling the most amazing makeup, and that it wasn't available to buy anywhere else. Mineral foundation, spray tan, but all at really reasonable prices. Anyway, I got in touch with her and bought a couple of things. And they said if I posted a review I got ten per cent off my next purchase, so I did. Next thing I knew, Michelle Rallie got in touch. She's one of the business leaders, you see. And then pretty soon Holly herself was emailing me."

Deborah preened. "She said I was a great ambassador for her products because of how good I looked. Well, I have always been blessed with excellent skin. Do you know, Liz, they used to think that I was Martha's sister, not her mother?"

Another snort from Bernie, but Deborah ignored it. She was

in full stream now.

"Anyway, Holly said I should come on board with the business. That she would be my direct 'upline' – I don't understand all the lingo, but it meant that I would be my own boss, and that I could recruit other people to work for me too. Well, I was between jobs at the time-"

"You got fired again, did you?"

This earned Bernie a proper glare from her mother. "You think what you like Bernadette. I'm sure Liz understands that when you're not twenty-one anymore it's not so easy to start a new career. What was great about Holly was that she saw that I was this bundle of unrealised potential. And it wasn't just the makeup business. The whole thing about dare2dream is that it's a lifestyle brand, you know?"

"I saw that on their website," Liz said. "What exactly does it mean?"

"Wow, it's hard to explain," Deborah shook her head, like the women in front of her would never be able to grasp such a unique concept. "It's as if every part of your life has to work towards your goals. You need to smash through any limitations, especially when you think about investing in your future. Early retirement without sacrificing your life right now, that's a big one. Property investment, that was one of the things that Bella talked about."

"Property investment? You're living on your friend's sofa," Bernie pointed out.

"Her spare room, actually. You're always so negative. That's the thing with dare2dream though, you don't have to have a lot of money to get started. It's all about helping each other. What did they call it again? Oh yes, working on your network. You are only as strong as your friends, and the best thing you can do is bring them along with you."

"Uh huh," Liz said, her suspicions raised. "And did you recruit many of your friends into this business?"

"As many as I could. Not all of them could stick it out, of course, but some of them saw results pretty damn quickly. The people that didn't, well, between you and me there's no cure for laziness, is there?"

How did you tell someone that they had bought into a dodgy business? And that they had brought their friends into the same trouble? Liz couldn't quite bring herself to shatter all of Deborah's dreams.

"Did you ever have any concerns about Holly and Bella?" she said gently. "I mean, selling a lifestyle brand is a bit... vague, isn't it?"

"I would have thought you of all people would appreciate what they're doing," Deborah said, hot pink spots appearing on her cheeks. "You're a mother to a small baby. Surely you appreciate a business that gives women back their independence."

"If that's what they were doing, then that's great. But my concern is that Holly and Bella weren't being totally honest with you. You know that dare2dream was funded by another company, Better Life Now."

"I wouldn't know anything about that," Deborah laughed and shook her head although Liz thought there was a flicker of recognition at the name.

"That wasn't what you were arguing with Holly about on Saturday night then?" Bernie asked.

Deborah waved her hand as if to dismiss the comment. "Not this again. I told you, it was just a silly argument. Over nothing."

"And the next day she was dead."

"Don't be so silly," was Deborah's only answer to that one.

"It's true," Bernie reminded her. "And the police are going to ask you about it, whether you want to answer or not. Come on, Deborah, I don't believe for one minute you went to this woman's house, your boss's house in fact, unless you had something major to argue about."

"If you must know, it was about the business. I think Holly was jealous of how quickly I was moving through the company. The two of them, Bella and Holly, they didn't like to share their success. I asked them if I could start my own franchise."

This earned Deborah raised eyebrows from both Liz and Bernie.

"You wanted to start your own brand? A competitor for dare2dream?"

"I saw it more as a partnership, but guess what? Holly thought the same as you. She accused me of poaching her customers. Well, I said to her that if they were happy to go with me then her company couldn't have been all that great in the first place. And I still stand by that. I'm going to branch out on my own, just as soon as I can work out how to set up a website."

"And you'll be doing what, lifestyle coaching too?" Bernie's voice was full of sarcasm.

"Why not? I have had a hard life. I'm a survivor, and a lot of people could learn from me."

Bernie's face was going from scarlet to a shade of purple. Liz knew they had to get out of there before there was a second murder.

"Thank you for telling us the truth about the argument," she said, getting up and pulling Bernie to her feet too. "You should tell the police as well."

Deborah shrugged, like she didn't think much of that idea.

"Give my love to Ewan," she trilled as they moved towards the door.

Bernie kept her mouth pressed into a thin line all the way out of the flat and into the car. Liz was a little worried her friend was going to give herself some sort of stroke, she was wound so tight.

"That was… well, we found out what the argument was about, didn't we?" Liz said, trying to fill the silence.

"If we can believe a word she says." Bernie shuddered. "I don't think this is over yet."

Liz had to agree. Until Holly Moore's killer was found, they wouldn't be able to get rid of Deborah. And what sort of state would Bernie be in by then?

Chapter 12: Mary

Mary had been waiting for news on the interview with Bernie's mother, but in the end all she got was a whispered phone call from Liz where she said it had been a 'total nightmare' and that Deborah hadn't told them much.

"Bet I could have got her to talk," Mary said to herself as she glared at the kettle while it got to the boil. She was still smarting from the fact that Bernie hadn't included her.

The doorbell rang and she was pleased to see Walker on the step.

"You could have used your key," Mary said as she gave him a hug. It was an ongoing discussion between them.

"Aye well, I wanted to give you a chance to hide your other boyfriends," he said, squeezing her back as they went into the house.

"I thought you might like some lunch before you pick up the kids," Walker said holding up a paper bag. "And I even brought you a bun."

A handsome man with cake? Mary was instantly cheered.

"Great, I'll make the tea," Mary said, leading them into the kitchen. "Have you had a busy morning?"

"Yep. I've just been interviewing the husband."

"And? How did it go?"

"It went," he said. "Am I still on for taking Peter to the ice hockey game this weekend?"

Mary just about managed to ignore his clunky change of subject. Peter had, for some unknown reason, become obsessed with watching ice hockey over the last few months. She reckoned it was because football just wasn't violent enough. It turned out that Walker also enjoyed the sport, and had heard that the local team was playing the Glasgow Clan at the weekend.

"Sure. Do you want me to get the tickets?"

"Nah, I'll get them. I think they do a VIP stadium tour, I'll see if I can get us on that."

It was nice that he was making the effort. Mary hadn't pressured Walker to assume any sort of 'dad' role. If anything, she had avoided it so far. The last thing she wanted was for them all to play happy families only for the relationship to end. The kids had been hurt badly by the breakup with their father and Mary would never do the same thing to them again. But ever so slowly, Mary was letting her guard down and allowing Walker to spend more time with the kids.

"I guess this case is proving to be tricky for you. I mean, if it was just a case of 'the husband did it' you'd have arrested him by now, right?"

"Right," Walker said, unwrapping his sandwich.

"I mean, we're not doing much better. We don't even know

the cause of death," Mary said, trying to be casual.

"Come on now, you know I can't tell you that."

She felt like reminding him that they had discussed these sorts of things plenty of times before. He knew by now that she would be discrete, surely. Mary bit her lip. What was it with everyone treating like an idiot today? She chewed on her roll.

"Let's sit down," Mary said once they each had a steaming mug of tea. They went through to the living room and moved the massive piles of laundry to one side so that they could actually take a seat.

Mary wanted to relax, but her mind kept going back to Holly Moore. "Does Macleod know if –"

"Look, I know the WWC are looking at this one, but I'd rather we don't let it ruin our lunch, okay?" Walker said in a clipped tone.

Mary couldn't help but be offended. "You're not really telling me to stay out of this case are you? You know that Bernie's mother is one of the suspects."

Walker sighed. "That's exactly why I'm asking you to keep your distance. Look, I know that there's nothing more that you lot love than solving cases that we're struggling with, but it's different this time. If Bernie's mother turns out to have been involved in this, even just as a witness, then you could all be in serious danger of being charged with interfering in the investigation."

Mary gave him a quick kiss. "You're so cute when you're being patronising."

"Patronising? I'm just trying to –"

"You're trying to tell me how to do my job," Mary said, trying to keep her voice light even though she was on the verge of getting annoyed. "It's not a hobby, you know. This is what I do for a living now. I'm a partner in the firm, something you encouraged me to go for, by the way. You have to trust me that I know where to draw the line."

Walker squirmed uncomfortably for a moment. "All right. At least I can tell Macleod that I said my piece."

"Macleod should tell us himself if he's that bothered," she said, causing her boyfriend to wince once more.

Mary could feel her neck growing hot. She and Walker rarely fell out, but when they did it was always about work. She decided to change the subject.

"Heard anything from your brother recently?"

"Ru? Oh, he's fine I guess. It's not like we talk all the time." Walker walked over to the fridge and went to grab another beer. He had effectively shut down the conversation and instead of feeling better, Mary was feeling more annoyed. He was so closed off about his family. After all, she had actually met Ruaridh. It wasn't like she had asked about Walker's mother.

"What about your parents?" Mary asked, anger getting the better of her. "Have they been trying to get in touch recently?"

As soon as she had said it she instantly regretted it. Walker winced, his shoulders twitching like she had hit him.

"I shouldn't have asked," Mary said, not able to bear the tension in his face. "I mean, I know that you don't speak. It's just… you're such a part of my family. I guess I'm interested in yours."

"I think all you need to know is that I don't speak to them," he said finally.

"Yeah, I get that. But if one of my kids never spoke to me again I'd be heartbroken."

Walker let out a dry laugh. "Trust me when I say you are nothing like my parents."

"Right."

The silence lengthened.

"You don't know what she's like," Walker told her.

"Because you haven't told me anything about her." Mary could hear the crack in her voice. She wasn't even sure how this argument had started, but now it felt like a serious fight. And she couldn't see how to get out of it. It *was* weird, wasn't it, that he kept so much of himself closed off. Didn't she have a right to know?

"I don't like talking about it," Walker said.

Mary knew she had a choice. Continue the argument, push home her point or back down. And maybe she was a coward, but when she saw the lines of tension around Walker's mouth, she just couldn't go any further.

"It's all right. I get it. I never even knew about Bernie's mother until this week. We don't have to talk about it if you don't want to."

Walker gave her a tight little smile. "Thanks. You want that bun now?"

"Sure."

He sat beside her and they ate their dessert. But the argument hung over them like a storm cloud and Walker ended up going back to work before she had cleared her plate.

Chapter 13: Bernie

It had taken Bernie a couple of days to work out where James Moore was staying. Clearly he wasn't allowed in his marital home which was currently a crime scene, but Bernie had put the feelers out in the Invergryff community to discover where he was based. It turned out that for the last six months James Moore had been living in a small flat in a newly built block near the river. And he hadn't been living alone.

"Funny how no one mentioned that he's been shacked up with another woman," Bernie told Liz when she phoned up about her latest lead.

"I thought it was Holly that threw him out?"

"Aye, it was, but not just because they weren't getting on. Invergryff gossip is that he was shagging this other woman for months."

"Who is she?"

"Her name is Leah Hill and she works in that big call centre out at the roundabout. Selling insurance or something. Pretty girl, about a decade younger than his wife, of course."

"Of course. But does it matter?" Liz had asked. "I mean, the police seem to reckon he has a watertight alibi."

"You trust those idiots in Invergryff police station to check out an alibi properly? I don't. I'm off to speak to one of his coworkers right now."

And so Bernie had found herself meeting Nadia Largs who was one of James Moore's admin assistants.

"I never liked him much," Nadia said while she poured two packets of brown sugar into her coffee. Bernie would have liked to tell her how bad refined sugar was for her gut health, but the other members of the WWC had told her never to mention other people's food while interviewing them. It was an irritating rule, although Bernie had noticed people were less likely to storm out of her meetings than they used to be.

"Why not?"

"He's a whiner. One of those guys who seems to think the world owes them a living and then complains when everything doesn't work out the way they want it. I mean, he's the boss so you would think he's doing all right. But he used to spend half the day moaning about his wife. And he was always complaining about people stealing his milk out of the company fridge."

To Bernie's eyes, Nadia had milk stealer written all over her. The woman was in her twenties, with one of those tattoo sleeves that seemed to be in fashion at the moment. Bernie wasn't sure if it was manga or anime, but it seemed to feature women with tiny mouths and big boobs and men with hair like starfish. Nadia had asked three times if Bernie was paying for lunch, even though they had arranged it all over the phone already. Yep, definitely a milk stealer.

"He won't be moaning about his wife anymore," Bernie

reminded the girl.

"No, I suppose not. Mind you, he hadn't been mentioning her as much since he got together with his new girlfriend."

"He talked about Leah in the office, then?"

"Oh, aye, he had no shame about it. Claimed he met her just after he left his wife, but everyone knew he'd been seeing her on the side. It was Holly that found out about it and kicked them out, you know."

"Did she?"

"According to Freddie who does the accounts, she lost the plot, threw all his stuff out the windows."

"Do you have any evidence of this?" Bernie asked, making a note of Freddie's name.

"Naw, but I'd love to see the pics if you find any. Always pretending he's the victim that one. I don't know how he ever got a girlfriend in the first place."

"He must have some good qualities," Bernie suggested.

"He's not bad looking. A bit like that lad that came third on X-factor that time. The one that butchered that Whitney Houston song."

Bernie was a little lost. She never watched talent shows if she could help it. Too little talent and far too much show, as far as Bernie Paterson was concerned.

Nadia was still staring into space, considering the merits of the widower. "Fake tan and shiny hair," she said finally. "I guess if that's your thing then James Moore might do it for you."

"He didn't do it for you then?"

The woman's face suddenly reddened. "Who's been telling you that?"

Bernie kept her face neutral. "Oh, you know, just the usual gossip. I'm sure there's nothing to it."

"We went on one date, that's all."

Ahah! Bernie thought. Gotcha. "Would this be before or after he left his wife?"

"Don't you be judging me," Nadia said with a wobble in her voice that made the couple at the next table start to stare.

"Not at all. As you said, it was only one date."

"Right," Nadia smoothed down her hair where it had started to escape the messy bun she had it in. "And not even a decent date at that. He didn't even pay for the dinner, I had to go halves even though I barely ate anything. Tight-arse."

"Did he mention his ex at all on your date?"

"You mean did he say he fancied murdering her?" Nadia laughed, a nasal sound that made Bernie's teeth itch. "Just the usual crap he said in the office about how she was obsessed with this business of hers. He said she didn't even care what he got up to. And he said her business was all a big con anyway."

"Did he?"

"Yeah. He said it didn't make her half as much money as she claimed. He had to keep bailing her out on her credit cards or something."

"Interesting," Bernie said, making a note on her phone. "And now he's shacked up with someone else."

"Aye. Good luck to her, that's what I think. What a creep."

Bernie didn't get much more out of Nadia and once she had paid for the woman's lunch, she left. Her coffee was cold, but Bernie didn't get up. She was thinking. So far, Nadia's intel on James Moore didn't seem anything more than the average office gossip. All that Bernie had learned was that the man was more than happy to go on dates while still married. That hardly made him unique, especially considering what Bernie saw in her line of work.

She needed to speak to the man face-to-face. She left the café and drove over to the new development next to the river where James Moore had his bachelor pad. There was a cloying smell of lavender as Bernie climbed out of the car. Someone had planted a whole row of the bushes along the front of the development. At least it would give the smokers somewhere to chuck their cigarette butts, Bernie thought as she made her way up to the door.

As was her normal strategy, she tried the services buzzer first to see if it worked and sure enough she was let into the building without even having to say her name. She double-checked the flat number and went up two flights of stairs to find Moore's place. Then she rapped on the door with her fist.

When the occupier opened the door, Bernie saw that James Moore had his coat on.

"Are you going somewhere?"

"Just back actually. Sorry, who are you?"

Bernie gave him a wide smile. "My name is Bernadette Paterson. I'm a private investigator.

"Bloody hell I'm just after finishing up with the police and now you're here?"

"Oh, I'm much worse than the police."

James Moore's forehead wrinkled, then he decided to ignore what she had said.

"Can't you come back another time? My wife has just died, for God's sake."

"I know. And I would say that I'm very sorry but I don't see the use in those sorts of pointless platitudes, do you? They don't really help anyway."

Moore shrugged. "No, they don't. What is it that you want?"

"To find out what happened to Holly. And if you weren't involved then I might just be the one that clears your name."

Moore ran a hand over his chin. "I suppose you better come in then."

"Leah not in today?" Bernie asked as she sat down on the brown leather couch.

"How do you... no, she's not."

"Did you mention to the police that you were living with someone?"

"No. It didn't seem relevant."

Bernie shook her head. "Classic mistake. It's a shame you're not my client. I would have told you that the more silly lies you tell the coppers, the more they get their backs up. They're a simple breed, and they tend to see the sort of man that lies about his Mistress as the same sort of man who lies about his alibi."

Moore flopped down into an armchair. "I just didn't want them to think I had a motive. Damn. You think I should have told them? Leah has nothing to do with any of this."

"So she never even met Holly?"

"Well, they met a couple of times. Holly had a bit of a go at her once."

Bernie smirked. "Because you were seeing her while you and Holly were still together, right?"

"No," Moore said, and Bernie knew that if he had lied like that to the police officers then even they would have seen through him. Idiot.

She decided to change tack. "One of the areas we've been

exploring is Holly's business venture. Do you think anyone from dare2dream might have been involved in her death?"

Moore nodded. "I've been thinking about this too, and it's the only thing that might make sense. You know the sort of people she employed, right? Complete losers. I mean, that was how it worked. Take some miserable, dowdy middle-aged woman with snotty little kids, probably fat and hating herself, and tell her she can be businesswoman of the year."

"They sound dreadful," Bernie said, and Moore must have been tired or just very stupid because he missed the sarcasm in her voice.

"Exactly. So what I'm thinking is one of those crazies went after Holly."

"It's certainly something to think about. From what I gather, the police are short of evidence."

"Aye, that's why they're so eager to blame it on me," Moore said, lapsing back into self pity.

"The husband is always the obvious subject. Lucky you have that alibi. But I suppose the question that the police will be asking is: would someone who ran a security firm be able to find a killer for hire. And the answer to that is clearly yes. So it seems to me that your alibi doesn't quite rule you out yet."

Moore let out another groan. "Do you always bring people such good news?"

"I don't believe in lying," Bernie said. "But if there's anything else you can think of, anything that might help us find who killed your wife you should tell me now."

"There's nothing."

For once, Bernie believed him. But she wasn't ruling out his guilt just yet. He wasn't the sort to get his hands dirty, but he might have been involved somehow. She just had to find some evidence one way or the other.

Chapter 14: Walker

Whether Macleod had mentioned his name to the rest of the team or Dianna had been working some behind-the-scenes magic, Walker found himself driving Suzie O'Connor to interview Holly Moore's sister.

"What is that smell?" Suzie asked when they got in the car.

"Ah, Neil had the squad car last night to pick up a couple of lads who were causing a disturbance after a stag do. We sent it for a deep clean but there is a lingering scent of kebab."

"Gross," Suzie said, winding down the window. "I thought you were going to make your way out of uniform? Less stag do's can only be a good thing, right?"

"Believe me, I've been trying. But no one seems to even want to look at my application form. I've completed all the training modules, everything." Walker hated that he sounded so whiny. "I don't know if it's the dyslexia thing or what, but I'm not getting anywhere."

"You should ask for a sit-down meeting with the Superintendent. Raise a grievance if you have to."

"You reckon so? Don't you think that would mark me out as a troublemaker?"

"Sometimes you have to make a little trouble," Suzie said with a shrug.

Walker didn't have time to ponder this as they pulled up outside a semi-detached house just outside of Invergryff in one of the more upmarket Renfrewshire villages. You could tell it was posh as the bakery across the road had the word 'artisan' written on the window, rather than the usual adverts for sausage rolls.

Walker killed the engine as Suzie checked her phone.

"Was there any new info on the sister since Macleod's last briefing?" she asked.

"Nothing note-worthy. She worked with Holly in the business as of a couple of years ago. Before then she was a beautician. Never married, no kids. No criminal record. No obvious motive to want her sister dead."

"Let's hope we learn something more when we get inside," Suzie said, leading the way forward.

They rang the door and introduced themselves to Bella Terrance. Walker found it a little eerie how much she looked like the pictures of her sister he had seen from the crime scene. It was like looking at a ghost.

"Come in. I suppose you'll want a cup of tea. Or is that only on TV that cops drink tea?" Bella had the exhausted look of the recently bereaved. Her skin had gone from a healthy tan to a grey colour and there were dark circles around her eyes. If nothing else, her grief was genuine. Of course, you could still be grieving even if you were the one that did the killing.

"Tea would be great, thank you," Suzie replied. "Did the family liaison officer get in touch?"

"Yes, she's just left. PC Little, wasn't it? She's gone over to my mum's. I told her the news yesterday, but she's got dementia so..."

Walker and Suzie didn't say anything to that. Nothing they would say would bring comfort anyway, not by the looks of Bella's face.

"We'd like to have a chat with you if that's all right," Suzie said. "Try and find out some more information about Holly."

"About her death?"

"If you know anything about it, yes."

"How would I know about it? I didn't even realise that she was... not until the knock on the door. Bloody hell." She wiped at her eyes.

"Anything you can tell us that might be even slightly relevant will help," Walker explained. "You didn't speak to her on Saturday night?

"No, I was at the pub with some friends. I already gave their names to the PC. I got home late, passed out about three and didn't wake up until you lot came knocking. At first I thought it was about the bloody car."

"The car?"

"Holly said some idiot had damaged it. I told her to report it to you lot. Should be in your files somewhere."

"She never reported an accident," Suzie told her.

"Oh. Well, maybe she hadn't got around to it before... before some evil sod killed her."

"What else did she say about the car?" Walker asked.

"I'm not sure now. It was a few days ago, maybe Thursday morning? She was meant to pick me up in the car so we could go to a meeting of property investors in Glasgow. But then she texted me saying we would have to get the train. She didn't tell me any details or anything, I just thought someone must have banged into it. Probably one of those delivery drivers, the maniacs."

Walker said nothing, but he would be surprised if a delivery driver had left the vicious scratch in the side of Holly Moore's car. It had looked deliberate and Walker made a note to check with forensics if they had found anything interesting on the car.

"Was there anything else unusual that happened in the last week or so? Anything that Holly was worried about?"

Bella shook her head. "We were both busy, but that's not unusual. You can't take the wins if you're not willing to put the work in, you know? And I guess there were always people that were jealous of how much success we've had. You know, the sort of people that give you a dirty look for being a size eight."

"Anyone in particular?" Suzie asked.

"There were a few nasty comments on the usual social media

sites. Trolling, that's what it's called isn't it? I can look up the names for you."

"Thank you," Suzie said, "that would be a great help."

Bella fiddled with the gold chain around her neck. "You said that James was at work when it happened?"

Suzie nodded. "He was doing a night shift. We're going to check it out, but it looks like there were plenty of witnesses."

"Huh."

Walker leaned forward. "If he didn't have an alibi, would you have any reason to suspect James?"

"Oh aye, a good half a million reasons," Bella said. "That's what their house is worth. And he'll get it all now, won't he?"

"I suppose so," Walker replied. "But do you have any reason to suspect that he wished Holly harm?"

"He has a mean temper on him. He shouted at her more than once."

"Ever violent?" Suzie asked.

"No…" Bella said slowly, as if reluctant to admit that the man had never hit her sister. "Not that Holly told me anyway. But they only have to snap once, don't they? And the last few months he really hated her. You know that he was shacked up with some young girl, don't you?"

Suzie raised her eyebrows. "No, we were not aware. You're saying he's living with someone?"

"He told Holly he met her after they split up. You can guess how true that is. Holly told him she would take him to the cleaners in the divorce. But he reckoned he was in for half the value of our business. You can talk to her lawyer if you like, Mitchell Howe, he's based in Glasgow. I know she had a meeting with him about all that stuff."

Walker made a note of the name.

"What about Holly? Was she seeing anyone?"

"Nah, she was too focussed on the business. We both were. Have you seen the website? We worked so bloody hard on all that, I can't believe that Holly won't be around to see how amazing it's going to become."

"You'll keep the business on then," Suzie said, "without your sister?"

"Of course," Bella replied, as if the very idea of giving up offended her. "We owe it to all those women out there that we're helping. Look, I'll give you my card. If you check out our socials you'll see so many testimonials of women who have had their lives changed by dare2dream."

"From selling makeup?"

Bella sniffed. "That is like... such a small part of what we do. We're a lifestyle brand, you know. That was Holly's vision."

Walker had been about to ask what a 'lifestyle brand' was when Bella broke down in tears. They decided it was time to leave.

"Funny that she said the car was damaged in an accident,"

Walker said as they walked back to the patrol car.

"Why?"

"You didn't see the pictures? Someone keyed down one side of it. Right down to the metal. No way that that was an accident."

"And Holly definitely didn't report it," Suzie said, climbing into the passenger seat. "So why wouldn't she want her sister to know that someone had attacked her car deliberately?"

"And was it the same person that killed her or just someone else with a grudge against the family?" Walker asked. "Considering that Bella told us everyone loved her, it seems like Holly had a fair few enemies."

"Let's not forget Deborah O'Flannery. She already said she had an argument with Holly. Did she seem like the sort to key a car?"

Walker thought back to everything he had learned about Bernie's mother. "She's got a reputation for causing drama, so it wouldn't surprise me."

"Let's get back to the station and see what forensics have to say about it," Suzie said. "And let's take another look at Holly Moore's finances. From what her sister said, there might be enough there to give someone a motive for murder." He went to put the radio on.

"You better not be about to play that indie rock crap that you like," Suzie said.

Walker turned on the sound, expecting that very genre to turn on. Instead, his ears were assaulted by a vintage Kylie Minogue track.

"Awesome," Suzie said, reaching past him to turn the volume up. "I didn't think you would listen to the classic 80's channel."

"I didn't. I gave Mary a lift the other day, she must have messed with the dial."

"Sure she did," Suzie laughed, then started singing along. Walker tried to ignore her all the way back to the station.

Chapter 15: Liz

Tuesday evenings were always booked in Liz's diary for the weekly WWC meeting. This time they had agreed to have it at her place. The emergency meeting the night before at Mary's house had not been a complete success.

"That off chocolate gave me a stomach ache," Liz explained to Dave. "And Bernie was not impressed when she put her shoes on and it turned out one of the kids had left her a little treat in them."

"Oh god, they hadn't –"

"No, not quite that bad. But Bernie said that the sensation of putting her toes into strawberry yoghurt was something she wouldn't forget for a while."

Dave laughed. "Got it. I'll take Sean over to my pal Fergal's. His son is in Sean's class and they've just got a new puppy."

"God, he'll be badgering us for a dog again."

"Lucky I'm allergic," Dave said. "Which reminds me, I should go upstairs and take an antihistamine."

"Great."

Liz tidied up around the house after the boys left. Baby Issy was sleeping well at the moment, so she was already down in her cot. Hopefully she would sleep through the meeting, but if not Liz knew that Mary and Bernie would be fighting over babysitting duties.

The kitchen was messier than usual with the baby paraphernalia threatening to take over. One of Liz's not-so-dirty little secrets was that ever since Issy had been born they had a cleaner come in once a week. She had never mentioned it to Bernie or Mary in the vague sense that they would disapprove, but the two hours a week when the lovely Sue came and made her house sparkle were the best thing ever. Unfortunately, by the next day the whole place was messy again. Liz had always liked an orderly house but the new baby was making it tricky.

Sean tolerated rather than adored his little sister, although he did play sweetly with her when no one was watching. So Liz had tried to hold her tongue when confronted with stinky football gear strewn across the house. Nagging wasn't always the best option, even though it was often tempting.

As she scrubbed at the countertops she wondered if she was being too easy on her son or if –

A face appeared at the window next to her.

"Ahhh!" On instinct, Liz threw herself backwards, whacking her elbow off the kitchen island. The figure in the window was already moving around to the side and let herself in the patio doors.

"Jesus Bernie you gave me a heart attack."

"Didn't want to wake the baby," Bernie said.

"I probably woke her up with my screams," Liz complained,

although there was no sound of a baby waking from upstairs. "Are you wanting a drink?"

"I think I'll stick to water tonight," Bernie replied. "I've had a drink every night since Deborah appeared and I don't want to make a habit of it."

"Fair enough."

At that moment the doorbell went.

"At least one guest knows how to behave," Liz said as she opened the front door.

"What?" Mary's round face wrinkled in confusion.

"Never mind. Can I get you a drink?"

"Just a fizzy water for me," Mary replied. "I've got to drive to my mum's place and get the kids later. She normally takes them overnight but she's got hot yoga tomorrow morning, whatever the hell that is."

"I quite enjoyed hot yoga," Bernie said. "Except that they got annoyed when I told them to hurry through all the spiritual crap. As if I need someone in leggings telling me how to breathe."

"Isn't the 'spiritual crap' kind of the point?" Mary asked

"Not for me. I want to stretch my hips out, not heal my bloody soul."

There was a brief pause while the others considered exactly what Bernie's soul would be like.

"I'd like to get us started if that's okay," Liz said, bringing them back to business. "I've barely slept looking at all this dare2dream stuff."

"This is Holly's company that she ran with her sister?" Bernie asked.

"Right. But it's not just a simple business. In fact, to all intents and purposes I think dare2dream is an MLM."

There was a moment of silence.

"Is that like the chocolate?" Mary asked.

"What?"

"An M&M?"

Liz narrowed her eyes. "Are you kidding me?"

Mary just squirmed. "Sorry Liz, I don't know what it is."

"An MLM? A multi-level marketing company. You haven't ever heard of them?"

"Don't think so," Mary said and Bernie shook her head as well.

"But you know about pyramid schemes, right?" Liz asked them.

"Something to do with people at the bottom of the chain sending money up to the bosses at the top, is that right?" Bernie was clearly trying her best, but Liz was surprised at how little her friends knew about these things.

"A pyramid scheme works by making money out of the workers they recruit, not the product they sell. So, for example, I have this great idea where every person in my business gets seven people to join for a joining fee of a tenner. And each of them gets seven people to join and so on. So it looks like you pay ten pounds in but get seventy back, right? But very quickly the number of people rising exponentially means that even once you get a couple of levels down, there aren't enough people to recruit. The newest recruits send in their tenner but never get anything back."

"That sounds really bad," Mary said.

"Right. And that's why pyramid schemes are illegal, in this country anyway. But Multi-level marketing companies are a loophole in this legislation. They claim that because they are selling a product or in our case a service like 'lifestyle coaching' they aren't a pyramid scheme, even though the whole thing relies on continual recruitment at the lower levels to keep funding the higher levels. The people at the bottom make nothing while the ones at the top…"

"Drive around in pink Range Rovers," Bernie said, catching on.

"Exactly. I know we want to solve Holly Moore's murder, and I'm sure we will, but I think we should do a side mission."

"Side mission?"

Liz paused. "I need to stop letting Ewan play so many computer games. What I mean is that solving the murder should still be our focus. But alongside that, I want to take this crappy company down."

Mary and Bernie exchanged a glance and Liz could tell they still didn't really understand what she was so worried about.

"Look at it this way, Holly's company was based on the exploitation of every single person she recruited into it. If that's not a motive for murder then I don't know what is."

"All right, I'm convinced," Bernie said. "You've done some good work here on the company. Can you put all the financial stuff in the file so Mary and I can look over it later?"

Liz nodded. "Will do."

"Did you two write up your interview with Deborah?" Mary asked. Her arms were folded and she gave Bernie a sideways look as she spoke. Liz wasn't too sure what that was all about.

"I haven't put anything down yet," Bernie explained. "As usual, Deborah is full of ten tons of crap so God knows what was the truth and what was a total lie. She says she had a meeting with Holly at her house on Saturday night. The so-called meeting seemed to have been a full-on row with Deborah wanting to split from the business and form her own company. After that, she went home to her flat in Glasgow. I'm sure the police have worked out that there are no witnesses to any of this and nothing to say that she didn't hang around to do a bit of murdering later on. So our main focus has to be to find an alternative suspect."

"Which we haven't done yet," Liz reminded them.

"What about the husband?" Mary asked.

"Your standard serial shagger," Bernie explained. "He's already shacked up with this other woman, Leah Hill. I'm hoping we can talk to her soon. He certainly has a motive, but there doesn't seem to be any chance that he committed the crime. He was working the night shift and there were plenty of witnesses that saw him there."

"I still think dare2dream is the key," Liz reminded them. "We need to look into the sister first of all. She's gone from being half of a company to being the only boss, so that gives her a motive. And judging by all the 'happy huns' on their social media, there are plenty of others that might have been ripped off along the way.

"Happy huns?"

"Sorry, that's what I've been calling them. People in these sorts of organisations love an emoji and they all talk like they're back on MSN messenger. You know, 'r u ok hun', and lots of 'hashtag blessed'.

"Ugh. I'm not sure I want to get involved with this," Bernie said. "The more I hear about it the more it sounds like my mother was deep into this crap. And I really don't want to have to go digging around her social media."

"I know," Liz said, squirming in her seat. "And believe me, I would rather we didn't have to deal with Deborah at all. But we need to do something about this awful company. Even with Holly murdered, the rest of them are still going to carry on. More people like your mother are going to invest in them and go broke. I just don't think we can stand by and let them keep pushing their dodgy business."

"What about you?" Bernie said, turning to Mary.

"Me? Oh, I'm sure whatever you decide is for the best."

Bernie's eyes narrowed. "You're a partner now and I would like to hear your opinion."

Mary looked a little pale, but she managed to find her voice. "I'm sorry, but I think I'm with Liz. From what she's saying, these companies target desperate women. Normal mums trying to make a bit of money to keep the wolf from the door. And that was me just before I joined the WWC. I think we need to stop these people and help the women escape from this awful situation. Um. But only if you want to," she added lamely.

Bernie folded her arms and the room went silent. Liz glanced at Mary who gave her a tiny shrug in response. The WWC was a democracy, of course, and they knew that because Bernie told them it was. They waited for the verdict.

"We'll do it," Bernie said. "I'm not going to interact with Deborah any more – Liz, you can do that if we need to – but I think we should look at this company. And how it might connect to the death of Holly Moore."

"Great," Mary smiled. "How are we going to go about it?"

Liz leaned forward. "I've got an idea about that one. I reckon we need to go straight into battle. Fight them from the inside."

All this got was two blanks looks.

Liz rolled her eyes. "I think we should join up."

"Brilliant," Bernie said. "We'll get our evidence straight from the horse's mouth. I should have thought of that myself. What do you think, Liz, you want to do it?"

But Liz had already considered this one and ruled it out. As she explained to the others: "The thing is, there's no way that if I go in there they're going to talk to me. These companies are super defensive, mainly because they know that they're such a con. They can smell a fake at a hundred paces. And besides, there's not many faces with melanin on their website, if you get my drift."

Bernie nodded in agreement. "You're right, they'll clock you a mile away. These companies are looking for naïve women, people who are desperate for money. The sort of person that hasn't bought new boots for several years."

"All right, I get it," Mary piped up from the sofa. "You don't need to be a dick about it, Bernie. And these boots are vintage, I'll have you know. And they only leak when it rains."

Liz grinned. "That's perfect then. Mary, you can be our undercover agent."

"I'm Bond, Mary Bond," Mary said, pointing her fingers at them.

"Oh lord," Bernie groaned. "What have we done?"

The logistics of setting up Mary's fake identity were not as tricky as they might have been. Due to their line of work, each of them had several social media accounts and online presences in false names. They just had to pick the right one.

"Can I be Talulah Makepeace again?" Mary said, bouncing up and down.

"No," Bernie replied. "We should never have let you make that one up. It's not even like we have a pole dancing club in Invergryff."

"Fine," Mary pouted. "Which one were you thinking of?"

"What about Brianna Grant?" Liz suggested, looking at the spreadsheet. "She's meant to be a nurse, so she probably fits the sort of income requirements that these shady businesses are looking for."

But Mary was already shaking her head. "I can't. Remember, they put her name in the paper after that case with the cheating wife and the bakery outlet."

"Right. The one with the discount buns." Liz updated the spreadsheet to colour Brianna Grant red for 'dead'.

"I think we should go with Maria Johnstone," Bernie said, peering over Liz's shoulder at the files. "You've not used that one much."

"That's because she's boring," Mary replied. "She's got four kids like me, she lives around the corner and she works in a bank. Apart from the bank part, she's basically me."

"That's why it's perfect," Bernie explained. "A single mum working part-time in a bank is just the sort of person that this business is looking for, am I right?"

Liz nodded in agreement. "To be honest Mary if you weren't a part of the WWC you would be a prime recruitment target just as you are. They look for women who are in need of money, who don't have a husband that could question their choice of employment, and who are vulnerable to flattery."

"I'm not vulnerable!" Mary pouted.

"You gave that guy sitting outside Markies twenty quid just because he said his dog needed surgery," Liz reminded her.

"So?"

"That's Big Jim that hangs out at the Hog's Head," Bernie told her. "He's got a bigger house than you and he definitely doesn't have a dog. Apparently he makes fifty grand a year from schmucks like you."

"Oh bloody hell."

"Liz, how do you think she should go about getting recruited?"

"First we'll need to build up this profile a bit. Make Maria Johnstone look a bit more desperate. I'll do some social media posts about how she's been 'let down by friends' or something. Then I think the best thing to do is to target one of Holly Moore's underlings. We don't want to go to the people at the top. That's far too suspicious. Leave it with me."

"I wonder what Walker will think of me going undercover," Mary said, tucking a loose piece of hair behind her ear. "We had a right row the other night."

"Tell Dalziel and Pascoe to mind his own business," Bernie

told her.

"I'm not sure that one quite works."

"Made Liz laugh."

Mary turned to Liz. "Did it?"

"Not at all," she lied.

Chapter 16: Mary

Mary woke up with a headache caused partly by the wine she had consumed when she had gone home and partly by Liz's complicated explanation of MLM companies. It seemed to have really riled her friend up, but Mary still wasn't too sure what dare2dream was doing wrong. Still, she was nothing if not supportive and had made sure to nod along in all the right places. And her earlier row with Walker wasn't helping her head either. They had exchanged goodnight texts, but it had all seemed a bit strained.

The kids had been in bed when she got home, with Mary's mother Nel snoozing on the couch until she arrived. Nel had told her that they had had a healthy dinner, but the empty ice-cream tubs in the recycling suggested that grandparent spoiling had gone on. It meant that the kids had awoken more grumpy than usual. Peter, her eldest son, had actually woken up before seven and was skulking in the kitchen while Mary ate a bowl of cereal.

"Everything okay?" she asked.

"Fine."

Mary knew her son and knew that all was not fine, but that there was no point in pushing it. Peter had gone through a difficult stage a couple of years ago. And the toddler years of course. And every six months from five to ten. But since he had turned twelve he had seemed to mature a bit. It was enjoyable not to be answering the phone to the school calling every day about his behaviour, and on one notable occasion the local motorbike learners' centre.

But despite the recent good behaviour, Mary's heart still dropped when he came into the living room with a sheepish expression and asked her if he could 'have a word'.

"Sure. Want a cup of tea?"

"Yes please."

Now Mary was worried. Normally when offered tea Peter would have tried for the forbidden fizzy juice and the unprompted use of 'please' suggested something was definitely going on.

Mary clicked the kettle on and turned to face her son. She fought off the urges to strip search him for illicit substances or to check for tattoos. Probably not something she needed to worry about at twelve. Probably.

"So what was it you wanted to talk about?"

Peter perched on the countertop but his eyes were staring down at his socks. "You have to promise not to get mad about it."

"You know that's not something I can promise," Mary said, coming over so that her shoulder was touching his. "But I can promise to listen."

Peter let out a sigh. "It's a thing at school. Or at least... some of the boys from school are doing stuff and... it's not very nice."

"What sort of not very nice?"

"Like… it's not bullying when it's your friends doing it, is it? I mean, I guess it's just sort of joking about only… I don't think it's very nice."

Mary could feel her heart rate increasing, but she tried her best to keep calm. "I'm afraid even your friends can bully you. It's horrible, but it happens."

Peter nodded. "That's what I thought."

She wanted nothing more than to pick him up and cuddle him, like he was still the toddler that had fallen over in a puddle. But he was nearly as tall as she was these days and the problems he had to deal with had grown with him.

"Why don't you just tell me? Tell me what happened to you."

He looked at her, his eyebrows raised in surprise. "It's not me, mum. They're not doing anything to me. It's just something I saw happening to someone else."

Relief flooded through Mary's veins, tempered by her need to know what he had seen that was so bad he felt the need to tell her about it.

Like he had been reading her mind, Peter said. "They'd be mad if they knew I told you."

"They won't," she said, not sure if that was true or not. "Please, just tell me what happened."

"It's been going on for maybe a couple of weeks now. There's four of them and they've been ganging up on this other kid. They stand with him at the bus stop and kind of... mess about with him until the bus comes."

"Mess about?" A thought had struck Mary. Had Peter invented this other boy? It was possible that they were bullying Peter but he didn't want to admit it. She bit down on her nail but he didn't seem to notice.

"They push him sometimes. Call him names, that sort of thing. They called him a geek once, and it reminded me how you said geeks rule the world."

"They do. Did you tell them that?"

"No. Jeez, mum, I'm not about to go and speak to them am I? Then they'll come after me."

"Okay. Was that all that happened?"

Peter slouched even further down into his dressing gown. "Yesterday at school they were messing about, like normal. But then there was this car coming fast up the road. And they just grabbed him and they held him out right in front of the car. They pulled him back at the last minute, and the car kind of swerved. But I thought... I thought for a second the car was going to hit him."

Mary felt an almost physical blow to her stomach. "They did this to you?"

"No. I really wasn't kidding about that. It's another boy they've been doing it to. Someone a bit older."

"Someone you know?"

"Not really," he replied. "Someone *you* know."

"What?"

"It's Ewan Paterson. That's the boy that's been getting all the stick."

"Oh god."

"Maybe I shouldn't have said anything," Peter's mouth sagged at the corners.

"No, you did the right thing. It's just..." Mary ran a shaking hand over her hair. "I've just realised that I'm going to have to tell Bernie that her son is getting bullied. And you really think he was in danger?"

"Yeah. I mean, I don't think the boys meant to do it, not really. But he could have slipped or anything. It was proper scary."

"Okay. Thank you for telling me. I'm going to speak to Bernie."

Peter rubbed at an ink stain on the table. "She's going to kill someone isn't she?"

"Of course not."

"Are you lying?"

"Maybe."

Chapter 17: Bernie

Bernie was just back from a particularly gruelling session at the gym. Normally she was strict not to allow emotions to influence her work-out, but her time with the punch bag was definitely more intense with the idea of Deborah floating around in her head. When she came out of the gym she chucked her bag in the car and then checked her phone. There was a message from Mary saying to call her, but more of a worry was that she had three missed calls from Martha.

"What is it?" Bernie asked as soon as her sister answered the phone.

"It's Deborah. She's only gone and got herself arrested."

"What?"

"I know," Martha's voice sounded strained. "The police picked her up an hour ago. She called me to get her out, but how the hell she thinks I can do that, I don't know."

Bernie massaged her temples. "Why didn't she call me?"

"She said she didn't want to bother you."

"Bullshit. She probably knew if she called you then all the sisters would be up in arms. And she might get some sympathy, which she sure as hell won't get from me."

"She is in trouble though, isn't she? I mean, if they've actually arrested her…" Martha trailed off.

"Well, it means they reckon they've got enough evidence to justify an arrest. But other than that, it doesn't prove anything."

"What if she was involved? It'll be in the papers, everyone will know about it and –"

"She didn't do it," Bernie said, shutting down her sister's rising panic. "God Martha, you know her, she wouldn't kill someone."

There was a silence on the other end of the phone that suggested Martha wasn't as convinced.

"Listen, I'm going to go to the station right now and sort this all out. I'll phone you as soon as I know something."

"Okay," her sister said.

Bernie ended the call. She was annoyed on two fronts: that the Invergryff police had been stupid enough to arrest her mother for a murder she clearly didn't commit. And on the other side, she was annoyed that Deborah had managed to upset Martha, getting exactly the reaction the woman would have been looking for. No matter what happened with this case, Deborah had somehow managed to worm her way back into her daughter's lives and Bernie was struggling to stay calm. But if there was one thing she knew how to do it was to channel her rage into action.

It only took five minutes to drive over to the station where she parked on the double yellow lines on the road opposite. She almost dared a traffic warden to come along and ticket her.

The mood she was in they would end up with their ticket machine shoved somewhere painful.

Bernie crossed the road and was all set to barge into the police station when she saw Mary's boyfriend standing outside.

"Oi Bergerac," she called, making the man drop the sausage roll he had been holding.

"God, you could give a guy a warning," Walker replied, scooping up the pastry and depositing it in the bin.

"Warning? You've arrested my mother!" Bernie didn't bother trying to keep her voice down and a few officers in uniform started walking towards them, eager to see what the fuss was about.

"Ah, yes," Walker cleared his throat. "The Superintendent was worried she might be a flight risk."

"A flight risk? She's skint, she's got no friends, where is she going to go?"

"She said she spent every summer in Spain."

Bernie couldn't help but laugh. "She took us to the Costa del Sol once for five days when I was ten. She got drunk, fell asleep on a sunbed and ended up with third-degree burns. I don't think she's even got a valid passport these days. Didn't want to update the photo to one that makes her look her actual age."

Walker frowned. "Then why would she say –"

"Because she is a liar." Bernie hated that her voice was high with stress. "She wanted you to think she was the sort of person that spent her summers abroad, so she just lied about it. She doesn't ever think twice, just lies any time it makes things easier for her."

"Look, I'm sorry you're caught up in this, but we need to do our job. And the fact that you think your mother is a liar, doesn't that mean we should be looking into her involvement in all this?"

Bernie crossed her arms. "A liar. That's what I said. Not a murderer."

"She could be both," Walker said.

"Can't I just talk to her? I've always been able to see through her bullshit. You give me five minutes with her and I'll find out exactly what happened at Holly Moore's house the night before she was killed."

Walker hesitated and Bernie knew she had him.

"I'll talk to Macleod. But there's no guarantee he'll say yes. Wait in reception for me and I'll get back to you as soon as I can. And no correcting the punctuation on the signs this time."

Bernie just grinned back.

Twenty minutes later Detective Inspector Macleod arrived with Walker in tow.

"Why don't we go to my office?" Macleod said.

"Sure," Bernie said. She managed to hold her tongue until they reached that room and the door shut behind them.

"Is it true? You've arrested her?"

Macleod looked older than the last time she had seen him. His skin sagged and he looked like he could do with a good B vitamin complex supplement. Although there was no way she was helping him by giving him nutritional advice while he had her mother locked up.

"You know that I can't discuss it with you. Yes, I can confirm Deborah O'Flannery is in custody, but that's it."

"And you couldn't extend the courtesy of giving me a call? After all the cases we've helped you with. You came to the WWC just a few months ago, hired us as consultants. And now this. It's… it's disrespectful."

Macleod's mouth turned down at the corners. "I have a good deal of respect for you, Ms Paterson and that's exactly why I didn't get in touch. I can't leave the force open to accusations of bias. We have to make sure that this investigation goes by the book."

"And you're quite happy to waste your time arresting Deborah if it makes it look like your investigation is going somewhere."

"I assure you that that is not why she has been arrested."

Bernie felt an urge to slap Macleod's face and she just barely managed to resist it. "Then why have you arrested her?"

"I can't –"

"Right, you can't say. But I can tell you this: that woman didn't kill anyone. Not like that. I know her. If she had murdered someone you would have caught her immediately. Hell, she wouldn't have been able to resist confessing, just to be the centre of attention. I've spoken to her, if she was involved in this, I would know."

"Bernie, we had a good reason to take your mother into custody."

"Some physical evidence then," Bernie surmised. "Something that puts her at the crime scene. Well, you might have found that. But I know that there will be some explanation for it. You just have to work your way around Deborah's bullshit."

"That's why I thought Bernie might be able to help us," Walker said. "She might be able to get her mother to talk."

"I can't do anything that would cause us problems in court."

"It's not going to get that far," Bernie said. "Surely there must be a way that you can let me help you. It would be better for all of us if you could deal with Deborah and get back to chasing proper leads."

The room fell silent.

"Your mother is getting on a bit," Macleod said finally, leaning back in his chair and staring at the ceiling. "Ever had any symptoms of dementia?"

"Why?" Bernie wasn't sure what the Inspector was getting at.

"If she was considered a vulnerable adult you could sit in the interview room with her."

Bernie grinned. She had always thought that Macleod was the least stupid of all the Invergryff police officers.

"Excellent. Can I see your face when you describe her as a 'vulnerable adult'?"

"Maybe we'll just not mention it," Macleod said. "Tell her I've let you sit in as an adviser or something. Wouldn't want to start the interview on the wrong foot."

"Probably wise," Bernie said.

Walker went off to sort out the interview. Bernie and Macleod sat in a silence that while not comfortable, didn't feel quite as charged with anger as it had previously.

When everything had been arranged, Walker returned to lead them to the custody suite. While some junior officers went to get her mother, Bernie followed the others into one of the interview rooms. The smell of stale sweat and overly floral cleaning fluids threatened to make her gag, but she managed to take small breaths.

After a few minutes, Deborah was led in by two young constables. Bernie was disappointed to see that they hadn't bothered with handcuffs. That would have been an image to treasure.

"Thank you so much," Deborah said as they showed her to her seat. Then she clocked Bernie.

"I wasn't expecting to see you here," she said.

Bernie fixed a smile onto her face. "I thought you might need someone with you."

Deborah sucked at her cheeks but didn't offer a reply.

The police officers did the usual business of getting everyone to say their names for the tape and explaining to Deborah what her rights were.

"Ms O'Flannery, we have arrested you in connection with the unlawful death of Holly Moore. Do you understand why you're here?"

"Well, I know that you think I'm involved in this dreadful thing, but I can't quite imagine why."

"You admitted to us that you had had a disagreement with Mrs Moore."

"A little fall-out between friends. I've already explained all that."

Bernie was glad to see that Macleod wasn't having any time for her mother's silliness.

"I think it was more than a little fall-out, wasn't it? We've found an email exchange between the two of you that got quite heated."

Walker pushed a set of printouts over to the other side of the table. Bernie scanned them and wasn't surprised to see that Deborah's attitude towards Moore had turned nasty very quickly.

"That was a business matter," Deborah said, not even looking down at the papers.

"You called her a selfish bitch," Bernie said, pointing to the offending sentence.

"I am very passionate about my work," Deborah said. "And so was Holly. I suppose you might say it was a clash of personalities. If you must know, I felt very let down by the whole episode. I gave everything I had to those ladies and I was upset that they weren't doing the same for me."

"And the argument on Saturday night?"

"Perhaps it was more heated than I said before. It's hard to remember these things."

Macleod glared at her. "You realise how important it is to tell us the truth, don't you, Mrs O'Flannery?"

Deborah took out a tissue and wiped at the corner of her eyes. "Dear me, I hope I haven't been too much of a nuisance. I've only tried to be honest. It's been such a traumatic time, I'm sure I don't quite know what I said."

"Did you threaten Mrs Moore."

"Of course not."

"But you did say in one email that 'she would wish she'd never been born'."

"Well, if it's on your little printout then I must have, but I'm sure I don't remember."

"Please do not lie to us, Mrs O'Flannery."

"I didn't lie. But maybe… well, I might have been a little confused."

She felt like rolling her eyes. Deborah O'Flannery had clearly decided on the Rupert Murdoch phone hacking approach: pretend to be a doddery old fool and hope that it gets you off. Mind you, it had worked for Murdoch so maybe she was on to something.

"Let's move on from the emails for a moment. I would like to show you some pictures of Mrs Moore's car."

"The car?" Bernie asked. "What happened to the car?"

"Why don't you let your mother tell us?"

Deborah looked at the ceiling and said nothing.

Ignoring her, Walker placed three enlarged photographs on the table. Each showed a close-up of a pink car. When Bernie leaned forward she could see there were scratches all along one side. She was getting a horrible feeling she knew what was coming.

"We found fingerprint evidence on the car. We matched those fingerprints to the ones you provided when you were arrested."

Deborah put her hands over her eyes. "Oh, I have been awfully silly, haven't I?"

"Criminal damage isn't 'silly', Mrs O'Flannery."

"I lost my temper. I don't even really remember it. Perhaps I blacked out or something."

"Are you admitting that you damaged Mrs Moore's car?" Walker probed.

"I think I might have."

"You idiot," Bernie said.

"That is not very helpful, Bernadette." Deborah turned to face the officers. "You see what I have to put up with? My daughter has always blamed me for everything terrible in her life. You know that she used to be so awfully fat. Dreadful it was. But look at her now! Skinny as anything. In fact, darling, you could probably put on a few pounds. Round out that figure a little."

Do not commit murder in a police station, Bernie told herself. Even you probably couldn't talk your way out of it.

"If we could return to the matter at hand," Macleod said sternly. "Now, my suggestion is that Holly Moore worked out that it was you that damaged her car. And when you arrived at her house on Saturday night she threatened to report you. And that's why you came back later in the evening and killed her."

"You are just telling stories now," Deborah said, her neck turning red. "I don't have to listen to this."

"You do," Bernie reminded her. "Come on, just tell them the truth and you might have a chance of getting out of here."

"Well, I can't see what more I can tell you. I did go around to Holly's house on Saturday night, around eight o'clock. And yes, we did have a little disagreement. She mentioned that car of hers. I shouldn't have lost my temper, but the thing is when I started dare2dream she said it would only be a few months before I was driving my own Range Rover. And of course, that never happened. Jealousy. I have spent my whole life fighting off jealous women. Holly was jealous that I was shooting up through the ranks and she must have seen me as a threat."

"Perhaps she saw you as a threat because you keyed her car?" Walker suggested.

"I apologised for that. You see, I had no reason to kill Holly. By the end of our meeting, both of us knew exactly where we stood. I wanted to strike out on my own and she wanted me to leave the company anyway. I won't say we parted as friends, but I certainly had no reason to come back and kill her later on."

"But my problem, Mrs O'Flannery is that you're not a credible witness. You lied to us about the car."

Deborah put her hands over her eyes again. "I just... I didn't want anyone to think I was a bad person. I just got carried away."

She started making little sobbing sounds. If Bernie had been in charge she would have told the woman to buck up, but Macleod felt it was time to end the interview.

Within a few minutes Deborah was back in her holding cell and Bernie was back in the Detective Inspector's office, feeling like she'd been in an hour-long boxercise class.

"She's quite something," Macleod said, slumping in his chair.

"Oh aye, she is that. But she's not a killer. You see that now don't you?"

Macleod grunted. "We probably don't have enough to hold her on the murder charge. We could have her charged with the criminal damage, not to mention wasting police time. Obstructing an investigation. Something like that."

"But then you would have to spend even longer with me in your office," Bernie said.

"True," Macleod said, running his palm over his eyes. "Walker, get the paperwork done. We'll get her released to you right now."

"No thanks, I'm not taking her home."

"What?"

"I don't want to spend another minute with her. Tell her to get a taxi."

It was funny what makes some people snap. Bernie was shocked at the language that came out of Macleod's mouth.

"I always thought Shetlanders didn't like swearing," she said once he was finished.

Macleod merely glared at her and walked out of the room. It seemed that he had left Walker in charge. That suited Bernie just fine. She had a bone to pick with the man anyway.

"I hear you've been messing our Mary about," she said once

they were alone.

"What? No, I haven't done anything," he said. "Where has this come from?"

"You've been avoiding her questions about your family."

"She told you that?"

"I overheard her talking to Liz. She sounded upset. You realise that I do not take kindly to any individual who upsets Mary Plunkett."

"I'm sure it was nothing major," Walker said, his neck turning red. "I don't like talking about my family. We don't get on. Surely you of all people can understand that."

"Oh yes, I understand. You've just spent an hour with my mother. And it might surprise you to learn that I used to be pretty screwed up about it all. But you know what I did?"

"What?"

"I talked to my husband, you dumbass. Talk to Mary. Tell her all your problems, even the ones that you don't like to think about. It might just make you feel better."

Walker didn't look convinced. It was infuriating when people didn't know what was good for them. Bernie, however, didn't see the point in saying anything else. If he couldn't fix things with Mary then he wasn't worth her time in the first place.

Chapter 18: Walker

After the Bernie Paterson incident at the station, Walker thought it might be best to stay out of the way for a while. So when Suzie asked him if he'd like to come and speak to the pathologist with her, he jumped at the chance.

"I want to check out the time of death with him," she said as they headed over to the mortuary. "If we have a definitive time frame to work on then I can look at the doorbell camera footage we got from the neighbours and see if there's anything conclusive."

Walker knew that Suzie was being optimistic. The fact was that they were chronically short on suspects. They had released Bernie's mother, and even though the Inspector had grumbled about it, no one thought she was the killer. Macleod seemed to still be hoping that they might find a hole in James Moore's alibi as he seemed to be the only person who benefitted from his wife's death. Then there was still the business angle, but according to the civilian contractor that handled these types of investigations, getting anywhere with their banking records was proving to be tricky.

Walker drove them to the central hospital in Invergryff. Like most mortuaries, this one was in the basement, for obvious reasons. It was hard not to find those sorts of places creepy. Especially as Mary had insisted on them watching a Stephen King marathon at the weekend. He half expected undead bodies to lurch around every corner.

The forensic pathologist met them in the mortuary reception area. Her name was Professor Ellie Rankin and Walker was surprised to see she was younger than he was. Once they got into the dissection room, however, the way she happily wielded the scalpel told him that she wasn't lacking experience.

"We've already done our preliminary incisions as you can see," Professor Rankin said, not feeling the need for any small talk. "Toxicology should be back soon, and there was some evidence of alcohol use in the liver. Not enough to kill her, but she drank more than the recommended amount."

"Cause of death?" Suzie barked.

"Patience please," the Professor said with a little shake of her head that indicated disappointment at the police officer asking to hurry along. "If you look at the wound site you're going to see where the main trauma is. We're looking at your traditional 'blunt object to the head', I'm afraid. Was there any sign of a weapon at the house?"

"No," Walker said. "We think the killer took it with them."

"Pity. You're looking for something around ten to fifteen centimetres across and at least twenty centimetres long, slightly curved. Heavy. If you do find it I should be able to match it to the wound with reasonable accuracy."

The pathologist continued for several more minutes but there wasn't any information they didn't already know. Walker was feeling both hot and cold, the weird recycled air getting to him. By the time they took leave of the Professor he was feeling light-headed.

"Ugh, that place always turns my stomach," Suzie said and they exited the hospital.

"Really? I thought it was just me," Walker said, taking a deep gasping breath of fresh air. "You looked fine."

"You can't let those medical types know you're squeamish or they're even worse. Once you've had a jar of stomach contents waved under your nose you learn to get in and out as quickly as possible."

"Yeah, that's not helping," Walker said, bracing himself against the side of the patrol car. Thankfully the fresh air started to revive him and by the time he got into the driver's seat, he almost felt human again.

Walker turned the key in the ignition. "You know, I haven't managed to get the lawyer on the phone yet."

"The lawyer?"

"The one that Holly had spoken to about her divorce. I was hoping he might know a bit more about the settlement she was after with James Moore. But every time I've phoned he's been out or in a meeting."

"Are they local?"

"Glasgow."

"Why don't we swing by?"

Walker was happy to drive them over to the lawyer's office. He knew that Suzie was still hoping for the breakthrough that she hadn't found with the pathologist. Neither of them wanted to go back to Macleod empty-handed. The senior officer's face was getting more miserable with every passing hour and Walker knew he must be facing pressure to get a result.

The motorway was busy as usual, but they made it to Glasgow before even a lawyer would finish work. Walker had to circle the street a couple of times before they found a parking space, but soon enough they were outside the offices of Central Legal Ltd.

Gone were the days were lawyers' offices were all dark wood and musty old volumes of books. The offices of Holly Moore's lawyer looked more like walking into a private dental surgery. The walls were white with uncomfortable-looking plastic furniture strewn around and some dreadful abstract paintings bringing a little colour. Walker had been spending most of his time in the maximalist chaos of Mary Plunkett's house and the lack of clutter was making him edgy.

Luckily, it didn't take long before they were shown into the office of Mitchell Howe, Holly Moore's lawyer. If the lawyer's offices didn't live up to the stereotype, Walker was pleased to see that Howe with his portly figure and tiny round glasses could have walked right out of a TV courtroom.

"I was so sorry to hear about Holly's death," Howe said, showing them to a pair of plastic seats in front of his desk. "She had been a client for less than a year, but she seemed like a good person."

"Her sister told us that she had been in touch with you

recently," Walker said.

Howe squirmed in his chair. "Ah yes. You see, I don't know how much I can tell you. My client may be deceased, but I still have a duty to her estate."

"We can get a warrant of course," Suzie replied. "But perhaps you could tell us anything that you think wouldn't be covered by client privilege. We know that she was getting a divorce."

"Well, I can tell you that Holly had started the divorce paperwork, but it was still in the early stages."

"Was James Moore aware of this?"

"As far as I know. We hadn't attempted to reach him yet. I think Holly was hoping they might be able to conclude the matter with the minimum of fuss."

"And she didn't mention any concerns or worries at all?"

"Nothing that suggested she might be murdered," Howe replied with a tight smile. "She was full of life. I must say that even though she was getting divorced, she was more excited about her business than anything else. I didn't get the feeling that her marriage break-up was slowing her down."

That was as far as the lawyer would go when it came to giving away any of Holly's secrets. After a few more minutes of fruitless questioning, Suzie and Walker stood up to leave.

"Hang on a minute," Walker said as they were walking out of Howe's office. "You said that you were the lawyer for her business as well. As far as we understood, they were just a small start-up company. What would they need a lawyer for?"

"I can't tell you that," Howe said, but it was enough to get Walker thinking.

"Why would a small business selling makeup and online coaching need a lawyer?" he asked Suzie when they were back in the car.

"I don't know. Why does any business need legal advice?"

"If they were in some sort of legal trouble. Maybe someone was suing them?"

Suzie nodded. "Could be. But there's no way that Howe is going to talk about it. We might get a warrant, but we'll need to provide a good reason for one."

Walker went quiet. He was sure that dare2dream's legal problems might be relevant to the case, but he wasn't sure how to convince anyone else.

Chapter 19: Liz

Liz had been scrolling through social media pages about dare2dream and Better Life Now all day and it was driving her mad. She was looking for someone that she could contact to spill the dirt about the two companies, but so far most of the messages had been irritatingly positive. All the online reviews, particularly of the larger company, were glowing, but Liz suspected they simply removed anything that wasn't five stars.

After a while she gave up on Better Life Now – it was simply too polished, too media-managed for her to find anything and went back to the earliest social media posts by Holly and Bella about dare2dream.

After another hour, the flood of sycophantic 'hun' messages was giving Liz a headache. She was becoming so numb to the heart emojis and love-bombing that she almost missed the crucial post as she scrolled past. It took her a second before her brain caught up with her eyes and she went back to the anomalous entry. It was a short post by someone called Kelly Macpherson.

Still waiting on my #refund biatches!

Liz's first thought was that Holly must have missed this message, as surely she would have deleted anything so negative. Then she read the replies:

Some people just can't hack the pace! Bella Terrance

Haters gonna u no what. Holly Moore

What was interesting was that other people had joined in slagging Kelly off, including a certain Didi (*losers gonna weep lololol*) until it looked like a landslide in support of dare2dream. Liz had to hand it to them, the sisters certainly knew how to rally their troops. And how to use social media trolling to their advantage.

Her interest piqued, Liz looked up Kelly Macpherson who it turned out lived in a small village just to the North of Invergryff. Kelly's social media pages were fascinating. Up until a month ago, she seemed to have been a fully-fledged dare2dream devotee. Most of her posts were gushing about how amazing the coaching was and what wonderful inspirational people Holly and Bella were. Then in March, the posts switched. There were cryptic references to 'false friends' and 'haters' and some posts clearly aimed at criticising the company.

Anyone think that people should sort their own lives out before advising others???

This was followed by an emoji with a hand over its mouth, like she had said something controversial.

There were a few replies to this, none of them from names that Liz recognised, but there were also some people who had clicked the 'angry' emoji reaction. Liz hovered over this to see what names came up.

Ahah! One of the people who had reacted angrily was Holly Moore. The other was someone called David Vincent, but when Liz looked him up he was in his seventies and seemed to react to every post that Kelly put up, so she figured he had probably just hit the wrong button.

It was enough, combined with the earlier mention of a refund, for Liz to search for where Kelly worked. Luckily, it didn't take too long. Kelly had written a post a year ago that she was 'moving salon' to a nearby town and gave the address of the hairdressers. Liz picked up the phone and placed the call.

"Hi, I'm looking for Kelly Macpherson, does she work here?"

"Yes, Kelly's in. Hang on a sec and I'll get her."

Liz listened to the hum of the hairdryers in the background while she waited for Kelly to come to the phone.

"Hello?"

"Hi Kelly, I'm Liz Okoro. I was wondering if I could talk to you about dare2dream?"

"You're not the bloody lawyer are you?"

"No. Why would you think that?"

"Because that cow Holly told me that she was going to set her lawyers on me. I said go ahead, waste your own time."

"You heard that Holly died, right?"

"Yeah. Very sad." Kelly wasn't even pretending to care. Liz decided it was best to be honest with the woman.

"I'm actually a private investigator. I've heard that dare2dream has some suspect business practices and I'm looking for anyone with information."

"You reckon you can get me my money back?" Kelly said, her tone more interested now.

"Probably not. But I can buy you dinner if you're willing to help me out. And you might be able to help me take down the company and make sure no one else is exploited."

There was a short pause, then Kelly said: "All right, I finish up in half an hour."

"Great, I'll meet you outside." Liz said and then she ended the call. She just had time to fix her makeup and grab her laptop bag before she had to drive out of town to find the tiny hairdressing salon where Kelly worked.

The salon was called 'Hair by Salome', and Liz had a feeling that it might be a made-up name. She didn't think any kid would survive their school days in central Scotland called Salome. But then, one of the kids in her son's class was called Badger, so maybe she was being too hasty.

By the time she pulled up, Kelly was already waiting outside.

"You still buying dinner?" The woman asked when Liz turned up. "Coz I'm bloody starving." She had a friendly face, the sort of person who laughed at the end of every sentence accompanied by a husky voice that sounded like she smoked forty a day.

"Yep, where do you want to go?"

Kelly chose a chippie over the road which had a few tables for sit-down customers. Liz, who was still trying to lose the baby weight, ordered a chip buttie and tried not to think too much about the calories. Kelly ordered a full fish supper and upended half a bottle of vinegar on it.

"God, I'm so hungry. It's been non-stop today. We do an OAPs discount on a Wednesday and we're always mobbed. And the stories they tell! Filthy doesn't cover it. I need a wash after."

On that disturbing note, Liz decided to turn the conversation towards the case.

"I said to you on the phone that I'm a private investigator. We're looking into dare2dream and Better Life Now. Were you a member of both these organisations?"

"Just dare2dream on the makeup side of things," Kelly pierced a piece of fish with her fork. "They never wanted me for the other stuff. Only their 'selected partners' got to do the investing side of things. Guess they knew I didn't have any more money they could nick."

"You think they stole your money?"

"I know they did. It just pisses me off that I didn't work it out earlier." Kelly went on to explain how she had started up by getting recruited through social media. "They sent me these dead nice messages, saying they really liked my 'look' and that I would be just the sort of person that would make a great 'brand ambassador'. They made it sound like I was going to be a model or something."

"When was this?"

"About six months ago. I went for a meeting with maybe six or seven other people in a café in Invergryff. Holly had this big case full of makeup and was showing us how great it was. I mean, at the time I thought it was great too, but what did I know? And somehow it went from being a bunch of free samples to us spending two hundred quid to buy a 'marketing pack'. You're going to think I'm a right eejit but I paid it. So did everyone else there, so it wasn't just me getting conned."

"Do you know the names of the others?"

"I can look it up for you later if you want. But they're still fully into dare2dream so I don't think you'll get much sense out of them."

"What made you change your mind about the company?" Liz asked.

"I think I always had my doubts. But the problem was, the more money I threw at this stupid business, the more I didn't feel like I could quit. I just about managed to sell the initial two hundred quid worth of stuff, mostly by begging my friends to buy it. And honestly, Holly and Bella made it sound like I'd done bloody brilliantly. They called me 'Seller of the Month', put my picture up online and all that crap. So yet, before you know it I've invested in the gold product pack and that was just over a grand."

"A thousand pounds?"

"I know. And I'd already fobbed off so much of this stuff on my family that they were all skint. Thank god I never got any of them to join the company. Holly kept saying that I should try and convince my mum and my sister to join, but I was already having doubts by this point."

Kelly paused to chew on a chip. "And then I did something really stupid. Holly said to me: well, why don't you think about selling to your customers at work."

"Uh oh," Liz could see where this was going.

"Yep. So I tried selling this crap at my old salon, and the boss there found out. And then I was out on my arse, with no job and nothing to show for it but a suitcase full of crappy makeup. I'm so lucky that one of my pals opened this salon here and took me on. But I'd learned my lesson, so I took all the makeup I had left back to Holly and asked for a refund."

"She said no?"

"Laughed in my face. If I couldn't make it work, well that was my fault wasn't it? It wasn't her crappy products. And that's where I am now, still stuck with this crap that no one would buy."

"And Holly threatened to put the lawyers onto you?"

"Aye. That was after I had sent her some nasty emails. And maybe a few not-so-polite phone calls after I'd had a few too many wines one night. But before you ask, I didn't murder her. I was visiting my mum in Cardiff at the weekend, only got back yesterday."

"Fair enough," Liz said. They chatted a little longer while

Kelly finished her chips, but there wasn't much she could add. She didn't know anyone else in the company that didn't get on with Holly, and she had been shocked when the woman had been murdered.

"Thanks for dinner," Kelly said, grabbing her coat.

"Oh, one more thing, just because I'm nosy," Liz said as the woman got up to leave. "Who's Salome?"

"Who?"

"The name of the hairdressers."

"Oh." Kelly cackled a laugh. "That was Sharon's idea. There was already a 'Hair by Sharon', see? I think she thought it sounded exotic."

"Thought as much. Thanks for your help"

Chapter 20: Mary

Mary had been undercover for the WWC before, but it had generally meant visiting a hotel and pretending to be a guest while a client's husband or wife was checking in with someone they shouldn't be. Those occasions had been short and hadn't needed much research. To infiltrate Holly Moore's business, she would have to put in a bit more effort.

As Maria Johnstone, Mary had spent the morning getting ready to look like the perfect person to be recruited into dare2dream. She sorted through some of her least garish outfits and made sure that they were well-worn, as befitted someone who could use a little extra money. In truth, that was basically what Mary had looked like when she first came to Invergryff, fresh from a split with her husband and becoming a newly single mother to four children.

Outfit acquired, Mary read back over the background file that she and Liz had put together. Maria, they had decided, was on the edge of big financial drama. She only worked part-time in the bank, and her ex had stopped paying her child maintenance. They had been sure to write a few social media posts slagging off the imaginary ex-husband, and Mary had started feeling outraged on her alter-ego's behalf. She had named the ex-husband Tam, which she had been sure to tell the others was practically Matt backwards. No one had laughed, but Mary had been pleased nonetheless.

The hardest part of her undercover plan was how to get

recruited. Their first idea had been to go after Bella Terrance herself, but Liz had mentioned that she had just lost her sister so they decided she might not be that interested in recruitment right now. Instead, Liz and Mary had persuaded Bernie to call her mother and find out the details of the woman who had first recruited Deborah.

Her name was Michelle Rallie and she lived in Hillend, a part of Invergryff that Mary didn't know well. When she drove over there she realised that it was one section of a sprawl of a housing estate that had been built in the nineties. The houses were nice enough but so close together that you would have to get on with your neighbours really well.

Mary wasn't going to turn up at the woman's house, so instead of turning into the estate she carried on along the road until she came to a small block of shops. Liz had found out through her research that as well as being an 'ambassador' for dare2dream, Michelle also worked in a natural health shop just around the corner.

It was interesting, Mary thought as she found a parking space outside the shop, that although everyone talked about how brilliant dare2dream was Michelle Rallie still had to work in a shop to supplement her income. Not that Maria Johnstone would have thought about that, she reminded herself. Her alter ego was ready to be convinced by anything. She took a deep breath, slumped her shoulders a little more than usual and opened the door to the shop.

The first thing she noticed was the sickly smell of incense. Mary had never been much of a fan of what Bernie Paterson would surely have called 'hippy shops' and Hillend Health seemed to be the archetype of that sort of place. There were shelves of orange salt lamps, a vast selection of crystals and more CBD products than you could shake a stick at.

Alongside all of this was a bay of Solaverse makeup. Mary didn't have to fake her interest in this. It was the first time she had actually seen any of the products apart from online. As she picked up a small bottle of moisturizer that was listed at over twenty quid, she heard the clack of heels coming towards her.

"Can I help you?" Michelle Rallie was slimmer than she had looked online, verging on gaunt. She had on one of those flowing dresses that Mary always thought looked cute on other people but made her look like a potato. Her hair was long and undyed so that grey peppered the black. Mary thought she looked kind of cool.

"Oh, I'm just looking. I heard that this stuff is really good, but it's a little out of my price range."

"It is fabulous," Michelle said. "I have some samples if you would like some."

Mary as Maria started gushing at the offer. "Thank you so much! I am having the worst week ever, that's so kind of you." She allowed Michelle to put some weird-smelling lotions onto her hands and wrists.

"Try some of this. It's great for the bags under your eyes."

Mary decided that the woman was referring to Maria's

Johnstone's eye bags, because Mary herself certainly didn't have any.

"Thanks, the kids have been keeping me up half the night. I only just came in here to buy a wee treat to cheer me up. Maybe one of your lovely, um, crystals?"

"Oh, I think we can find you something nicer than that," Michelle said firmly. "Try this age spot remover on your hands."

Mary did as directed. She had decided that Michelle was the sort of woman it was very difficult to say no to.

"There you are now, you can hardly tell your hands are those of a mother. And did you say you're doing it on your own?"

Mary nodded.

"It's so hard being a single parent, honestly, I think all of you guys are absolute super-stars."

"Thanks," Mary said, genuinely touched. Not everyone appreciated what it was like raising kids on your own.

"You know," Michelle gave her a wide smile. "I think you might be just the sort of person that my friends are looking for. I know this sounds a bit weird, but you seem like someone with a lot of skills that are just being wasted sitting at home."

"Well, I do work, actually," Mary said, trying not to seem too keen. "I do my sixteen hours in the bank so I can still get the benefits. I bet working here is more fun though!"

"Working in the shop? Yeah, it's fine. But I was thinking of something you could do from home. And you could still work in the bank, it would just be like a side hustle."

"A side hustle?"

"Exactly. I mean, you can see already how amazing these products are, right? They practically sell themselves."

Mary hoped that even for someone like Maria Johnstone that phrase would have rang alarm bells. "I don't know if I could commit to something like that. I mean, I'm pretty busy already."

Michelle squeezed her shoulder. "Don't do yourself down! I bet you would be amazing. It's all on your phone anyway, and we all spend plenty of time scrolling, right? Now you could make some money from it."

A headache from the incense combined with the floral scents on her skin was probing at Mary's temples. "I'm not too sure. I mean, it sounds great but…"

"Why don't you give me your number and I'll send you some more info. Absolutely no pressure."

"That would be great!" Mary said, happy that there was the possibility of exiting the shop in the near future. She gave her Maria Johnstone's burner phone number and Michelle practically glowed with joy.

"I think you're going to love it. Here, take one of these on me."

She popped the moisturizer into Mary's bag.

"Wow, thanks."

It wasn't until Mary arrived home that she managed to shake off a feeling of guilt for deceiving Michelle. The woman had seemed perfectly nice, friendly even. And she had given Mary free stuff that would presumably come out of her wages. Maybe Liz was wrong about the whole MLM thing. If everyone was enjoying being in the company then it wasn't hurting anyone, was it?

The kids were still at school so Mary made herself a cup of tea and a chocolate biscuit from the secret stash she kept under the sink. She had just settled down on the sofa when the doorbell went.

"I thought you were off chocolate before lunch," Bernie said as she walked in and hung up her coat.

"I think that was your idea," Mary said. "I never agreed to implement it. Would you like a coffee?"

"Yes please. I can't stay long as I've got weights training in half an hour but I wanted to know how you got on with Michelle. And I need to tell my sisters that Deborah is out of custody."

Mary's mouth fell open. "They arrested your mother?"

"Yep. I had an interesting chat with your boyfriend. Don't you worry, I didn't bust his balls too much."

"Thanks for the image," Mary grimaced. "Did you at least

convince them to let her go?"

"Eventually. But she doesn't help herself. If she only managed to tell the truth for five minutes then even the Invergryff plods wouldn't think she was capable of murder. But she kept inventing more and more ridiculous stories. Anyway, let's get back to your meeting with Michelle."

"Right." Mary tried to tear her mind away from Bernie giving Walker a bollocking. "Well, I'm not so sure she's going to turn out to be as bad as Liz was making out. I mean, she really seemed like she wanted to help me make a bit of money. And she gave me some free moisturizer. Smells a bit funny, but it goes on nicely."

"Looks like she hooked you straight away," Bernie said.

"She hooked Maria, don't you mean? I'm much more savvy."

Bernie rolled her eyes to let Mary know exactly what she thought of that. "You reckon she bought your identity?"

"Do you mean did I play the desperate single mother accurately enough? Yeah, I think I managed that one okay. She asked for my number and she's already texted me some stuff about the business. I forwarded it on to Liz for her to take a look at it."

"You did well," Bernie said and Mary was pleased. Then she remembered how Bernie had left her out of the meeting with Deborah and the pleasure at the compliment disappeared.

"Maybe I should come and see Deborah with you now that she's out of the police station," Mary said, testing the waters. "I mean, I could try and befriend her, that sort of thing."

"God no," Bernie said. "I can't think of anything worse."

"Right. Of course." Mary's heart sunk. "Do you know, I think I might have another tea? Be back in a second."

She retreated to the kitchen and stared out of the window. Why did she always feel the need to poke at an open wound? First she had asked Walker about his mother, now she was testing Bernie's commitment to their partnership. Mary opened the cupboards in search of sugary consolation. The thing was, surely she was right to find out about Walker's family? And her status in the WWC. It was all a bit of a nightmare.

A search of the bread bin revealed some yellow-stickered cakes she had picked up a few days ago. Moving quietly so that Bernie wouldn't hear her, Mary grabbed a cinnamon swirl and slowly peeled off the outer layer. Truly, she was an éclair girl. The crisp pastry with the confectioner's custard was always her go-to snack. But she had recently discovered that one of the supermarket bakeries on the high street made their own cinnamon rolls and now she was getting through half a dozen a week. It would have been more if she'd ever got around to sharing any with the kids.

"Are you eating something?" A voice shouted through from the other room.

"Nope," Mary said, stuffing the rest of the bun into her mouth. She grabbed her cup of tea and went back to sit with Bernie.

"I hope that's sugar on your top lip or I'm going to have a word with you about your lifestyle choices."

Mary rubbed her sleeve over her face. "It's sugar. Look, Bernie, I've got something to tell you and I don't want you to overreact."

"Is it about Deborah? Because if it beats her getting arrested I'd be impressed."

"It's not Deborah. It's about your Ewan." Trying to stick to the facts and not make things worse, Mary told Bernie what she had heard from Peter about Ewan and the other boys. When she had finished Bernie sat unmoving. Like one of those deep sea fish that hid under the sand until their prey went past and then they dragged a poor unsuspecting minnow into their jaws.

"Why are you looking at me like I'm about to pounce?" Bernie asked.

"Oh well, it's just, I thought you might be a bit angry. And people think – not me, of course – that you're a bit frightening when you're angry."

"I'm just going to think about it for a while," Bernie said, with all the appearance of a normal human being and not a psychopath. "Thank you for telling me."

"You're not mad at me?"

"For God's sake, why would I be mad at you?"

To her embarrassment, Mary could feel the tears forming

behind her eyes. "It's just… well, I never know what you think of me."

"What the hell are you getting so emotional for now?"

Mary sniffed. "The thing is, you only wanted Liz with you to go and interview your mother. And I guess I felt like now I'm a partner in the WWC you should be including me in stuff. I don't just want to be the one who always goes and gets the coffees, you know?"

"I always let you get the coffees so that you can buy yourself a muffin without me having to tell you off," Bernie said.

"Oh. Right."

"You did get a muffin the other day didn't you?"

Mary wiped her eyes. "Yeah. Blueberry and oats."

"And if I'd gone in with you I would have had to explain for the thousandth time that just because something has 'oats' written on the label it does not mean that it is healthy. That actually that muffin you wolfed down on the walk over with the coffees had more calories in it than a cheeseburger. So I thought it would be better for both of us if you just went in yourself."

"I guess… well, that's considerate of you," Mary said, her cheeks growing red. "But you still excluded me from the thing with Deborah."

"That's what you think, is it?"

"Well, yeah. I thought you didn't think I was up to it so you went with Liz instead."

"Honestly, woman, it must be exhausting being in your head with all the self-flagellation you get up to. I just didn't want another person to witness what the horror that is my mother. I mean, I want you to respect me. And when I'm around her…" Bernie winced, like this conversation was causing her physical pain. "I'm not myself. I'm that little girl that couldn't do anything right. And I hate being so weak."

"Bernie, you are an absolute monster. I mean… everyone I know is scared of you. Half of the police force hides under the desks when you walk into the room."

"Do you really mean that?"

"Of course."

"Thank you," Bernie said, and her face was cheered by the sort of grin that had police officers dropping to the floor.

"Why don't we get back to the case," Mary said when the silence grew a bit too long. "I know it's a tricky one because of Deborah, but we've never been beaten by an investigation before. If we work the case just like we always do, I'm sure we can get it solved."

"Of course. You have a think about our next moves. I'm going to head home to talk to Ewan."

"You will be careful, won't you? He's probably embarrassed about the whole thing, even though it's not his fault. Teenage boys are tricky."

"I will be my usual diplomatic self," Bernie replied.

"Great."

Chapter 21: Bernie

It was two hours since Bernie had found out that her son was being bullied and she hadn't done a single thing yet. To those who knew her as merely an acquaintance, that might have been surprising. But those who knew Bernie well knew that she liked to plan every move when she went on the attack. Like a cobra, she always waited until the correct moment to strike.

Not everyone seemed to have confidence in her ability to deal with the situation. Bernie had been fielding calls from Mary and Liz, each of them eager to offer their advice.

"Don't go off on him for not sticking up for himself," Liz had warned her. "You know that not everyone looks at the world like you."

Mary had been just as quick to judge, in her own roundabout way. "They're all just kids, really. I'm sure no one meant to hurt him."

That sort of thing was very easy to say when it wasn't your child that was involved, Bernie reflected. And she had seen Mary when her kids were threatened: the proverbial mongoose versus serpent sprung to mind.

It was funny, but Finn had been the one who had gone off on one when he found out. She had called him at work to tell him – making sure he wasn't up on a roof at the time – and he had blustered about 'giving the lads a piece of his mind.' But Bernie knew how that would look if the little arseholes reported a six and a half foot tall man threatening them. No, much better if Bernie dealt with it, nice and quietly.

When Ewan came home from school, Bernie was waiting in the kitchen. Her first instinct had been to sit at the table and force him to sit down too, interrogation style, but Liz had warned her 'not to go all Gestapo on him'. So she had tried to make it look a little less like an ambush.

"Hi," Ewan said, dropping his bag at the door and moving towards the stairs.

"Why don't you come in and chat with me," Bernie said, plastering a smile on her face. "I've bought cookies."

Ewan stiffened, pausing with one foot off the ground. "Cookies? What's up, is someone dying?"

"No, just a wee treat," Bernie said. Was she sweating? Why was this parenting thing harder than facing down murderers?

Enticed by the smell of sugar despite his wariness, Ewan came into the kitchen, grabbed a cookie and perched on the counter. He was almost as tall as she was now, his dark hair flopping over his forehead like he was trying to hide from the world. Bernie decided she needed to get on with it, or she would start feeling those soppy emotions that everyone else always had.

"I heard something funny the other day, and I wondered what you thought about it. Someone told me they had seen some kids pushing you around at school. So I wanted to know, are you having any trouble with the other kids?"

Ewan scrambled away, like a wounded animal. He sped

towards the patio door, reaching for the handle, only to find it was locked.

"Did you lock the door?"

"I knew you were a flight risk." Bernie reached into her pocket and held out a set of keys. "In fact, I've locked all the doors."

"Oh Mu-um," Ewan whined, flinging himself into one of the kitchen chairs. "I knew you were going to go mental about this."

"I am not going mental. If I'd been going mental I'd have tracked down exactly who these kids were, where they lived and gone around to have an intimate discussion with their parents. And then reported the lot of them to the police."

Ewan had his head in his hands and groaned.

"But I'm not doing that, am I? I mean, for one thing it's pretty hard to track them down until I know all their names. I don't suppose…"

"No, Mum, I'm not giving you their names."

Bernie took a deep breath. "You know what, Ewan, I think I'll eat a cookie."

Ewan's eyes went wide. "You? A cookie?"

"Yep. And it's full of refined sugar and hydrogenated fat, so I'm going to chew it slowly. And while I'm eating the cookie I won't be able to talk, right? So I want you to talk. Tell me everything that's going on and I won't be able to say a word.

Understand?"

"There's got to be a catch," her son said, peering at her from under his hair.

"Nope. Except for the damage to my gut health."

She picked up the cookie. It had chocolate chips and they weren't even dark chocolate. She took a small bite and waved at her son to get started.

Ewan slumped even further down in his chair, like his shoulders were eating his neck. "Ok, well it has kind of been building up for a while, you know? There are a few messaging groups, and they're meant to be used for homework and stuff. And then when the homework got handed in the groups kept going, and they would share memes and stuff. And then they started saying some nasty stuff. And I guess they thought it was funny to direct it all at me."

Bernie sucked a piece of chocolate out of her teeth. This was not what she had expected. Was this the same group of kids that had been physically bullying him? She wanted to ask, but instead took a second bite.

"The worst though was that they got some photos of me and started editing them, making it look like I did all this gross stuff. I mean, the edits weren't good, so you could tell they were fake, but then they started sending them to a bunch of different people and now everyone in the school has been laughing at them. At me, I guess."

She was crunching the cookie so hard that she was in danger of cracking a tooth.

"And I know you're going to say: tell the teachers! But the teachers don't give a crap. Unless it's some sort of 'ism' like racism or homophobia, then they can't do anything. Being mean doesn't really matter."

Bernie really wanted to argue this one, but she still had half a cookie left. She shoved it into her mouth.

"I just couldn't make it stop, mum. I kept thinking they would get bored, but it's like they know other people will laugh if they make fun of me. And now they've started pushing me around too. I don't know what to do."

Ewan hid his face in his arms. The cookie was gone, but Bernie still didn't speak. She didn't know what to say. It wasn't often that Bernie Paterson was speechless, but it was happening right now.

She got up from her chair and went over and wrapped her arms around him.

"I'm sorry this is happening to you. Kids can be right arseholes and it's nothing to do with you. That's the key thing. It's not your fault that they've picked you for their target."

"What am I going to do, mum?"

"I'm not sure yet. But I reckon we can work it out together. As a team. You don't have to solve it all on your own."

Ewan managed a weak nod.

"How did you find out anyway?" he asked, wiping his eyes on his shirt.

"It's Invergryff," Bernie shrugged. "You know that there are no secrets here. And besides, I'm a PI. It's kind of my job."

"Wish you didn't have to do your job with me," Ewan sniffed.

"Me too."

Chapter 22: Walker

There was an air of excitement at the police station when Macleod called them into the incident room. Walker could see that Macleod had something from the way he was ushering them in as fast as possible. It was about time: leads had been hard to come by so far in the Holly Moore case.

"All right everyone, sit down where you can see the smartboard," he said. "We've just got a decent result on the doorbell footage from the neighbours. DS O'Conner has pulled it out of the hat on this one."

Suzie O'Conner preened a little in her seat. "It wasn't just me, sir, the techs did a really good job on the video. There were hundreds of hours of footage to go through before we got something."

The last few stragglers arrived and Macleod shut the door behind them. The atmosphere in the room tingled with anticipation and Walker leaned forward so that he got a good view of the screen.

Macleod brought up the video file. "Suzie, why don't you take us through what we're looking at?"

She joined him at the screen. "All right, we're going to start with Saturday evening. Unfortunately, the victim herself didn't have a doorbell camera. They had an alarm system, but that wasn't set at the time of the murder."

"We asked her husband about that," Macleod interjected. "But apparently they never bothered to set it."

This wasn't uncommon, Walker knew. People thought just having the alarm sign on the outside of their house was deterrent enough. Perhaps if Holly had set the alarm, she might never have been murdered in the first place, he thought, knowing that everyone in the room was thinking the same.

"So what we did was get a few PCs to take all the footage from properties on the streets around the house. We found four doorbell cameras that had useful footage. I've marked them on a map that's in the file to show how they relate to the scene of crime and you can look at that later."

"Can we go through them chronologically?" Macleod asked.

"Sure, that's what I was going to suggest." Suzie pulled up the first video. "This is from one of our best vantage points. Three doors up from Holly Moore's house, this is the Stevenson household and you can see that their doorbell cam records the junction which is the only entrance to South Park Avenue for vehicles. Now, it is worth bearing in mind that to the north end of the street, there is a pedestrian walk-through that leads to the main road. We don't have any CCTV or other footage on that path, unfortunately, so if our assailant entered by foot, we could have missed them."

There was a murmur at that in the room.

"I know, but we've got some more positive results on the roads. So on the Saturday night we've got a list of the cars that came and went past the Stevensons' camera. Uniform is working through the list at the moment. Most of the cars belong to residents of the Avenue, but we've got half a dozen that we're still identifying. Unfortunately, several of the cars that pass are at the wrong angle to see their license plates."

"How inconsiderate," Macleod smiled.

"Right. But if I fast forward the footage I can show you one car that we can identify. At twelve minutes past eight on Saturday night we have this black Nissan Micra passing, positively identified as belonging to Deborah O'Flannery. The same car passes back past the camera at eight forty-seven."

They all leaned forward to see the grainy image of the car going past, but there was no way to tell who was driving or even how many people were in the car. "That seems to back up O'Flannery's story that she visited Moore, argued with her and then left," Macleod said. "Although the fact that we can't see her face means we can't let her off the hook yet."

"Any other cars after that?" Neil asked, saying what everyone else in the room was thinking.

Suzie nodded. "After O'Flannery's car leaves and before seven in the morning when people start going to work, we have a list of seven cars captured on the Stevensons' camera. Now we've identified three of these as belonging to residents. That leaves four cars unidentified. Is it all right for me to take you through them?"

Macleod inclined his head to give assent.

"All right. The first car is a blue or grey estate. It passes the camera just after ten o'clock and then doesn't go back the other way until two hours later."

"Would that fit with the time of death?" Macleod asked.

"It's on the earlier edge of our window, so we'd have to check with the pathologist if the time fits."

"Okay, we'll keep it as a possibility."

Suzie clicked play on another video. "This next car is interesting because it looks like it might have a private cab plate. If you look closely it's the rectangle just there. Now again, we're chasing that up with the local taxi companies but no hits yet. It enters the street at ten thirty-two and leaves two minutes later."

"Dropping someone off?" One of the Detective Constables asked.

"We assume so. We know from the other cameras along the street that the cab stops between house numbers four and seven, but we can't see if anyone got out. Here's the footage of it leaving."

Again, there wasn't much to see, and certainly no chance of identifying anyone in the car. A small furry dog with a flashing collar went past the camera, drawing a few 'ahs' from the dog lovers in the room, but that was the height of the excitement.

"Another one for the list. What about the last car?"

"This one passes by just twenty minutes after the taxi. No number plate again, but take a look at this image."

Walker found himself squinting at the screen, trying to see what Suzie had spotted. It showed the left-hand side of the car. Was there something on the wheel?

"This is your standard Audi, probably black or a very dark green or blue. But what's interesting is that it's got some custom hubcaps. We might be able to match these to the car if we find out who it belongs to."

"Excellent," Macleod said. "Get onto the local garages. And upload those images to the files so that everyone's got a copy. Is that it?"

"Almost." Suzie clicked to the last image which showed a white van. "Now, this guy comes in at seven in the morning. It looks like a trade van, but there's no logo on it. Could even be a hire. It's right at the outer end of the time-of-death, but we've got to count it as a possibility. As you can imagine, it's not going to be the easiest to trace."

Macleod grunted assent. An untraceable white van was not going to fill anyone on an investigation with joy. "All right, thanks for that Suzie. At least it gives us some leads to run down. Divvy it up between the constables and let's hope we can track these vehicles down."

Walker went back to his computer to go through the images that Suzie had uploaded. Was he looking at the transport that the killer had used after they murdered Holly Moore? It was a small chance, but better than nothing. He pulled up the files and got to work.

Chapter 23: Liz

It still felt weird for Liz to be out and about with no baby attached to her hip. Dave had taken Issy for the day, with only the minimum of grumbling about missing the golf on his day off. Enjoying the quiet, Liz had driven to Glasgow to meet with an old friend.

Doctor Naomi Floyd had been Liz's idol when she started her accountancy course in Glasgow. It was her first lecturing job so Naomi was only a little older than the students, which made her more approachable than the white-haired Profs in other classes. And the fact that the American Naomi was a loud black woman in a very white conservative campus had made her instantly compelling to Liz.

"Thank you for meeting with me," Liz said. She still felt like a student meeting an intimidating lecturer, even though Naomi was being perfectly friendly.

"No problem," Naomi said, her eyes crinkling at the corners. She had barely aged in the last twenty years and she was still the most stylish person in the room. "Always happy to meet with a former student. Although I was surprised to hear from you. Someone had told me that you left your firm last year."

"Gossip travels fast."

Naomi shrugged. "I like to hear how my students are doing, especially the brilliant ones. Now, am I right that you started some sort of research business?"

"Not exactly," Liz smiled, more pleased than she would admit at the compliment. "We do a fair bit of research, but it's actually a private investigation firm."

Naomi's smile wavered for a second. "I do hope you're not investigating me."

Liz laughed. "No, you don't need to worry. I'm just doing some background on a case that has turned out to be more complicated than we first assumed. I was hoping I could pick your brain about some of the financial aspects of it."

The other woman's smile returned. "That does sound interesting, more interesting than marking a hundred undergraduate papers on Keynesian Economics."

They both ordered some lunch. The café in Glasgow's west end had been chosen by Naomi and Liz was pleased to see that it wasn't too pretentious. A lot of the student dive bars had gone upmarket since she was here last, but you could still get a bacon roll in this place at least.

"There's a woman that's been killed," Liz explained once the waiter had left. "You've probably seen it on the news. She lived in Invergryff and she was the head of a company that I'm pretty sure was operating as an MLM. The company is called dare2dream and they branch off into all sorts of things, mainly selling makeup and some links to property investing. Lots of mention of 'coaching' on their website, without much information about what it is actually supposed to teach you."

"I know the type," Naomi said. "True MLMs have never had a firm foothold over here. Even companies that used the MLM model in the US like Avon and Tupperware were much more concerned with selling products rather than recruitment over here. But there has been an uptick in companies, particularly those that are mainly based online, using more predatory MLM practises. It sounds like you've come across one of them."

"Right. Holly and Bella – that's the woman who died and her sister – had this whole spiel on the website about how amazing it is, but it's the people at the bottom that have joined up that are losing money. I'm speaking to several of them now, and they're willing to testify against the company.

"What good will that do? Do you think you can take them to court?"

"I was hoping so," Liz replied. "They've stolen these people's hard earned cash. And these are single mums, elderly people, lots of them have mental health issues…"

"That doesn't mean you have a legal case."

Liz took a gulp of her coffee. "You're telling me there's nothing I can do to stop these people."

Doctor Floyd shrugged. "I guess my question to you would be why would you want to?"

"Well, because they need help. I mean, first of all, we want to solve Holly's murder. But I can't help but think that she wouldn't have been killed if her company hadn't been so dodgy."

"Do you have any evidence that she was killed because of this MLM business?"

"Not yet."

"So this is what... a personal crusade?"

Red heat crawled up Liz's neck. "I mean, you could see it like that. But don't you think someone needs to do something about these people? If nothing else, it's an exploitative business practice."

"Isn't Capitalism?"

"You're teasing me."

"A little," Naomi grinned. "I know that you're not a naïve kid, Liz, but it does sound like you've chosen an odd battle to fight. Yes, these companies are shady, but are they any shadier than that investment bank you used to work for? Do they do more harm?"

Liz thought about this for a moment. "I think they are."

"All right, convince me."

"Well, take the bank for example. Yes, they were ruthless and out to get every penny they could. But they operated within a set of rules that anyone could look up if they wanted to. Nothing was hidden about the business and it wasn't pretending to be something else."

"Point one against the MLMs," Naomi said, holding up her

index finger. "Next?"

"The sort of people they recruit are calculated to be the most vulnerable. People who are not the most educated, financially unstable, and desperate for any opportunity that comes their way. And those are exactly the sort of people who don't have a safety net when the MLM collapses. Which it will."

"Point two," Naomi was clearly enjoying herself. "Do you have a third?"

"And third they're on my patch. Recruiting people I know. And that just pisses me off."

The table shook as Naomi roared with laughter.

"Liz, you have turned into a badass since your student days. I have to say I'm here for it. Look, I can't tell you that it's going to be easy, but I understand why you want to take them down. Send me over all the details and I'll have a look into these suspect companies of yours. Hell, I might even make it a research project for some of my brighter post-grads."

"That would be amazing, thank you."

"No problem. But I will warn you about one thing. Don't do anything to libel these companies. Nothing that exposes you to being sued. The sketchier a business is, the more likely they are to get legal on you. And they won't have the moral compunctions you are so bothered by."

Liz understood the warning. But the truth was she was going to do anything to shut these guys down. She just had to hope that Naomi could help her do it.

Chapter 24: Mary

Maria Johnstone was sitting in a café waiting to be recruited and Mary Plunkett had come along for the ride. She had dressed in her dowdiest outfit and scraped her unwashed hair back into a bun. In fact, Mary was quite enjoying playing the Maria character. Since working with Bernie and especially the always well-turned-out Liz Okoro, Mary had felt she had to smarten herself up a bit when working. It was nice to dress down instead. She had sadly left off some of her more quirky items from fandom as Bernie said she had to dress 'normal', whatever that was.

She had ordered a tea and decided to forgo any of the cakes. This was disappointing, but she wanted to make it seem like money was tight for Maria, so she couldn't justify spending four quid on a muffin. She had just put the third sachet of sugar into her tea – it was a big cup – when the door opened and Michelle came into the café.

Mary was surprised to see that Michelle was not on her own. Walking in next to her was one of the most handsome men she had ever seen. He was around forty, wearing a tight black t-shirt and dark blue jeans with a tanned face and the sort of hair you normally saw presenting morning telly. He was like a beautiful Ken doll.

"I'm Tom Field, I work with Michelle," the man said. He pulled a chair over so that the three of them were sitting at the same table. Michelle gave her a smile and Mary noticed that the other woman was decidedly pink in the cheeks whenever Tom spoke to her. Mary was glad she could keep her composure rather better.

"I'm Mary – I mean, Maria. Maria Johnstone." Mary let out an embarrassed laugh that had nothing to do with her alter ego. He really was exceptionally handsome.

"It's lovely to meet you Maria," Tom said. "Michelle told me what a natural you are and I just had to come and see for myself. I hope you don't mind me crashing the party."

"No, of course not," Mary grabbed her cup to give her hands something to do and slopped some tea onto the table. Tom Field didn't seem to notice.

"Michelle tells me she already sent you some of our marketing material."

"She did," Mary nodded. "Although I must admit, I found it a bit confusing. I didn't really understand how the selling bit works."

"It's quite simple really. You'll be a Junior Star Seller for our fantastic Solaverse makeup range. You can start off with our low £199 seller's pack and from there the sky's the limit"

"Sellers pack? I don't…"

"But you don't think I came all the way up here just to talk about selling makeup, did you?"

"Um, well…"

"Solaverse is just the beginning. When you join dare2dream you get access to our holistic brand of lifestyle coaching. Pretty soon you'll be the CEO of your own personal empire."

Despite Tom's smooth exterior, Mary noted that the man's calf was jittering as he sat at the table. It wasn't until his t-shirt sleeve rode up a bit exposing a nicotine patch that she understood why.

"The thing is, I'm pretty busy with the kids and my job and everything," Mary was trying to seem reluctant. "And I wouldn't want to commit a lot of money to something that might not work out."

Tom shrugged to indicate these were minor matters. "For starters, you can pay in instalments. I'll get Gail in the office to call you about that. But what we're offering you here is the key to the door. Today you're selling one of the top beauty brands in Invergryff. Now, that in itself is not to be sniffed at. Dare2dream started off just like you, selling one brand. Now it's a premiere lifestyle destination. The founders have gone from strength to strength and now they are coaching others in all sorts of upskilling including property, investing, you name it."

"Poor Holly," Michelle said.

A flash of irritation swept over Tom's face although it was gone an instant later. "Yes, poor Holly," he added a little too late.

"Who is Holly?"

Michelle leaned forward. "Holly was one of the co-founders of dare2dream. She was killed just a few days ago."

"OMG!" Mary put on her best shocked face. "I saw on the news that someone had died. I had no idea she was involved in this business."

"Not just involved," Michelle said, her face animated by the sharing of gossip. "Holly was the founder of dare2dream."

Tom cleared his throat. "It is very sad. She was one of my best students. It's an absolute tragedy." Despite his words, Tom didn't seem overly upset. Although perhaps he was just hiding it well. "But here's the thing: Holly has left an incredible legacy. What she did here in Invergryff can be replicated by female entrepreneurs like you."

"Really?"

Tom reached over and held her hand. To Mary's disappointment, it was slightly clammy, like a used tea-towel.

"Take your time to think it over. I know I for one would like to have you on board."

If it was just for the joy of seeing Michelle's jealous face while Tom held her hand, Mary would have signed up then and there. But she knew that Maria Johnstone would not be in the position to easily get hold of two hundred quid, so she left the others in the café with a promise to get in touch later.

As Mary walked out of the door and turned in the direction of the car park, she noted that Tom and Michelle were now in a furious discussion. Tom's handsome face had turned grim with a sneer pulling at his mouth. Michelle looked surprised and more than a little upset, her body language screaming get me out of here. Mary didn't stay any longer in case they looked up and saw her but as she pulled her hood to stop the drizzling rain, she couldn't help but feel that Michelle was getting a right telling off. Most likely for bringing up the death of Holly Moore. The murder of the founder of their business did cast a bit of a damper on recruitment.

Still, even if it didn't go any further Mary knew that she had some good info to bring back to the others. For all the sisters claimed that dare2dream was an independent business, the very presence of Tom Field suggested otherwise. She couldn't wait to see what Liz could dig up on the man.

Chapter 25: Bernie

Bernie's mother had described her as a 'hot-head' after one of their many rows. It just went to show how little Deborah understood her daughter. Yes, Bernie was not afraid to stand up for herself, but her rage never ran hot. Instead, when she was angry she turned it into cold calculation, her furious brain working out exactly how to turn the situation to her advantage. It might even have been Deborah that she had to thank for that lesson. Even as a toddler she knew there was no point in crying. Her mother would never pick her up even if she did.

If she had ever felt like crying then it was when Ewan showed her the messages that he had received from his so-called friends at school. Instead of tears, she embraced the cold ice in her stomach and kept that feeling with her throughout the day. Now that it was the next morning, she was having crisis talks with her son in the kitchen.

"I think we need to talk to the school," Bernie said to Ewan once they had gone through everything in the messaging groups one more time. "I know you don't want to, but it is either that or I go whoop-ass at these lads' homes."

Ewan managed a half-smile. "Whoop-ass does sound good."

"I know. And believe me, if it was just me involved I would do it. But you still have to go to school with these kids. So much as I generally favour the nuclear option, maybe it's not the way to go right now."

"Wow mum, you're totally maturing," Ewan said.

"Cheeky." She drummed her fingers on the table. "You know that I was bullied at school, right?"

"Were you?"

"I was fat and it was the eighties." Bernie shrugged. "That was all it took back then. And because I was clever, that made it worse somehow. I think they would have liked me better if I had been stupid. But the fat girl coming top of the class? They couldn't have that, could they?"

"They don't like that I'm clever either," Ewan said. "Call me a swot."

"Wow, I didn't realise they even still used that word. I thought it was all 'bro' and 'skibiddi' now."

"Please don't ever say that again, mum," Ewan said, with the agony of embarrassing parents etched on his face.

"All right then."

They sat quietly for a while.

"How did you deal with it? The bullying I mean."

"At the time? Well, I mainly found some better friends and ignored the bullies until they got bored. They do get bored eventually. And then when my bully grew up and turned into an adult I got her sent to prison for fraud and extortion. But that's a story for another day."

"You really are tough, mum, aren't you?"

"Yes. That's the one thing those little pricks that are messing with you don't realise, Ewan. Every time you survive something like this it hurts. But the scar tissue makes you stronger. Makes you tougher. And it'll be the same for you."

She took a deep breath. "Now if I call the school and set up a meeting, what do you want to get out of it?"

Ewan stared at the ceiling. "I guess I just want it to stop. I don't want like a big public apology or anything like that. I just want the messages to stop."

"Okay, then that's what we'll tell the school." Bernie didn't add that she was going to employ her own very special whoop-ass when it came to the teachers. Because they should be aware of this sort of crap going on under their noses. And she was going to find out why nothing was being done about it. And then heads would roll, or if not, at least tilt awkwardly.

Ewan went off to school with the meeting arranged for three o'clock. Bernie had almost been tempted to let him stay off, but she knew that it only made things worse if you prolonged the agony. But if any of those little cretins tried anything with her son today, she would definitely lose the cool she had been working so hard to maintain. Bernie opened up her laptop and tried to concentrate on the case.

Just as she had downloaded Liz's latest file on dare2dream, Mary's number came up on Bernie's phone. She considered leaving it, but she didn't want to miss something important.

"I wanted to tell you about the meeting I had with Michelle today," Mary said when Bernie picked up the call. "It was so weird. There was this guy there called Tom and he was very charming but the long and the short of it is I need two hundred quid on expenses."

"Two hundred quid? I'm not paying for that many cakes."

"It's not for cake. It's for my introductory sellers pack. And, to be honest, I'll probably be able to pay it back once I sell the stuff."

"And how are you going to do that?"

"Well, Maria Johnstone will do it, won't she?"

"How exactly will she do that?" Bernie said, feeling her frustration growing.

"She's got her own social media, doesn't she? I'll sell it on that."

"Let me guess: hey hun, come buy this pile of crap, hashtag girlboss hashtag blahblahblah."

There was a long pause down the other end.

"Are you all right, Bernie?" Mary asked. "You don't sound yourself. Well, I mean you do, but you sound like you but even *worse* somehow."

"I'm not really in the mood to talk right now," Bernie replied.

"What happened? Is it Deborah?"

"No. It's Ewan. You were right about the other boys. And I've just found out some of those crappy kids have been bullying him online as well as shoving him around in person. They've been sending messages to his phone every single day after school."

"And what are you doing about it?"

"Well, my first thought was to find out their names, track down where they live and raise seven levels of hell on them and their weasely families."

"That's... that's one way to deal with it."

Bernie stifled a laugh. "I thought you wouldn't be impressed with that idea. I've gone with talking to the school. The softly-softly approach, even though I don't reckon it'll do any good."

"I'm glad. You need to let him fight his own battles," Mary said.

Bernie rolled her eyes. "I guess you've never had any problems with any of your kids, Supermum."

"I'm definitely not Supermum."

"Oh come on. Your kids adore you. You even do crafts. I hate crafts."

Mary shrugged. "You just have to be prepared to get a little messy."

"Gross. Look, I might not be the best mum where cooking or crafting or even hugging is concerned. But I can sure as hell protect my son from this little prick who wants to ruin his life."

"But they need to fight –"

"Their own battles. Yeah, you said," Bernie let a slow grin spread across her face. "But that doesn't mean I can't supply him with the weapons. I will try it your way. I will try the school and if they step up, then great. But if not, it's the nuclear option. And can you guess what the nuclear option is?"

She heard Mary sigh down the phone line.

"Is it you?"

"That's right. It's me, Bernie Paterson, nuclear bomb. And don't you forget it."

Chapter 26: Walker

Walker was finding it hard to see what James Moore's type was when it came to women. Leah Hill, his new girlfriend didn't seem to have much in common with Holly Moore. She was younger, that was the first obvious thing to notice, at least ten years younger than Holly. A slight figure made her look younger still and the sharp bob of dyed black hair suggested an edgier look than Holly Moore had.

Maybe that was the point, Walker thought. Perhaps Moore wanted someone completely different from his wife. It would have been interesting to know what Holly thought of the new woman. Leah certainly didn't seem shy about telling them what she thought about her predecessor.

"She was a nightmare," Leah Hill said as she leaned back on the sofa. She was wearing the sort of outfit that was designed for people to go to the gym in but instead was worn for buying ice-cream and watching telly. Walker wondered if she knew that you could see the outline of her underwear through the skin-tight leggings, and if she was bothered if she did.

"You didn't get on, then?" Detective Inspector Macleod asked.

"I mostly stayed out of her way. I mean, it's not like they were still together when I met James. Couples break up all the time, she didn't have to be such a bitch about it."

"Can you give us some examples of her bad behaviour," Walker asked. "Something concrete for us to go on."

"It was all about that stupid business with her. I tried some of that makeup once, it brought me out in a rash. She was always saying that James was trying to take her business away, but he didn't care about it. Why would he? He earned a whole lot more than she did."

Walker noticed Macleod was checking the time on his watch. It didn't feel like they were learning anything interesting from the woman. When Macleod had suggested Walker join him to interview Moore's new woman they had both hoped they might learn something relevant to the case. Not just name-calling between the current and ex-partners.

"Honestly, I don't know why James didn't report her to you guys," Leah said. "She was trying to ruin his life."

Walker wondered if the woman realised that she was making it sound like James Moore had a motive to murder his wife.

"Marriage break-ups can be difficult," Walker said.

"Aye, but she didn't need to be so horrible, did she? She was just bitter because he had moved on and she hadn't. She was totally delusional. I mean, one time just a couple of weeks ago she turned up here, shouting and screaming. I mean, you would think by her age she would be a bit more dignified, know what I mean? Everyone was looking out of the windows to see what was going on."

Leah's mouth twisted up at the corner, as if she had quite enjoyed the attention.

"What was she so upset about?" Walker asked.

"She said that James had been stealing money from the business. Said she could prove it. Total crap, of course."

"Of course," Macleod said, raising his eyebrows at Walker. "I suppose James told you that he hadn't stolen anything."

Belatedly, a wrinkle of concern appeared on the young woman's brow. "Well, of course he told me that. Because he would never steal from that woman. I told you, he didn't need to, did he."

"It's funny, because we've been looking into James Moore's finances as part of the investigation," Macleod told her. "And it doesn't seem like he's got that much money at all. Between paying off his wife's credit cards and paying the bills here, he seems to be pretty skint."

"What?" Leah's brow furrowed in annoyance. "Nah, you must have that wrong."

"Maybe you should ask him yourself."

She shook her head, like she was getting rid of what they were telling her.

"Can I ask you about your whereabouts on Saturday night into Sunday morning?"

"Well, I was out with my pals in the Crown bar until two-ish. But after that I just went home."

"By yourself?"

Leah jumped to her feet. "Just what exactly do you mean by

that? I've got a boyfriend who was working nightshift, remember? I wasn't out picking up other blokes."

"We have to ask these questions," Macleod said, unmoved by her outburst. "There's nothing personal about it. From what you've told us, your life will be easier now that Holly Moore is out of the way."

"That doesn't mean I'd kill the stupid cow," Leah said, sitting back down. "Wow, I never thought I'd be a suspect in a murder trial. It's like one of those social media things about true crime. Maybe they'll make a podcast about it."

Macleod's face showed exactly how he felt about that one. Walker felt it was time to step in.

"Do you drive, Ms Hill?"

"No."

Undeterred, he showed her pictures of the cars from the doorcam footage and asked if any of them were familiar. Leah Hill just shook her head.

"And none of these belong to James either?"

"Are you kidding? He drives a Range Rover, not any of those piles of crap."

Their last hope dashed, Macleod and Walker took their leave of Leah Hill. They already had another meeting with James Moore booked for the next day, but Walker could tell that neither of them was happy about where this lead was going.

"If James Moore did kill his wife then he's a lot cleverer than he seems," Macleod said as they began the drive back to the station.

"The WWC seem to think that someone connected with the dare2dream business might be responsible," Walker told him.

"They haven't given up investigating this then?" Macleod asked although he already knew the answer.

"With respect, when have you ever known Bernie Paterson to give anything up?"

"Fair point," Macleod said, his tone morose. They drove back to the station in miserable silence.

Chapter 27: Liz

Liz and Mary were having a brainstorming meeting about the case. They absolutely had not arranged to meet at Liz's house to order a takeaway pizza and discuss the situation with Bernie's son.

"Do you honestly think Bernie will be able to resist going off on one," Mary asked as they each grabbed a piece of piping hot deliciousness.

"I'm not worried about her losing her temper," Liz explained. "The thing is, even though she's hard as nails, she doesn't tend to scream and shout. It's much more calculated than that. I'm not worried about her causing a fuss today. I'm worried about her causing a catastrophe in about a week's time."

"That's not too comforting," Mary said. "Why don't we get to work? I need to get the idea of a Bernie Paterson catastrophe out of my head."

Liz took out her phone where she had made some notes on the case and started sorting through them.

"How are you getting on with the background on the business?" Mary asked.

"I'm waiting to hear back from one of my old lecturers," Liz explained. "She's going to see if there's any way we can prosecute these bastards. Although she did say that these sorts of companies are very careful to make themselves look legit."

"You don't think that you're —"

"Don't tell me I'm obsessed with this. I've already heard it all from Bernie. The thing is, we still don't have the first clue about who might have killed Holly Moore. And if we don't find another suspect then they'll keep on looking at Deborah. The MLM angle is the only other thing we have to go on."

Mary didn't look convinced. Liz was about to continue her little speech when there was a cry from upstairs.

"That's Issy wakening, I'll go and get her."

Baby Issy needed a quick change before she was ready to come downstairs and meet a member of her fan club.

"Ooh, give her over," Mary held out her arms as soon as she spotted them and Issy went over to her, happily burying her face into Mary's chest. "She's even cuter than ever. Aren't you sweetpea?"

"She wasn't so cute this morning when she was chewing on the skirting-board," Liz replied.

"Just getting her fibre in," Mary said, jiggling Issy into baby giggles. "I hope you don't mind me working here today but I wanted to tell you about my meeting with Michelle face-to-face."

"Did she get you to join her cult?"

"It's not a cult."

"That's what cultists always say," Liz told her.

"Well, the interesting thing about our meeting was that she didn't come alone. There was this guy with her. Very handsome but ever so slightly creepy."

"Guy? What guy?"

"He said his name was Tom Field."

Something nagged at the back of Liz's mind. "Tom Field? I've definitely seen that name somewhere. Can you watch Issy while I grab the laptop?"

By the time Liz had found her laptop and returned to the living room, Mary was sitting on the floor wearing a tiara and having a teddy bear tea party with Issy who looked like she was having the time of her life.

"Don't mind us," Mary said. "We're the princesses and the King is coming for dinner."

"I didn't think Princesses were very 2024," Liz said with a smile.

"As long as they do their own rescuing and fighting dragons, we're cool with it, isn't that right Issy?"

"Da-gons," Issy said, waving her tiara in a threatening manner.

Happy that her child was occupied, Liz turned on the laptop and found the case file for Holly Moore. With all the research she had done on the business side of things it was by far their largest document yet. Liz knew that Bernie and Mary thought she was going a bit over the top about the MLM angle, but she just hated the idea of people being exploited.

"Got you!" Liz called out, making Mary jump and spill her imaginary tea. "Remember I said that dare2dream was connected to this larger company, Better Life Now? Tom Field is one of the Directors."

"He did seem like one of the entrepreneur-type bosses. He was heavy on all the 'it's not a company it's a lifestyle' stuff. Very charming though. Maria Johnstone would be totally suckered in."

"I don't suppose he asked you for money, did he?"

Mary squirmed. "How did you know? It's a two hundred quid signing up fee and that gets you enough products to start selling."

"And I bet you don't get a refund if you don't sell any."

"Honestly, I didn't ask." Mary pretended to enjoy a plastic slice of pizza. "Delicious. It was funny really. I was expecting Michelle to be giving me the hard sell on the toiletries, but she didn't really mention them. In fact, she barely spoke at all. It was mainly Tom going on about the other opportunities, like the coaching programs."

"Another way to get money out of you."

"I guess so. Michelle was looking at him like he was God's gift. I mean, he is very handsome."

"You mentioned that already."

"Did I?" Mary flushed. "I just think that Maria Johnstone would have been attracted to him, that's all. He certainly knew how to turn on the charm."

Liz was suddenly glad that Mary was happily in a relationship with her cop boyfriend. It sounded like this Tom Field was a bit of a temptation. Liz had no doubt that someone involved in this sort of business would use any means at their disposal to exploit others, including a handsome face.

"Have they been in touch since you left the café?" Liz asked.

"Yep, both Michelle and Tom have been pretty much messaging constantly, despite them saying they would give me time to think. Do you think I should sign up for the selling pack for Solaverse? Bernie is already moaning about the two hundred quid."

"Maybe we could stall for time for a few days. But ultimately I'm sure Bernie would see that the money was going to a good cause."

"There's another thing you might find interesting," Mary said. "Tom messaged me to say they're having a zoom meeting tonight for the property business. He said I could listen in if I wanted, just to get a feel for it."

"Excellent, send me over the link."

"He might not like it if a stranger dials in," Mary said, a little unsure.

"That's okay, I'll come over to your place. I'll just be out of camera-shot somewhere."

"Oh. Right."

"You weren't looking forward to seeing his handsome face again on your own, were you?"

"Not at all," Mary said, ducking her head over Issy's dolls so that Liz couldn't read her facial expression.

"That's sorted then. I can't wait to see what fascinating insights they're going to give me about the world of property investment."

"And don't forget lifestyle branding," Mary said, the humour returning to her face.

"Aye, that too. I've always felt my lifestyle could do with a bit of branding."

Chapter 28: Mary

The whole situation was very weird, Mary thought. Not least because Liz was hiding in her wardrobe.

"You have a lot of hoodies," Liz said, although her voice was muffled from being surrounded by fabric. "Do they all have geeky slogans on them?"

"Not all of them," Mary said, fixing her mascara where it had smudged. "Some of them have geeky pictures."

"Does this one have an angry hamster on it?"

"That's Gordon the Gopher," Mary said. "He's an icon."

"Sure. Did I tell you I dug up some interesting stuff on your Tom Field?"

"Really?"

"His Companies House record is quite the long list. He's had more failed businesses than you've had pistachio eclairs. He was based in London for a while, but he seems to have moved up here. This Better Life Now has only been around for a couple of years. If it follows the pattern of his other companies he'll be looking for an exit strategy soon."

"A lot of entrepreneurs go through that though, don't they?"

"They can do. The problem is all the suppliers and clients that they leave in their wake every time one of these companies folds. I'm going to see if I can find anyone to dish the dirt, but it'll take some time. How's the login going?"

"It says that the 'host knows I'm waiting' so I guess it'll be starting soon. And you will have to be quiet then, right?"

"You'll forget I'm here."

"Hmmn." Mary wished that Liz had stayed home. It was one thing to think herself into the Maria Johnstone character, but quite another to stay in character with Liz Okoro hiding in the background. Besides, she couldn't help but feel that Liz disapproved of Mary's attitude to investigations. Mary liked to ingratiate herself with the people they were investigating. She was good with people, something she always found surprising, but you couldn't rush those sorts of relationships. Bernie and even Liz were much more direct. Which meant Mary was better at being undercover, in her humble opinion.

"Ooh, it's starting up," Mary said, glancing over at Liz to make sure she was off-camera. Her friend made a zipping motion across her lips, and Mary thought that would probably have to do.

There was the usual faffing about with mute buttons and camera screens. Mary had already made sure that the picture she was showing to the others was a carefully curated one. She had put on some makeup, figuring that Maria Johnstone would have wanted to make an effort too. She was sitting on her bed but she had made sure to clear the wall behind her of its usual retro prints and photos of the kids, just in case she gave too much of herself away. The kids themselves had been taken swimming by two of Bernie's nieces, so at least the house was quiet.

"Hello everyone," Tom's face popped up on the screen, large and slightly shiny. "I'm so happy to see you all."

There were maybe twenty people on the call. Only a third had turned their cameras on, but it was interesting to note they were all women. Mary took a sneaky screenshot so that they could track them down later.

Mary found herself scrutinising Tom's background. He was filming himself in front of some bookcases, and he had put up some self-help pop-psychology type books so that they faced forward. She took another screenshot even though she could already guess what Liz would say about book titles such as 'Coach Your Way to a Better Life'.

"Wow, I'm so glad to see so many of you here today," Tom said, showing his dazzling smile. "Some of our returning guests, shout out to Louisa from Newtonmore!"

A woman in her twenties with a high ponytail waved from one of the squares. He called out a couple of others, neither of whom had their cameras on.

"And we've got some newcomers. I'd like you to all extend your welcomes to the very wonderful Maria Johnstone."

Mary didn't have to act her awkward smile as the other squares started clapping.

"I have high hopes for Maria who is just starting out on her Better Life journey."

It was weird how quickly she had gone from Solaverse makeup, to dare2dream, which was ostensibly Holly and Bella's company, to this other business. As the presentation started there didn't seem to be any mention of the makeup brand that Mary thought she would be selling.

"I'd like to talk investments today. Now I know from last week's feedback that some of you were asking for a crypto deep dive, we're going to get our good friend Davos to come and do that another time for you. I'm going to start with what I think is the easiest and most reliable way to make money by investing for minimal risk and that is property hacking."

A slide appeared with a block of flats that looked like it was somewhere local. A diagram appeared that showed how one simple flat could provide multiple income streams.

Mary tuned out a bit when Tom started to talk interest rates and return on investment and other dull things, but she knew Liz would be taking notes. While she was daydreaming, Mary wondered if Tom Field could be their murderer. Was there really a person that could kill someone and then sell people on property investing a couple of days later? It was possible, Mary knew. She was always surprised by the ability of the truly wicked to compartmentalise their lives. Maybe he had killed her by accident, and he really didn't feel any guilt. Maybe...

There was a flaw in her thinking, Mary knew, stopping herself before she got too carried away. They had found no reason whatsoever that Tom would want to kill Holly. From what they knew they weren't even friends. If anything, the business structure suggested that Holly was making money for Tom, so why would he want her dead? Could they have been having a torrid affair? Mary made a mental note to follow that up.

On the screen, Tom had moved on from property development to the promotion of coaching in all aspects of a person's life.

"I know some of you have already signed up for our premiere plan where you have access to one-to-one coaching sessions, along with the pre-recorded talks that you will have lifetime access to. I'm so proud that we can help you make a positive change in your life. And for those of you that haven't signed up yet, I know what you're thinking: a zoom meeting can't change your life. And it can't. But maybe *you* can."

Mary could feel Liz rolling her eyes so hard she was surprised that the wardrobe wasn't vibrating. But Maria would have been totally suckered in, and Mary herself, even though she was already mortgaged up to her neck, was thinking if she should find a way to lease out a flat somehow. It couldn't be that hard, could it?

The thing was, Mary *did* want to be financially independent. Since joining the WWC she was managing to pay her mortgage and bills, but with four kids there was never much money left over. Her ex-husband Matt and his secret gambling habit had led to masses of debt, some of which had ended up in her name. She could feel the pull of 'passive income' and not just as Maria Johnstone. It was hard to believe it was all a scam. After all, there were twenty-odd people on this call who believed they could make some money.

It was all very well for Liz Okoro with her optometrist

husband and her big fancy house to laugh at this sort of thing. Mary understood why people wanted to believe that they could better their lives, even if that was through selling overpriced makeup.

"Maria, I think this might be an opportunity that suits you, if it's something you would be interested in?"

She glanced over to Liz who was shaking her head so hard she was threatening to dislodge Mary's collection of novelty hats from the top shelf.

"Sure, why not?" Mary said firmly.

"What?" Liz cried out and tried to climb out of the wardrobe, a futile attempt that left her nearly smothered by winter coats.

"Everything okay over there?"

The laptop was shaking as Liz tried to grab her leg.

"Think there's a problem with the signal," Mary said loudly to cover Liz's muttering. "You're breaking up, but I'd love to find out more about this opportunity."

"Great, I'll send you over the details. All right everyone, that's our session over for today. If you want to ask me any questions personally, just stay on the line."

Mary turned off the call.

"What was that all about?" Liz said, pulling a pair of leggings off her head. "And you really need to Marie Kondo this wardrobe, by the way."

"We need to find out everything we can about this company. You said so yourself."

"Yeah, but I don't think Bernie's expenses budget is going to stretch to whatever the handsome Tom is going to charge you for this next 'opportunity'."

"I haven't said I'll do it yet."

Liz sighed. "Don't you see how much easier it is to succumb to these people once you've invited them in?"

"Like vampires," Mary said, suddenly getting it.

"What?"

"Never mind. Look, I'll be careful. There's no need to worry about me." Even as Mary said it, she wasn't sure if that was true.

Chapter 29: Bernie

It was time to go to Ewan's school and if anyone else had seen Bernie Paterson's face, they would have thought she was anxious. But Bernie had always believed that anxiety was something that happened to other people, like that wet lettuce Mary Plunkett. So she probably wasn't feeling any sort of anxiety. Instead, it was concern for her child, appropriate motherly concern in fact, along with more than a little eagerness to give his teachers a right good bollocking.

Part of her knew that the teachers weren't to be blamed for all this trouble, but she wasn't allowed to vent her anger on minors, so they would have to be the ones to get it in the neck.

Invergryff High School was an uninspiring boxy building with tinted windows that made it look more like a prison than a school. She had been there a handful of times, most recently when they had asked for parent feedback on the new lunch menu. Bernie had been disappointed to learn that despite her long list of nutritional requirements, the other parents had voted for chicken nuggets and fish fingers.

Probably the same parents that let their horrible sons bully other people, Bernie thought as she parked up in one of the staff bays just outside reception. She went up to the door and headed straight for the office.

Talking to the woman in the office through the tiny plexiglass window reminded Bernie even more of a prison. Mind you, she had seen plenty of prisons that were more cheerful than this place. Why were high schools always so horrid? She remembered that when she went to the High School it had been the old building, full of asbestos and subsequently knocked down. The whole place had been painted in surgical pink. This new place was stark white and chrome and it didn't seem to Bernie to be much better.

The woman at reception told her to take a seat in the waiting area. There were posters advertising cooperation and kindness – ha! – besides posters for the school talent show and adverts for Planned Parenthood. Nothing changed, she thought, not where school was concerned.

"Mrs Paterson? We've got someone to see you."

As she was turned around she spotted the last person she expected to see.

"Hello darling!" Deborah clicked along the corridor towards her. "I'm just here to sort out a tiny bit of trouble that's been happening with Ewan. I don't suppose he's mentioned it?"

Bernie wasn't often speechless, but bumping into her mother at Ewan's school was enough to dry the words right out of her mouth.

"What the… why are you here?"

"Ewan asked me to come, of course," Deborah said. "You were just so awfully busy and he needed someone on his side, so I volunteered."

"You don't have any right to be here!"

"Any right? You're the one who said I should make more of an effort with Ewan and here I am. You can't possibly complain about that now, can you?"

Bernie pressed her lips together. She could see the women in the office leaning towards them to see what all the fuss was about. "Where's Ewan?"

"Just having a quick word with his teacher."

"So you just went into the school and what? Arranged a meeting all by yourself? I had arranged to see them at three."

"That's right, I moved the meeting to two o'clock. Much handier for me. The teacher seemed so happy to see me. She said you weren't really involved in the school spirit."

"Um, that's because I said I didn't want any more cheap-ass toiletries from their raffles." Bernie was getting one of her Deborah headaches. The whole thing felt like some dreadful dream, only dreams didn't smell like BO and disinfectant. "I sent them a detailed list of how they could improve their fundraising, but they never got back to me."

"Oh Bernie, still trying so hard to make friends and never quite managing it."

"Actually I don't try," Bernie said. "But somehow they work their way in anyway."

Her mother's nostrils flared and things might have got nasty if Ewan hadn't appeared out of the doors at that moment. He was accompanied by one of the teachers who was in charge of pastoral care, a harassed-looking woman who needed her roots done.

When Ewan saw his mother standing next to Deborah he blushed scarlet.

"I guess you told your Granny all about this, right?" Bernie said, her muscles tense.

"She asked me and it kind of... just happened."

"And nobody thought to tell me that the appointment time had changed?" This question she barked at the hapless teacher.

"Oh, um, I thought your mother was going to let you know."

"Must have slipped my mind," Deborah trilled.

The pastoral care teacher had the look of realisation slowly crossing her face that happened to everyone when they had spent time with Deborah. The realisation that they had been duped.

"Can we just go home please, mum," Ewan said, tugging on Bernie's arm.

"Fine," Bernie said, struggling to keep her temper in check. But she knew from Ewan's face that the last thing her son needed was a full-on family drama enacted inside his school.

"If you could just fill in one of our feedback forms..." the woman trailed off when she saw Bernie's face.

"You'll be getting feedback soon enough," Bernie said, a false lightness in her voice. "Don't you worry about that."

They walked out of the school into a shower of rain that had just started up to perfectly match Bernie's dour mood.

"See you later Ew-bear!" Deborah said as Bernie marched her son towards the car.

"Let's get home," Bernie said, hoping she wouldn't crash the car on the way back due to the surge of adrenaline she was currently experiencing.

"Mum…"

"You can tell me later. Did it at least go okay in there?"

"Yeah. Granny did a good job."

Bernie snorted her disbelief at that one.

"You can tell me all about it once I've had a chance to calm down. And then I'm going to have a word with the teachers about having a meeting about confidential issues with someone who is not on their list as a care-giver for their student. See how they like that coming up at their next inspection report."

"Mum!"

"All right. I'll think about it for a bit."

"Before you go nuclear?"

"Nuclear? I'm going anthrax island, chemical warfare and whatever that thing was that people got from eating funky burgers."

"Great," Ewan said.

"That's right young man," she added, just in case he hadn't twigged how annoyed she really was. "I'm going apocalyptic."

Chapter 30: Walker

Walker had spent the whole of Thursday afternoon looking at car ownership records. So far, no one connected with the case had been linked to any of the cars that Suzie had found on the doorcam. There was still some hope, but the initial enthusiasm in the office was fading fast. Feeling like he needed to stretch, Walker decided to take a walk and see how the Detective Inspector was getting on.

When he got to Macleod's office he saw that the Inspector was sitting at his desk with his head in his hands.

"Everything okay?"

"My head is killing me. Got any paracetamol?"

Walker looked at his boss. The man was rubbing at his eyes and his skin had gone a blotchy colour.

"You don't look too good," Walker said. "Have you been eating right?"

"Probably not. Knackered too. This case has me working all hours. You couldn't grab me a chocolate bar out of the machine could you?"

"How about I go to the van over the road and get you something a bit more decent? Soup and a sandwich?"

"If you must." Macleod stretched his back. "Did I tell you that toxicology finally got back to us? Holly Moore's last meal was a takeaway, some noodle-type dish. We're chasing that up with the local restaurants. Small amount of alcohol in the system, probably a couple of glasses of wine, but not enough to incapacitate. Might suggest that there was someone else with her for dinner, or it might just have been she liked a glass of wine by herself."

"So nothing very useful then?"

"Nope."

Macleod looked miserable as Walker left to get him something to eat. When he got to the snack van across the road from the station, Walker found it easy to avoid the temptation of a bacon roll for once and bought himself and Macleod some virtuous chicken wraps and soups.

When he got back to the station he bumped into Sergeant Neil Mickelson in the reception.

"Still waiting on those spreadsheets," Neil reminded him.

"Crap. Sorry. I'll get on it today."

"Too busy sucking up to the DI?" Neil said with half a laugh.

"Give me a break, won't you?" Walker said, matching Neil's light tone. "I mean, it's a Major Investigation, got to be more important than those spreadsheets."

Neil frowned. "Both need done. Isn't that kind of the point of the police force? And you are still in uniform, unless you've forgotten."

Walker wasn't sure what to say to that that wouldn't lead to an argument, so he snapped his mouth shut.

"Look, I'm not having a go," Neil said as they walked up the stairs in awkward silence. "I just don't want you getting a bollocking for it."

"Of course. I'll give this to Macleod and then I'll get to work."

"Thanks," Neil said and the tension was broken. "I've got a report to deliver to him anyway. We've checked out Leah Hill's alibi and it's just as she said. She was seen by multiple witnesses in the pub until around one on Sunday morning, but no one to vouch for her after that."

They had made it to the DI's office, but there was no one behind the desk. At first, Walker thought that Macleod had already left.

"He's not here, hang on…" Walker was just turning to leave when he spotted the shadow of something behind the desk.

His heart hammering before he even understood what he was seeing, Walker rushed over to the rear of the room.

"Neil, get over here!"

Macleod was on the floor, lying half on his side and half on his back. He was making horrible little gasping noises with his mouth and his eyes were glass and unfocused.

"Sir?"

As Walker bent down to loosen his shirt, Neil appeared beside him.

"Oh crap."

"Phone an ambulance," Walker told him.

"Right." Neil moved around to the phone on the desk and dialled the emergency number. Walker was vaguely aware of him talking in the background as he tried to get Macleod to respond. He called his name a few times and tried squeezing his hand, but the man didn't seem to be capable of answering.

Walker manoeuvred him into the recovery position while Neil relayed questions from the call centre.

"An ambulance is on its way. They're asking if he has a history of heart conditions," Neil said.

"I don't know," Walker said, trying to keep calm. "I know he said he was pre-diabetic, so I don't know if it's blood sugar. Or…" Walker looked down at the man's face which was turning an alarming grey colour. "Crap. Maybe it is his heart."

The commotion had drawn some other people from the office who were crowding around the door. Suzie came over and ducked down beside them.

"What's going on?" She asked.

"Don't know, we just found him like this. You're emergency treatment trained, right?"

"Yeah, but it looks like you've done everything right so far." She checked his pulse and put her cheek next to Macleod's mouth to feel his breathing. "He is breathing shallowly, and there's a pulse even if it is a little thready. I think we just wait for the paramedics."

It was the longest five minutes of Walker's life. Nobody said anything, which made the gasping noise of Macleod's breathing sound even worse.

When the green-dressed paramedics ran into the room Walker was almost shaking with relief. They quickly got the DI onto a stretcher and put an oxygen mask on him.

"We'll take him to the main hospital," one of the medics said. "He can have someone in the ambulance along with him."

"Mind if I go?" Walker asked straightaway.

"Of course," Suzie said. "Let us know as soon as you hear anything."

The ambulance sped away. It wasn't Walker's first time in one – it was unfortunately quite a common event in his line of work – but it was the first time that he's felt like a useless spectator. Feeling a little self-conscious, he reached out and took Macleod's hand. It was just about the only thing he could do for him.

Chapter 31: Liz

After the zoom call with Tom Field, Liz ramped up her investigations into dare2dream and its related businesses. She didn't like the idea of Mary being exposed to these people for any longer than necessary.

Bernie wasn't answering her phone again, which was driving Liz a little crazy. She was sympathetic, of course, to the problems that her friend was having with her mother and her son, but they still had a murder case to solve. Liz decided she would need to press forward on her own.

She was still tuned to the hideous toxic positivity of the dare2dream which if anything had only ramped up since news of Holly's death had filtered through to the online world. There were so many RIP posts, each more gushing than the next, that they were starting to make Liz's eyes twitch. Any hint of negativity that had appeared from people like Kelly Macpherson on other posts was absent from the hordes of people rushing in to praise the deceased woman.

One thing that had interested Liz was that Bella, Holly's sister had taken a central role in this outpouring of grief. At first, it had seemed natural enough, with Bella posting a personal tribute to Holly on her page. But as of today, things had taken a different tack. Bella had gone back to business.

We are mourning our wonderful founder but safe in the knowledge that her brave legacy will live on.

Underneath were links to their website and the sign-up pages for selling Solaverse. Liz found it distasteful at best, creepy at worst. And she was wondering if it gave Bella the motive they had been missing: would someone kill their sister just to make a few sales? It seemed ridiculous, but then everything about these companies was so out of whack it was hard to tell.

Once Dave was home to take over with baby Issy, Liz decided to visit Bella's house. Bella lived in a village just outside town which was opposite an artisan bakers. Liz made a note to pop in on the way home to pick up some sweet treats for Mary. It might distract her from Tom Field and his charming business proposals.

She rang the bell on Bella's neat little semi-detached house and was pleased when the woman herself answered. Her face was more sun-lined than it had seemed in her online photos, but Liz guessed that was due to the judicious use of filters.

"So you're telling me that you're a private investigator looking into Holly's death?" Bella had led her into the kitchen where she had offered her a filtered coffee. Bella herself was drinking some sort of nasty herbal smoothie that smelt like freshly mown lawns. "I thought at first you were a journalist. There's been a few of them asking for me to do a piece in the paper."

"You don't have to do that, you know," Liz said, thinking that she would have hated that sort of intrusion into her privacy.

"Oh, I know that. But it might be good publicity. I have to

run the business by myself now and it's not going to be easy."

"I understand," said Liz, who wasn't sure that she did. Surely any business that can't survive without cashing in on a murder wasn't worth saving?

"If you're investigating Holly's death, then I don't understand who hired you?" Bella asked, showing that she was sharper than she looked.

"I'm afraid I'm not at liberty to divulge my clients," Liz said, which was something she had seen someone say on a bad TV cop show once.

"Huh." Bella sipped on the horrible green juice. "Well, I don't know what I can tell you. The police don't seem to have a clue about what happened to Holly. I still think they should be looking at that arse of a husband of hers but apparently he's got an alibi."

"We often find we can discover things that the police can't," Liz explained. "People feel more comfortable talking to us."

"You certainly couldn't do any worse. But I still don't see who… Hang on, that Deborah woman, her daughter is an investigator isn't she?"

Uh oh. "I'm not at liberty to…"

"Bullshit. Now you can't be Deborah O'Flannery's daughter. Unless you were adopted."

Liz laughed in spite of herself. "No. Look, you're right that my business partner is Deborah's daughter. But that doesn't mean that we're biased."

"Too right it does. You know that Deborah hated Holly, don't you?"

"Why would you say that?"

"Because Deborah was a total nightmare. She wanted to be right at the top of the business, you know, so she kept pushing herself forward. But no one liked her. She kept stealing other people's clients and I'm sure she was fudging her sales figures. Holly told her to buck up her attitude or she was out of the company."

Bella paused to draw breath, then put her hand to her mouth. "It's her, isn't it? She's the one who killed Holly."

Liz wished she could say for definite it wasn't, but of course they had no proof of that. "We're still not sure who's to blame. I was wondering if dare2dream might have something to do with it."

"And what do you mean by that?"

"Well, you see, I'm an accountant. I used to work in fraud detection."

"Really. How interesting." Liz was pleased to see that the word 'fraud' had had its desired effect and Bella looked decidedly nervous. "And why is an accountant involved in this investigation?"

"Well, you could say that dare2dream's structure exposes itself to harm."

Bella's face was pinched with irritation. "In what way?"

"Don't you think it could be viewed as exploitative? Like a kind of pyramid scheme? I mean, it's only you guys at the top that really make any money, isn't it?"

"What rubbish. Only the haters ever say things like 'pyramid scheme'."

Liz sighed. There was no arguing with crazy. "But don't you think that someone to do with dare2dream could have done this? Some disgruntled customer or recruit?"

"No. I mean if you're saying it isn't Deborah... Which it still could be as far as I'm concerned. But, you know, at first I was convinced it was James," Bella said, picking at the edge of her nail. "He was pretty pissed off about the break-up. But then the police said he had an alibi, that it couldn't be him. So I guess it must have just been some pyscho. A wannabe burglar, probably off his head on meth or something."

"Could be," Liz said. "You don't think that anyone who knew her might have had a motive?"

"God no. Everyone loved Holly. She was the life and soul of every party. That's why I thought it had to be James. He's the only person she ever argued with."

"It must have been such a shock," Liz said. "Especially as she didn't have any enemies, like you said."

"Exactly," Bella said, ignoring any edge of sarcasm that Liz had in her voice. "God, the whole thing is such a mess. I called the police station today and they can't even tell me when I can collect my car."

"Your car?"

"It was in Holly's garage but for some reason the police have impounded it. They're saying it's evidence, but how can that be if she was killed in the house?"

Liz frowned. "Oh, I thought that was Holly's car in her garage."

"No, it's mine. Or... I mean, I let her borrow it."

Wheels were turning in Liz's mind. "You mean that you shared the same car?"

"Yeah." Bella chewed on her nail.

"But from your social media, you definitely gave the impression that you each had one of those pink cars. Because the business paid for it, right?"

"We did have two. But it seemed like kind of a waste, so Holly sold hers."

Liz felt like punching the air, although she made sure to keep her expression neutral. This was the first admission from the woman that their business was not doing as well as they claimed.

"She was my sister, you know? We shared pretty much everything. God, it's going to be a nightmare sorting it all out. And no doubt James will want his paws on as much of her money as he can get."

"You think so?"

"I know it." Bella tucked some stray hair away behind her ear. "I mean, they were separated but they were still married. So he gets the lot right?"

"I suppose it depends if she wrote a will or not," Liz said, making sure to watch the other woman's face.

"A will?" Bella glanced up at her. "Do you think she might have written one?"

"I have no idea. You could check with her lawyers."

"I will. If there's any chance I can stop that man getting all our money, then it's got to be worth a shot, right."

"Right."

Chapter 32: Mary

Mary was starting to believe that she had missed her calling as a property mogul. After all, one of her favourite pastimes was nosing around other people's houses. It was kind of a requisite skill for a private investigator. And now Tom Field was explaining to her how she could use it as her next side hustle.

She wasn't too sure why Tom had decided she was going to be his latest protégée. Despite Liz's worries that she was far too naïve, Mary knew that the man would happily throw her under a bus if it meant he could earn a few quid. But that didn't mean that she could ignore the appeal of a quick buck. And if she was honest, she liked the attention a little too. She was committed to Walker in whatever state their relationship was currently in, but she still found it flattering to be chatted up by a good-looking guy. It didn't happen that often when you were running around covered in sticky handprints and tea stains.

If the WWC ever came to an end, maybe she could grow to love the 'girlboss' stuff. Although the trouser-suit she had bought for today's seminar was a little too shiny for her liking. It wasn't very breathable either and she had already had to reapply deodorant in the toilets.

There were only ten of them this time, in a room that Field must have rented from some other business as there were pictures of car engines on the walls. Bella Terrance was there too, which had surprised Mary. Would Mary have gone to work just a couple of days after a sibling's death? Probably not. But then Bella would need to take over Holly's role in the business, so perhaps she didn't have any choice. Mary still wasn't sure what the hierarchy was between Tom Field and the members of dare2dream, but Bella seemed to be treating him more like a boss than an equal.

Liz would be able to make sense of it, Mary hoped. That was why she was recording everything on her phone which was tucked away in her handbag.

Looking around at the others Mary noticed that Michelle Rallie wasn't there. Maybe she had been banned after their meeting in the café. Or maybe because she was more on the makeup side of things she wouldn't have been there anyway.

At the front of the room, sitting casually on one of the tables, Tom Field was telling them all about the opportunities that were available in property investment. It seemed to involve a lot of slides with funny memes on them and not a lot of actual financial data. The way Better Life Now worked seemed to involve setting up property renovators and managers with those with the money to invest. Mary was sure she was missing the catch somewhere but she couldn't quite get what it was.

Tom Field was still incredibly handsome, but the more she watched him, the more she realised there was something desperate about him. He was like a gameshow host, trying to enliven the audience into a state of excitement. He was having a hard time of it. People in the West of Scotland weren't prone to exuberant displays unless it was a football match or someone had tripped over in a bar.

"Now we currently offer this coaching plan for the low price of just seventy-nine pounds. You've spent that on shoes, haven't you girls, own up! And after eighteen monthly payments that's it. You're free to go off and start your new business."

"Um, did you say eighteen monthly payments?" Mary asked, holding up a hand.

"That's right. You can discuss with our finance department if –"

"It's just that eighteen times seventy-nine makes more than fourteen hundred pounds," Mary said with an apologetic smile. "I used the calculator on my phone."

There was a murmur from the other people in the crowd as this sunk in.

"Can I just say I am loving your new clothes today, Maria," Tom Field said in what was clearly a clunky attempt to change the subject.

"Oh, thanks," Mary said. "But I –"

"Do you know what I like about it? You're manifesting this new career. By looking like the person you want to be, the perfect model of success you are making it happen. Can I get a huge round of applause for Maria?"

There was a small amount of clapping, but it allowed Field to go back to his presentation, which was probably the idea.

Mary was quickly bored once more. Maria Johnstone might have still been interested in this spiel, but Mary had checked out. Liz was right. It was nothing more than a scam. She looked around the room and saw that Bella was glaring at her.

Uh-oh. Mary gave her what she hoped was a friendly smile then turned back to face the front. She had probably drawn too much attention to herself, something that was never good when you were meant to be undercover. She pretended to be engrossed in Tom Field's sales pitch once more.

After he was finished, there was a round of tea and biscuits, but even the little packets of shortbread couldn't persuade Mary to stick around. She started to head for the door.

"Leaving already?" Tom appeared beside her, his face shinier than ever.

"Oh, I need to get back to the kids," Mary said. "It was all very interesting."

"I sense that you're being Little Miss Sceptical," the man said.

"I guess I am," Mary said, beginning to seriously dislike him. "I guess I don't really understand what your role is in all this? Or, rather, the role of Better Life Now."

"Well, apart from the instructional element, I'm a facilitator. I connect the investors on the one side and the property hunters and managers on the other."

"Right. And I guess you take a cut from both sides?"

Tom Field raised his eyebrows. "Very smart." He didn't look

particularly happy that he had called her out.

"I think I better go," Mary said. She had seen Bella heading in her direction and she didn't want Holly's sister to overhear any drama. "I will think about it though," she said, not wanting to burn her bridges. "I really would love to be a 'mumtrepreneur'."

Field broke into a genuine smile. "That's the spirit. I'll be in touch."

Horrified that she had used such an ick-inducing word, Mary hurried out of the conference centre. She would have liked to stay and hear what Bella and Tom were going to discuss, but there was no way to do it without drawing attention to herself. She just had to hope that Liz would have better luck with her background sources.

It didn't take long to drive home. Her mother had picked up the kids already from school which is why she could hear children yelling out in the garden before she even got out of the car. Mary decided to walk around the house and go and see them straight away.

Vikki and Peter were chasing each other with water pistols and Johnny and Lauren were playing in the sandpit. It was one of those moments where everyone was looking adorable. Mary ran over and hugged them all before they could spoil it by speaking.

"Did you have a good day?"

"Yep," Johnny said, showing her a newly skinned knee. "Only

Gran said we couldn't go into the house because she needed a nap."

"Really?" Mary was surprised. Her mother, Nel, was normally the uber-granny; baking cakes, ironing shirts and reading storybooks, often all at once.

"She's on the sofa snoring," Lauren giggled.

Mary let herself in through the patio doors in the kitchen and saw that the children were correct. Her mother was fast asleep on the sofa and Mary was horrified to notice that she looked like an old lady. She wasn't wearing make-up and her hair was sticking up all over the place.

Mary tiptoed away and put the kettle on. A few minutes later she heard her mother get up.

"I've put the kettle on," she said as Nel came through from next door.

"Thanks," her mother was smoothing down her fringe. "I didn't expect you back for a while."

"There was only so much investor-speak I could handle." She gave her mum a cup of tea, then decided she needed to say something. "Mum, I hope you don't mind me saying, but you look kind of tired."

Nel flinched. "Well thank you very much."

"Sorry, I just meant…"

To Mary's horror, her mother's lip began to wobble.

"You're right, love, I am tired." Nel sniffed. "I think maybe… it might just be a little much for me sometimes. Looking after the little ones."

A pang of guilt tugged at Mary's heart. "No wonder. God, I know. I'm permanently knackered. Looking after four kids is bloody hard work. They can be little monsters at times."

"Oh, I wouldn't go that far. I mean, they're angels most of the time."

Mary could see that Nel was visibly struggling with the idea of admitting that her grandchildren were anything less than perfect.

"Peter set up a fake social media page for his teacher the other day," Mary told her. "I only just caught it before it went live. He had listed her profession as 'child-torturer' and said in her description that she was in need of a tummy tuck."

"Oh god," Nel covered her eyes.

"The woman is a size eight, by the way. And Johnny still likes to pee outside wherever we go, Lauren got two pieces of Lego stuck in her nose last week and Vikki said I was too old to wear pink. It's okay to say that they're hard work sometimes."

Her mother smiled and it stopped her from looking quite so tired. "I suppose I don't want to sound ungrateful. I love looking after the kids. But maybe three times a week is a little too much."

Mary felt terrible. She had been relying a lot on her mother this week while the WWC were so busy. It hadn't occurred to her that Nel might be struggling.

"I should have realised. I'm sorry."

Nel's mouth turned down at the corners. "Please don't be. I never... well, it seems silly to object to granny duties. I really do love it most of the time. I just didn't want to cause trouble."

Mary sighed. "The women in our family never really learned to complain, did we? Took me a decade of living with Matt before I realised that life might be better without him."

"Families are difficult. You know, your dad's mother never liked me one bit."

"What, Granny Fletcher?" Mary could barely remember the woman who had died before she was five years old. "I always thought she seemed like a nice lady."

"Oh, she was lovely to her grandchildren, but a right cow to her daughters-in-law. And her own children for that matter. Just because you're a mother, doesn't mean that you're nice." Nel patted her arm. "I don't tell you enough but I'm so proud of you. I've never seen happier children and they are an absolute credit to you."

Now it was Mary's turn to feel tears in the corner of her eyes. "Thanks, Mum. But I never feel like I'm doing all that well. Most of the time I'm barely holding it together."

"If you were a terrible mother you wouldn't question yourself," Nel said firmly.

"I just don't want my kids to hate me, like Bernie hates her mum," Mary said. "I can't think of anything worse."

"That would be Deborah O'Flannery, wouldn't it? I can tell you that you are nothing like that woman. Two-faced, that was what she always was. And I heard that she's still up to her old tricks."

"What do you mean?"

"You know my neighbour, Andi, the one with the husband who ran off with the flute player, do you remember."

Mary rolled her eyes. "Let's just say that I do."

"Well, anyway, Andi signed up to this makeup business that Deborah was running. Gave her two hundred quid, and Andi's not exactly well off. Stan left her with nothing, you know, and she never had a pension of her own. I drop off the odd casserole, but there's only so much you can do."

"You were saying about this two hundred quid," Mary prompted.

"Oh yes. So Andi hands over the money and then hardly sells any of it. Deborah had told her there was a thirty day refund guarantee, but ever since Andi got in touch to ask for her money back, Deborah has been ghosting her."

"Yeah, Bernie always said she was a liar."

"It's like a sickness really," Nel said. "I remember when she was a teenager, she was always telling fibs. I was much younger but even I knew not to trust the girl. And how she treated those children of hers was disgraceful."

"But no one ever stepped in?" Mary asked. "Called the social work or anything?"

"I suppose we didn't really in those days. I mean, she wasn't beating them black and blue, so anything else didn't seem worth bothering over. Different times."

Mary wasn't so sure about that, but she had already upset her mother once today so she didn't take it any further. Instead, she asked Nel for the details of her neighbour Andi to pass on to Liz. Any person who had a grudge against dare2dream was worth investigating. And then she treated her mum and the kids to a takeaway dinner. It seemed like the least she could do.

Chapter 33: Bernie

Bernie was struggling to control her temper. In general, her attitude was that it didn't do kids any harm to know that grown-ups got pissed off too and sometimes liked to show it. But the sort of anger she was feeling made her want to smash the place up or scream until her lungs bled. Probably best not to show her son that.

"I just needed someone to help me, and Granny was right there."

"Right there? Can I ask how your Granny was 'right there' in the first place?"

Ewan hung his head. "Remember when she came around the other day?"

"Uh huh."

"She got me to give her my phone number."

Bernie banged her hand down on the table. "I knew she was up to something."

"You said that you wanted me and her to have a relationship," Ewan complained, "and now you don't want her to have my number?"

"Bloody mobile phones. There's something to be said for going to live in the forest in a mud hut. Wouldn't have to deal with this crap then."

"Mum?"

Bernie tried to think how to explain. "The thing is, if she sends you a message through me, then I can filter through some of her... well, her crap before I pass it on. This way you are exposed to her full Deborah-ness. And it's not always very nice."

"She's always nice to me."

"So far," Bernie said darkly. "And I suppose you just happened to mention the whole bullying thing to her."

"I wanted to talk to someone."

Bernie had been ready for this, but it still hurt. "And you thought she would be the best person, right?"

"Well, she got it sorted. I mean, she said she did anyway."

Bernie wasn't so sure of that. Ewan's bottom lip started to wobble and he looked much younger than the teenager he was.

"Are you mad at me?"

"Why would I be mad?"

"Your lips are doing that thin thing. And your left eye is twitching."

"Maybe I am a little mad, but not at you."

"You're mad at granny, right?"

"A little."

"Please don't be mad at her. She was just trying to help."

Bernie shrugged. "The thing is, your granny... well, we've not got the best history together, put it that way."

"I know. But just because she was a crap mum doesn't mean she's a crap granny, does it?"

There was some logic to this. "I suppose you could be right. Did she really help you?"

"Yes. She was amazing. I mean, she still treats me like I'm five half the time, but she did a good job on this one. She sort of *flirted* with Mr Greives, you know the head of year? It was total yuck, she was saying how a strong man like him would sort it out. That he was far too smart to let this sort of thing continue when he was in charge. And he was well pleased, because he said he would stop the messages straight away, and post someone in the playground after school to keep an eye on things."

"That's good," Bernie managed.

"Yeah, she knocked it out of the park. So do you think you guys can be friends again? You and granny?"

"Probably not. When you're an adult things get a hell of a lot more complicated. Bullying is... well it doesn't exactly stop after High School, it just gets a bit more sly and sneaky. I didn't realise at the time that sometimes the bully can be your own mum. And you might have to do things to protect yourself. Difficult things like avoiding certain people who make you feel pretty damn terrible about yourself." She took a breath. It was exhausting trying to be diplomatic for the sake of her son. "But I'm happy that you and Deborah can have a good relationship. That you guys can manage something me and her never did. And I'm super proud of you for managing that."

"Thanks."

Other mums might have brought him in for a hug. But there had been a lot of hugging recently and she was feeling touched-out. Instead, Bernie gave Ewan a hearty fist-bump.

"I still want you to tell me if this bullying crap starts up again. If those guys don't quit I'm happy to show him what retaliation looks like, Bernie Paterson style."

Ewan laughed. "Yeah, I can just imagine that. I'd prefer to deal with it without anyone getting punched in the face."

"Huh. Interesting. Are you sure you're my child?"

Chapter 34: Walker

The quiet in the office when Walker got back from the hospital was unnerving. At first there had been a crowd of people coming up to him and asking for news on the DI. Once that initial rush was over, however, the room had fallen silent.

"Macleod's all right," Walker said, raising his voice so that everyone could hear. "They've stabilized him. They think it was related to his high blood sugar. At the moment, they reckon they caught it in time and he should wake up soon."

He found he couldn't quite join in the sounds of relief around him. Macleod had still been unconscious from the seizures when he left the hospital. His wife had arrived down from the Highlands, along with his brother, so Walker knew he wasn't needed at the bedside. Still, it had been hard to leave his boss like that. A big strong man, suddenly vulnerable.

He sat down at his desk, turning on the computer and hoping to lose himself in the Holly Moore case files.

"We're waiting to see who they're going to send to lead the case," Suzie told him, coming over to perch next to his monitor.

"You could do it," Walker said.

"Nah, not senior enough. So far we've just been told to continue our list of enquiries, but we're just holding water until they assign another Senior Investigating Officer. I wonder if –

"

At that moment Superintendent MacKinnon entered the office. For once, the Edinburgh man looked flustered, shirt crumpled.

"I've just heard from the hospital. DI Macleod is doing well, he regained consciousness a few minutes ago and was speaking to the Doctors. They've given him a sedative now so his body can recover."

MacKinnon cleared his throat. "And I know he would want to thank you all for your swift assistance, in particular Sergeants Mickelson and Walker for responding so quickly."

A round of applause was taken up around the room.

"All right, thank you," MacKinnon continued. "Now, we still have an active investigation to manage here. I'm afraid that Macleod chose a very poor time to collapse."

There was an awkward chuckle from the troops at this, as no one was sure if he was joking.

"We currently have no Chief Inspector to assign because they're all over in Glasgow on that trafficking case that's been rumbling on all week. There's a chance we might get DCI William Stratham over from Lothian but he's in court for the next two days. I have therefore decided to take personal supervision of the case alongside Detective Sergeant O'Connor. In addition, I've asked for Detective Sergeant Tonny who was working over in Greenock with the coastguards this week to help us out. They're not going to be happy we're stealing him away but never mind."

Walker saw Suzie trying to hide her surprise. It effectively meant that she would be the lead investigator. A good result, Walker reckoned. She was a solid detective, even if she didn't quite have Macleod's flair.

"I'm going to read through all the files just now and I'll give an official briefing this afternoon."

MacKinnon started walking away and everyone went back to their computers.

"Walker, can I have a word?" The Superintendent had appeared beside him.

"Of course, sir."

Walker had been hoping he could attach himself to Suzie again, but instead he found himself following MacKinnon along the corridor to his office.

"I wanted to check that you knew which actions you were working on," MacKinnon said once he was seated in his swivel chair.

"Well, I have been working through the car registrations and trying to find one of the vehicles on the doorcam near Holly Moore's –"

MacKinnon held up his hand. "I believe you were asked to focus on the statistics that Mickelson needed help with. Crime in the Invergryff North postal district, isn't that correct?"

"Yes sir. I am doing that as well. But I was hoping I could continue to work the murder case," Walker said. "I'm sure that Macleod would want me to –"

"I'm afraid we don't know what Macleod wants at the moment," the Superintendent reminded him. "And while our Senior Investigating Officer is out of commission, I think it's more important than ever to follow procedure. Therefore I would like you to leave the MIT case to the detectives and go back to the burglary figures."

"But…"

"It is not up for debate, Sergeant."

Walker fought down his complaint. "Of course. Understood sir."

He was very careful not to slam the door on his way out.

Chapter 35: Liz

Liz was sorting through her son's clothes and wondering what it was that boys did at school that ripped the knees out of their trousers. She and Dave were not badly off, even with the cut in wages she had taken to join the WWC, but she reckoned if she could invent trousers that lasted for more than a term they could afford an extra holiday every year.

Mind you, there were worse things than ripped trousers. The thought of Bernie's son, Ewan, being bullied chilled her heart. She knew that her own son had faced similar things, although thankfully not as severe. Still, Invergryff would always be a majority white town and lads like her Sean would always stick out. It was horrible knowing she probably wouldn't be there with him when he faced that stuff. She missed the nursery days when you just had a quiet word with the other mums if anyone was causing trouble. But at thirteen it wouldn't be some snotty kid stealing his toys.

She shook her head, trying to get rid of the thought. Sean seemed happy enough and had a group of friends who seemed marginally less idiotic than most of the kids their age. That was all she could hope for, at the moment anyway.

Liz put the basket of laundry on the stairs, where it would inevitably live for several days until the men of the house noticed it was there. She put the baby's clothes away herself, enjoying the softness of them. She knew that she would blink and Issy would be a teenager too. How quickly it all passed.

In her meditative mood, it took Liz a few moments to realise that her phone was buzzing on the kitchen counter. She picked it up to see that an unknown number was calling. Liz clicked to answer hoping it wouldn't be some crappy call centre asking if she had had an accident with her car/pet/workplace. Instead of the tinny sound of a minimum wage slave, she heard a familiar female voice.

"Is that Liz Okoro?" The voice whispered.

"Yes."

"It's Bella. Bella Terrance."

Why was Holly's sister phoning? And why was she doing a weird whispering voice?

"Can I help you Bella?"

"I bloody well hope so. Look, I don't have time to talk. Two coppers have just turned up and they said they're going to arrest me for Holly's murder."

"What? Why?"

There was the sound of a tap running.

"I need to be quick. I'm hiding in the toilet."

"What?" Liz was still trying to get her head around what the hell was going on.

"Yeah, I told the police constable there was no way I could hold it in. I've only got a few seconds."

"I don't think they're going to be happy about –"

"That's why I've got to be quick. Look, I'm hiring you, okay? Whatever it costs. You need to get me out of prison."

"Prison? I think you're getting a bit ahead of yourself."

"I don't think so," Bella said, her whispering growing more urgent. "They must have found out about the money I was skimming off from Holly's account."

"You were doing what?"

"You heard me. Now they're going to think I murdered her. But I didn't do it! And you and your weirdo friends need to prove that for me."

"I'm not sure –"

"Ssh, that's them, got to go." She hung up just as the noise of someone hammering on the door echoed through the phone.

Liz pinched the bridge of her nose. A new client. Well, in some ways Bernie would be happy. It wasn't too great that she was a thief and a possible murderer, however. Mind you, they always made sure to charge a retaining fee, and by the sound of things Bella could afford it.

Liz opened up a new client file and typed Bella's name into the heading. She had just inputted her contact details when her phone rang again. This time it came up with Bernie's name.

"You'll never guess who's just been taken into Invergryff police station."

"Oh I think I might have some idea," Liz explained about the phone call from Bella.

"Excellent," Liz could hear Bernie grinning down the phone. "I don't have to tell you that doing this case pro bono was giving me chest pains."

"Hang on, how did you know she'd been arrested?"

"She only lives two doors up from that Pam who works in the shoe shop."

"Ah yes, Nosy Pam. That explains it. So what do you think we should do?"

There was a pause while Bernie was thinking. "It's a bit difficult having a new client that's just been arrested. I don't suppose they'll let us in to see her?"

"I reckon you've probably used up any goodwill you had at Invergryff police station."

"You could be right. I'll get Mary to try and chat up Hamish Macbeth just in case."

Liz looked back over her notes. "We could look into what Bella said about skimming the books. If that's true – and I don't see why she would lie about it – then it should tell us something about the way they were running the company."

"Doesn't help our client though, does it."

"Well, if she did commit the murder we would have a responsibility to report that too, wouldn't we?"

"I suppose," Bernie didn't sound too convinced. "I reckon we need a proper sit down WWC meeting to go over all this. Any idea what Mary's up to?"

"Selling overpriced makeup somewhere, probably. I'm a bit worried she's getting sucked in by this stupid company. She really seemed to fancy that creep Tom Field."

"She wouldn't do anything stupid there, would she?"

Liz wanted to say definitely not, but there was something a tiny bit flaky about Mary Plunkett.

"Your silence speaks volumes," Bernie said. "We'll have a word with her tonight. God knows, I'm not the biggest fan of Sergeant Broadchurch but this Field bloke sounds even worse."

"If he's as bad as I think he is, then he's much worse than Walker. Holly and Bella might have been running a crappy business, but it looks like this Field guy has a whole corrupt empire. I've been preparing the file on him for you."

"Add it to the list. We'll have an emergency meeting tonight. All right to have it at your place?"

"Sure. Don't suppose you fancy doing some ironing for me?"

"Not a chance. I'll be there at eight."

Chapter 36: Mary

Mary arrived late to the WWC meeting and it wasn't until she walked into Liz's dining room that she realised she hadn't had time to change.

"What in the 1987 is that trouser suit?" Bernie asked.

"Oh, yeah, Tom said we had to dress like the person we wanted to be."

"And you wanted to be Business Barbie?" Liz jumped in.

"Harsh guys," Mary said, although she was finding it hard not to laugh. The suit was navy, shiny and if she was honest, probably one size too small. "I got it reduced, if you must know. I was thinking of your expenses, Bernie."

"Does it seem a little creepy to anyone that Tom Field has started dressing you," Liz said as she made Mary a cup of tea.

"I mean, you could see it that way," Mary replied. "It's hard to tell with Tom. Sometimes he seems super nice, but other times he seems like he's just acting a part, you know? I actually have no idea whether he believes all the stuff he says or not."

"Classic conman," Liz said. She certainly seemed to have made up her mind about Tom.

"Like I said, I haven't decided yet." Mary caught Liz's eye. "I know, you don't have to look at me like that. I'm not in danger of drinking the Kool Aid, but I just want to find out if he's just an ambitious, ruthless businessman or a full-on fraudster."

Liz turned away and Mary was frustrated to see that neither she nor Bernie seemed to trust her judgement on this one. Yet again, she was reminded that she was very much the junior partner.

"Oh, I did find out something from my mum," Mary said, remembering what Nel had said about her neighbour. "She told me about another person who had been let down by dare2dream. Her name's Andi Catto and I've got her number for you. She was signed up by... well, by Deborah actually."

Bernie's face stayed neutral.

"Anyway, Andi tried to get a refund but Deborah ghosted her. It sounds like she was pretty mad about it, so I thought you might want to call her, Liz."

"Thanks, I will do."

"Let's focus on the Bella Terrance situation," Bernie chimed in. "Now that she's officially a client I want to make sure our profile of her is as comprehensive as it can be."

"I still can't believe she phoned Liz while she was getting arrested," Mary said. She was dying to ask Walker about it but she hadn't heard from him that day. She was trying her best to pretend it had nothing to do with their almost-fight about his family. "That can't have made her popular with the police officers."

"Yeah, she must have been feeling pretty desperate," Liz

replied. "The only problem is, how do we get started on her case? Given that she's in the police station and we can't even speak to her."

"I have an idea about that," Bernie said. "I think we should take a visit to our client's house."

For a moment, Mary didn't understand what she meant. "But Bella's in the police station, isn't she?"

"Exactly. The perfect time to have a jolly good snoop around."

Mary didn't like the sound of this at all. "Is that something that she has okayed?"

"I'm sure she would have, if she hadn't been arrested."

Liz chewed her lip. "I don't know Bernie, isn't that a bit risky? Plus the police might not see it quite the way that you do. If she's a suspect – which she must be – then they might see it as tampering with evidence. As well as the usual breaking and entering of course."

"What else are we meant to do," Bernie said, "just sit around and wait for her to be released? How is that going to help? Bella called us because she had no other choice. I'm sure she'd want us to do everything in our power to help."

"I'm not sure that included rummaging through her private possessions," Mary said.

"There are no private possessions when you're accused of your sister's murder," Bernie said, in the tone of voice that invited no argument.

"But —"

"If anyone has a better idea, I'm happy to hear it."

And so it was that half an hour later they were sitting outside Bella Terrance's house arguing about whether or not they should break a window.

"This is bloody ridiculous," Liz said, sitting in the driver's seat with her arms folded. "We're going to get arrested. And Dave is not going to be happy if he has to bail me out. I told him we couldn't afford a cross-trainer this week, how the hell am I meant to ask for bail money?"

"Do they do bail here or is that just an American thing?" Mary asked. "I remember there was this episode of CSI where…"

"I don't suppose the episode of CSI had any suggestions for focussing on the matter at hand and getting into a locked house," Bernie asked.

"'Fraid not."

"Then it's up to me. Again. I'll go around the back and see if there's any windows open or anything. You two can keep a lookout. If you see the cops coming then beep the horn and I'll come running."

With that, Bernie jumped out of the car and ran towards the house.

"If I see the cops coming I'm getting out of here," Liz said, staring at Bernie's retreating figure. "She can try talking herself out of this one if she wants."

Mary sort of felt like they should be supporting Bernie, but she was also more than happy not to get arrested. Besides, Liz was driving, so as far as Mary was concerned that made her boss of the car. It was a moot point anyway as just a couple of minutes later, Bernie arrived back in the back seat, a little out of breath.

"We're going to need a rethink. There's a nosy neighbour twitching the curtains over at number twenty-seven. I couldn't even climb over the fence without her noticing. Had to pretend I'd lost my phone or I'm sure she would have been phoning 999 there and then."

Mary was more than a little relieved. "All right, so we'll come back tomorrow and —"

"What do you mean 'come back'? I'm still going in there. I could see from the street that Bella has left the kitchen window ajar. I just need you guys to distract Nosy Parker 27."

"But —" Liz began.

"Come on," Mary said, bored of the arguing. "It might be fun. If we play our cards right we might get a cup of tea."

"Fine," Liz replied. "But don't try the Jehovah's Witness thing this time."

"I'll think of something else," Mary said. The truth was, she was happy to be out of the car and doing something. It would look less suspicious when the police did turn up if they weren't sitting in the car right outside the house.

As Mary got out of the car, she grabbed her handbag and inspiration struck.

"I've got my Solaverse stuff in here," Mary told Liz. "I could offer her some free samples."

"And what has the woman done to deserve that?" Liz hissed back. "No, let me take the lead this time. You don't need any more cult members."

Mary was sulking by the time they got up to the door. She had been hoping to at least try out her sales pitch. She was going to have to buy some of the dreadful stuff herself at this rate.

Liz rang the bell and a woman with a pinched face and a small dog that looked like a tiny moving wig answered the door.

"Yes?"

"Hello there. I'm from a charity group. We wanted to talk about setting up a Neighbourhood Watch in this area. Would this be something you would be interested in?"

Mary was always impressed at how professional Liz seemed, no matter what she was claiming to do. If Mary had tried to say the same thing the woman would have shut the door in her face. Instead, the Nosy Parker broke into a grin.

"I would, yes. In fact, I saw a very strange woman hanging around here just a few minutes ago. I'm sure she would have been nicking stuff if I hadn't scared her off."

Liz smiled. "You sound like just the sort of person we're looking for. Mind if we come in?"

Chapter 37: Bernie

With the bare minimum of help from her friends, Bernie had managed to break into Bella Terrance's house. Breaking in was probably a stretch. A window at the back of the house was open and she only had to use her metal nail file on the latch and one quick pull-up got her in. Once in the house, Bernie reached into her pocket and pulled on a pair of latex gloves. She had nicked half a dozen boxes from the care home on her last day and they often came in handy. Not that she would be able to avoid leaving evidence if the police were looking for it, but considering that Bella's place wasn't a crime scene, she reckoned she was safe.

Bella's home reminded Bernie of her sister Martha's place. Was there some sort of middle-class, middle-aged women's décor shop that they both used? Lots of overly positive signage impelling the viewer to laugh or love, two things that Bernie didn't particularly feel like doing at that moment.

Along with the terrible inspirational quotes, there were several photographs on the wall of Bella and Holly. Would you keep your sister's picture on the wall if you murdered her? Bernie wasn't sure. She wasn't one for pictures. She liked clean, plain walls without too much clutter on them. In her own house, she had her wedding photo, one of Ewan as a baby and a photo of Bernie herself completing her first marathon. That was all she needed.

The living room was a little untidy, with a pile of papers that had been tipped onto the floor. Bella must have been in the middle of doing her paperwork when the police arrived. Prepared for any eventuality, Bernie reached into her backpack and brought out a bag for life. She scooped all of the papers up and dumped them into the carrier. Liz could sort through them later and see if there was anything useful. She looked longingly at the laptop on the sofa but decided the police might be a little grumpy if she took that one too.

Bernie moved into the kitchen, taking a quick peek out of the window on the way to check that Mary and Liz were still next door. There was no sign of the nosy neighbour so she just had to hope that the other members of the WWC hadn't chickened out.

The kitchen was pretty standard. Bernie opened a couple of cupboards but there was nothing of interest apart from the amount of ultra-processed foods and a concerning lack of fibre. She made a note to speak to Bella about it once they got her released from custody.

Downstairs covered, Bernie moved upstairs. She was careful to close all the curtains before turning on the lights, just in case the neighbour happened to peek out of the window. There were only two bedrooms upstairs. Bernie discounted the spare room fairly quickly as it looked empty and unused. Instead, she focussed on Bella's bedroom.

Again, the décor was a little too glittery for Bernie's liking and there were far too many pillows on the bed. Not supportive for the lower back either, she thought. She scanned the room for something useful. Next to the bed was some more paperwork and a notepad, so that went into the bag as well. Even Bernie didn't relish rooting through another woman's underwear drawer, and she had just started looking through the bras when there was a noise downstairs.

Bernie's head whipped up and she slammed the drawer shut. She moved as fast as she could towards the top of the stairs.

At that moment, Bernie heard the front door open and someone thumped up the stairs towards her. She shoved the plastic bag into her backpack and called out a 'hello?'

"What the hell are you doing in my house?" Bella Terrance did not look happy when she reached the top of the stairs.

"What the hell are you doing out of prison?" Bernie always believed that the best defence was a strong offence.

Bella put her hands on her hips. "None of your goddamn business. Who the heck are you anyway?"

"Ah, we haven't been introduced. I'm Bernadette Paterson, I'm the founder of the detective agency. Liz Okoro's friend," she finished a little lamely.

"Right. But I still don't get what you're doing in my house."

"We thought you were still at the police station."

"They released me. No thanks to you. I thought you were private investigators, not burglars."

"Sometimes we need to be both," Bernie explained. She wanted to keep the woman talking so that she wasn't tempted to call the police herself. "When you were arrested we didn't get a chance to speak to you, to hear your side of the story. We wanted to do everything we could to get you released so we decided to look for evidence of your innocence."

Bella glared at her. "Well, what did you find?"

"We didn't find the murder weapon covered in blood," Bernie told her. "So that's a point in your favour."

"I just... you know, it's been a really long day. I don't think I can deal with you right now." Bella pinched the bridge of her nose, a stressed facial expression that Bernie found was surprisingly common when she was speaking to people. "Those stupid cops have let me go but they said I am still a 'person of interest'. I got the feeling they were just looking for a reason to keep me in there."

"You said that they had some evidence that you had been cheating your sister, is that right?"

"I'd rather talk to Liz about this."

"She's busy pretending to be a Jehovah's Witness."

"I really don't understand your sense of humour," Bella snapped.

"Most people don't," Bernie said, but she was glad to see that Bella had relaxed her shoulders. It didn't look like anyone was calling the cops, not tonight at least. "Liz is busy right now, and you would only get bogged down in financial jargon. I want you to tell me straight: you were cheating your sister, so how did you do it."

"I didn't plan for it to happen," Bella said, slumping against the wall. "Holly was always talking about how amazing the business was, but it only seemed to be her getting rich. I'm single, right, so I have to pay the mortgage, all the bills and everything myself. So I started borrowing a little money out of the account. Honestly, if she'd found out about it I would have told her it was just what I was owed. I was meant to be a partner, after all. Not to mention her bloody sister."

"How much?"

"A few thousand. Less than ten. You really think I'd kill my own sister for that?"

"People kill each other for all sorts of stupid reasons."

Bella rolled her eyes. "I thought you were meant to be helping me. If I'm the client, why are you accusing me of being the one who killed her?"

"I'm only following the line of enquiry that the police will take. The best way to defend yourself from them is to make sure that you have an explanation for everything."

"Makes sense, I guess. Look, I'm tired and I really want you out of my house now. Or were you planning on staying to watch me sleep?"

"I think I'll pass," Bernie replied. "Although I could stay and give your bathroom a clean. That silicon has seen better days."

Bella pointed to the door. "Out. Now."

Deciding not to push her luck any further, Bernie hurried back down the stairs. She strode out of the front door to find Mary and Liz standing like lemons right outside.

"Bella came back!" Mary said as Bernie stormed past her towards the car.

"Thank you Captain Obvious. Where was my warning signal?"

"We were busy distracting the neighbour. That Nosy Parker made us some really good coffee," Liz explained. "She had an Italian blend, it was awesome."

"You don't even like coffee, Mary, what in the hell distracted you?"

"She had a dog," Mary said, and that explained everything.

"You guys would both be sacked if there was any chance I could hire two private investigators in the next five minutes."

"And I'm driving you home," Liz reminded her as they got into the car.

"That too."

"Well, that was a total bust," Mary said once they were on their way back home. "Did Bella fire you?"

"No, but she was close. I think I persuaded her to keep us on. Anyway, I wouldn't say it's a total bust."

"Why?"

Bernie held up her trusty bag for life. "Because I nabbed some of her paperwork before she got back. That woman is far too trusting. I'll be letting her know about home security too. Just as soon as we've finished our investigation."

Chapter 38: Walker

Walker felt utterly drained by the time he got to Mary's house late on Friday night. The flood of adrenaline when his boss had collapsed had passed and left him washed out. Macleod would be okay and the DI was in the best place he could be. But the fear that had settled in his stomach hadn't left yet.

Really, he should have just gone home, but he didn't want to be alone. As soon as he opened the door and hugged Mary into his chest, he knew he had made the right decision. She might drive him crazy at times, but Mary Plunkett always managed to make him feel better. Selfishly, he was glad that all the kids were asleep. He wanted her to himself for once.

"I'm so sorry about Macleod," Mary said as they walked into the house together.

Walker twitched his shoulders in a half-shrug. He wasn't sure what to say. According to the hospital, Macleod was on the mend but it was hard to shake the image of him collapsed on the office floor.

"He's going to be okay," Walker managed to say. "But it was all pretty horrible."

"He's lucky you were there."

Walker didn't think there was much about the day that had been lucky. But just having Mary next to him was easing a little of the tension.

"Where have you been?" Walker asked, finally realising that her face was flushed and she had the guilty look she got when she let the kids watch nineties action films.

"Um, out jogging."

"Jogging? In that?" He stared at the weird shiny suit. "What on earth are you wearing anyway?"

Mary looked down at her outfit. "Don't you like it?"

"I mean, it's fine... It's just not you."

"What, can't I be a businesswoman now?" Mary asked, laughing as she said it.

"Of course you could be a businesswoman, but wearing something a little less, well, trouser suit. A t-shirt with some obscure eighties pop band on it or something. I mean, you still look cute," Walker belatedly realised his girlfriend might not be pleased with this conversation. "It's just not the Mary that I know."

"That's because I'm not Mary. I'm Maria. And Maria would not wear anything as cool as my Bewitched t-shirt. I'm undercover."

Walker groaned. "Let me guess: this is something to do with the Holly Moore case."

"I can't possibly divulge that to a member of the constabulary," Mary said with a wink.

"Wouldn't matter anyway," Walker said, slumping further

down the sofa. "I'm off the case."

"What? Why? It's not because of me is it?"

He reached over and pulled her next to him. "Not because of you, don't worry about that. I suppose it's because of me. Macleod was only ever indulging me by letting me into the Major Incident Teams as much as he did. Now that he's in the hospital there's no one to advocate for me. And MacKinnon basically told me that I needed to wise up and know my place."

Mary rested her head on his shoulder. "I'm sorry to hear that. But if they don't recognise what an amazing detective you would be then they're just as idiotic as Bernie always says they are."

"I'm not sure if I'm doing the right thing, staying in the force," Walker told her, voicing his biggest worry. "If they're not going to make me a detective then I don't know how long I can stick it out."

"Why would you stay somewhere that makes you unhappy?" Mary asked, as if it was that simple.

"It doesn't most of the time, that's the thing. And I know I would make a great detective. It's just frustrating not to get that opportunity."

He looked down at his police-issue boots. Was it time to move on? It was a hell of a thought. And there were other reasons why he found the idea of leaving the force so difficult.

"It's funny, until you asked about my mum the other day," Walker said. "I hadn't thought about her for a while."

Mary shifted awkwardly next to him. "I didn't mean to cause a row. It's just... I hate that there are parts of your life that I know nothing about."

"It's not that I deliberately lie about it or anything," Walker said, trying to explain something that he didn't understand himself. "It's just easier not to talk about it. But I think it all feeds into this police thing. Mum and dad really hated it when I left the army. Which was funny, because they weren't exactly over the moon when I joined. But they have this thing about quitting. Like it's admitting failure. All the way through school they used to get me to do harder and harder subjects. They never accepted that I just couldn't do some stuff. And even when I say that it makes them sound like great parents, doesn't it? Ru certainly thought they were, pushing him forward to excel at school. But for me the more they pushed the worse I did. And of course it didn't help that I couldn't read half the stuff I was given."

"And they didn't realise you were dyslexic?"

"They just thought I wasn't trying," Walker said with a shrug of his shoulders. "I mean, I probably did give up a bit by the end. It's kind of depressing to spend days reading a textbook that someone else flicked through in an hour. But my parents just couldn't get it. Going to university for them was not just a plan, it was expected. And Ru lived up to that expectation, whereas I didn't."

"You don't think... I mean, you wouldn't ever try and reconcile with them?" Mary asked, and he could tell how much she wanted him to say yes.

"It's not that I haven't tried over the years. But it always ends badly."

Mary was quiet now, and Walker worried that she was disappointed in him. It was so hard to explain quite how damaging his upbringing had been.

"The thing is, I never thought I was worth much," Walker's throat was getting dry from talking so much, but he wanted her to understand. "Certainly nothing like as much as Ru or my parents. I didn't think I was anything special really. Until."

He started laughing.

"What?"

"It just sounds so cheesy." He pulled her in for a kiss. "But there is no better way of saying it. I never thought I was worth anything until I met you."

"Oh." Mary sounded shocked. "That's kind of lovely but kind of sad too."

"I don't think it's sad. Not anymore."

She reached out and took his hand and he didn't release it until they went up to bed.

Chapter 39: Liz

It was Saturday morning and instead of having a lie-in, Liz Okoro was working through a bunch of stolen paperwork. There were a million documents to go through and simply not enough time. So like many parents over the years, Liz had decided to utilise under-aged slave labour.

Sean sat at the kitchen table sifting through the envelopes and printed paper. "What am I looking for, Mum?"

"I want you to sort it into three piles. Anything that's just junk like takeaway menus, stick in one section. Another is for anything relating to the business but not financial, so like makeup branding, all that crap, put it together. And the final pile is anything financial. Bills, bank statements, anything that relates to the money side of things. That's the most important one."

"Got it."

Thankfully, Sean hadn't asked how the WWC had got hold of all this stuff. It would have been a little awkward to explain to her son that it had been stolen from Bella's house. It didn't help that Bernie had handed over the plastic bag in the car like it was contaminated.

Liz had already grabbed some of the more promising items before Sean started doing the sorting. The first was a bill from a local supplier, Lolo Printing, which had caught Liz's eye due to the heading in red ink at the top of the page. According to the note, it was a third and final reminder for payment of an invoice and the letter was threatening to take them to court if non-payment continued. The invoice amount was for just under three thousand pounds, not a small amount, but not the sort of money that a person would normally risk a legal judgement for. Another thing that had struck Liz was that the bill was addressed to Holly. Had she given it to her sister? Or had Bella obtained it without her sister's knowledge? Something to ask their client later.

A quick search on the internet later and Liz had the telephone number for Lolo Printing, a shop in Invergryff near the college. It took her five minutes on the phone to explain exactly why she was calling, but eventually she got put through to the manager, Chloe.

"I saw in the news that that woman died," Chloe said once Liz had told her she was investigating the firm. "And God help me but the first thing I thought was: there goes any chance of us getting our money back."

"Can I ask what it was that they hadn't paid for?"

"Marketing materials. A couple of hundred tote bags, big banners for doing shows, flyers, leaflets, all sorts of stuff.

"And you didn't take payment up front?"

There was a pause on the other end. "We usually do."

"Then why…"

"My husband took the order. Let's just say he fell for a pretty face. I was pretty cross when he took the order, so you can imagine just how I felt when they never bothered to pay up."

"Ah, I see."

Liz finished the conversation with Chloe quickly as apart from failing to get paid, the woman had no other information on dare2dream. But it was all causing alarm bells to go off in Liz's brain. At first, she thought that dare2dream were traditional scammers in that only the people at the top were making money. But if Bella was having to steal from her sister to pay the bills and Holly couldn't even pay a fairly standard supplies invoice, where was all the money going?

There was a jangle of keys that signalled Dave was back from his walk with Issy in the buggy.

"It's just started spitting rain," he told Liz when he came into the kitchen, reaching over to grab a banana from the fruit bowl. "Issy's fast asleep so I've left her in the hall. Only got five thousand steps done so I'll have to go out again later."

Dave's latest obsession was a step-tracker on his wrist. He seemed to think that everyone wanted to know how many steps he had taken at any given moment. He was wrong.

"That's nice," Liz said, still focussed on the endless pile of papers.

"I see you have a new assistant," Dave said, giving their son a high-five.

"Yep. I thought it would save me money but he's probably costing as much as paid help in chocolate biscuits."

"Harsh," Sean said. "I only had four. What do you want me to do with printouts of Holly Moore's emails? I'm not sure if it counts as finance or just general business."

"Pass them over here," Liz said, holding out her hand. She scanned through them. "This is very weird. It seems to be to do with a commercial property sale. A unit of shops by the sound of things. But dare2dream is all online, what would they want shops for?"

Dave shrugged. "No idea love. Want a coffee?"

"And why would you bother to print out emails in the first place?" Liz mused, speaking half to herself. "I mean, no one does that anymore do they?"

"I do at work if I need to show someone something important," Dave said. "People pay much more attention if it's in their hand."

"So I guess that means these messages are important for some reason," Liz said. She read through them a bit more closely.

The emails seemed to be regarding Better Life Now and in fact the subject of many was someone called Gail Carrer, and Liz was sure that Tom Field had mentioned a Gail that worked in the office on the zoom call the other day. As usual it was hard to work through all the pseudo-business jargon, but there seemed to be some confusion over a property sale that had happened six months ago. The email thread was titled 'RE: Skelton Street' and there were lots of messages about outstanding charges back and forth. The tone got a little heated by the end.

The agent that put us in touch is still asking for their fee. One email read, then the next replied:

We are happy to avoid this expense if you are. Ms Moore will call to discuss.

And that was the end of the conversation. Sure she was missing something important, Liz went online to a house sale website and took a look at the historic transactions. Sure enough, a large commercial unit of a dozen shops had been sold in October of last year. The sale price was 3.2 million pounds.

"Woah, that's a lot of money," Sean said, peering over her shoulder.

"Enough to kill for?"

"Yup."

Liz agreed.

Chapter 40: Mary

Just as Mary was thinking she might have a quiet Saturday morning to catch up on her reading, with Walker out for a run and the kids in the PJs watching telly, Bernie Paterson turned up at the door.

"Are those cowboy pyjamas," Bernie asked as she shook off her coat.

"It's *Firefly*, a show from... never mind. Why don't you make us a tea while I go and get changed," Mary said as she hurried upstairs. Five minutes later she was back downstairs where she found Bernie tipping a bag full of assorted chocolate bars onto the table.

"Chocolate? That's not like you," Mary said.

"I know, but I didn't think protein bars would do the trick. These are for the kids."

"Oh, that's nice of you but I don't like to give them chocolate before lunch."

Bernie scowled at her. "Come on, it'll give us five minutes peace. I want to talk shop."

"All right," Mary said, giving in as usual. "But give me one of those chocolate bars over here before the kids eat them all."

"Really?"

Mary unwrapped the bar while Bernie distributed the rest to the kids and shut the door.

"I didn't sleep too well last night," Mary explained. "Walker was upset, he's going through a lot with his work at the moment. And he actually talked about his mother to me for once."

"Imagine that," Bernie said, looking bored. But Mary needed someone to talk to and there was no one else available.

"I hate that he doesn't speak to his mum," Mary explained. "It's all so sad. They gave him such a hard time about his academic stuff at school, and they just didn't understand what it was like for him. I can't help but think that if Walker's parents understood about dyslexia at the time they might have been a lot closer."

"Or they might not," Bernie said, her brows lowered. "From what you've told me, dyslexia wasn't the only issue there."

"I guess so," Mary said, but she wasn't convinced. Bernie saw the world through her own perspective and insights and she never saw that a different point of view might be relevant. Mary on the other hand was always in two minds about everything. She wasn't too sure if that was better or worse.

"I've read through everything that Liz has put up on this case file and I still can't get my head around all this pyramid scheme stuff. But I'm inclined to think that's where we're going to find our killer, only because we don't have any other suspects."

"Maybe you could ask Deborah about it again?"

Bernie narrowed her eyes. "And why would I do that?"

"She's an expert on dare2dream. And, well, it might give you something to talk about. She did try and help Ewan after all."

The room went quiet apart from Bernie's trainer tapping a rhythm on the floor.

"Let me guess," the woman said slowly. "You're thinking there will be some sort of happily-ever-after moment where my mother and I will make up and everything will be fine."

"No, I just –"

"Is this what the problem is with Walker too? Jesus Mary, sometimes families break up for a reason. Did it ever occur to you that it is better for both me and Deborah if we stay away from each other? That if we tried to play happy families we would end up hating each other even more?"

"I…"

"You need to respect people's boundaries. Mine and your stupid boyfriend's. God, now you've made me feel sorry for the copper."

Mary went quiet and her cheeks turned pink.

"I'm sorry if I've upset you," Bernie said.

"No you're not."

"Not really. But do you understand now that not everyone can have the lovely relationship with their parents that you have? Not everyone's childhood was happy. Just because it wasn't technically abuse or neglect, you can still have some utterly crap parents that you want nothing to do with. And unless I'm wrong – which I never am – then that's what's going on with Walker too. The more you try and 'fix things' for him and his family, the more he'll push you away."

Mary sniffed. "I thought you would be on my side."

"I am. And I've already told that man of yours to be nice to you. But I can't help if you're going to sabotage everything in a mistaken need for everyone else's life to be perfect."

Bernie reached over and put her finger on Mary's mouth.

"Ssh. That's enough now."

Mary was so shocked that she did indeed shush.

"Now I want you to get into this pyramid scheme like a bloody pharaoh. Find out who had the best motive to kill Holly and do it today. Because any more time spent with Deborah and I'm going to lose the blooming plot."

Mary raised her hand. "Do I speak now?"

"Of course you do," Bernie rolled her eyes.

"Can I have the money for the lifestyle coaching? I reckon if I wave a grand under Tom Field's nose then everyone is going to be much friendlier."

"A grand? I should bloody well think not. But I'll give you one of those fake cheques we used in that corporate case. That way he'll think he's getting the money but it won't be denting my expense account."

"You do think of everything, don't you Bernie?" Mary said weakly.

"And don't you forget it."

Chapter 41: Bernie

It was lunchtime on Saturday and for the last few weeks, Bernie had spent her Saturdays in training for her latest distance running challenge. This Saturday however, she was sweating for a different reason.

After speaking to Mary it had become clear that they needed to force this investigation wide open. All of Liz's investigations into the company's financial details seemed to have given Bella a motive and no one else. This was frustrating as Bernie found that clients were less likely to pay their bills when imprisoned for murder.

Mary's weird obsession with everyone making friends with their parents – something that Bernie hoped she had made the woman reconsider – had given Bernie an idea for how to go forward. She realised that she had been making a mistake where Deborah was concerned.

Just because she didn't like the woman, it didn't mean that she couldn't use her. Where this case was concerned, Deborah was an untapped asset. Once Bernie looked at things that way it made the prospect of meeting up with her mother more tolerable.

Deborah had got the best of her where the meeting with Ewan's teacher was concerned, so Bernie knew that she needed to start this meeting off on her terms. That was why she was sitting in Martha's kitchen. Everything was ready when the doorbell rang.

"Come in?" Bernie said, offering her mother the sort of warm smile found in rivers in Florida.

"I didn't know you were going to be here," Deborah said, not even pretending to play nice today. "Where's Martha?"

"I sent her on a spa day. She should be getting a relaxing massage right about now." Bernie shook her head. In her opinion, massages shouldn't be relaxing. If you weren't shouting out in pain then they weren't doing it right.

"Then why…"

"I wanted to speak to you myself," Bernie said.

"Is this about Ewan? I do hope he's doing better."

"You did well there."

Deborah's overly plucked eyebrows shot up. "Really?"

"Yeah. If only you had run it by me first."

"Would you have let me go to the school?"

"Hell no," Bernie laughed and Deborah managed a smile too. Then there was a knock at the door.

"I better get that," Bernie said.

Bernie had never met the woman at the door. She was in her sixties, small and round with nervous hands that never stopped moving. Bernie showed her into the kitchen where Deborah's mouth had dropped open.

"You remember Andi, right? You recruited her into your stupid MLM company, took all her money and then refused to give her a refund."

As if acknowledging the woman was too much, Deborah turned instead to Bernie.

"What is this, an ambush?" she asked.

Bernie shrugged. "You could call it that. Andi here was telling me that you were ghosting her, so I thought let's unmask the ghost, Scooby-do style."

"What?"

"Sorry, been hanging out with Mary Plunkett for too long."

Andi had been standing, looking from one woman to the other.

Deborah let out one of the sighs that she reserved for when the whole world was against her. "I'm sure I meant to phone you back, Andi, but as you can imagine it's been a very busy week. And poor Holly's passing has set everything back."

"But you didn't talk to me at the party last Friday, and Holly was alive then," Andi said, her voice barely above a whisper.

"What party on Friday?" Bernie asked.

"Holly had a little get-together for some of the top reps," Deborah said.

Bernie scowled. "There was a party at our murder victim's house on Friday night and no one thought to tell me about it?"

"It wasn't like a proper party," Andi said, her face apologetic, "I mean, it was one of those pep talks that Tom Field does sometimes."

"He's so inspirational," Deborah said.

"I know," Andi said, nodding her head vigorously.

"You know that these crooks took your money, don't you?" Bernie reminded her.

"Deborah said it was an administrative error," Andi said. "And I'm sure that Tom would never be involved in something like that."

Bernie slicked her eyes to the ceiling. There was no helping some people.

"Tell me about the not-quite-a-party," Bernie said.

"Well, there was a bit of a commotion, wasn't there Deborah?"

"I'm sure I don't remember."

"Mother, please," Bernie said, her frustration mounting. "The sooner we get this sorted out the sooner you can get back to bingo and bus trips or whatever it is that you do with your free time."

"Always so unpleasant," Deborah said, with another sigh. "I suppose that Andi is referring to the fact that Holly and Bella decided to have a go at me because of my new business idea.

They had this whole strop about the fact that I was leaving to strike out on my own. I was hoping Michelle would back me up, but she left early. And Tom didn't seem too interested either, which was frustrating. I'm sure if I'd been twenty years younger it would have been a different story"

"Oh, I love Michelle, she was so nice to me when I joined," Andi said.

"For god's sake, she was stealing your money, just like Deborah here," Bernie snapped. "You need to get better friends."

"Right," Andi said, snapping her mouth shut. "I might just head home now, if I'm not going to get my money."

"I'll make sure she gets you it as soon as possible. Thanks for your help," Bernie said as the woman shut the door behind her.

"What a drip," Deborah said. "Come on, I know you're thinking the same."

"She is a drip," Bernie agreed. "But that doesn't make her a bad person and it certainly doesn't give you the right to exploit her."

"You are tiring me out, Bernadette. Are we finished here?"

"Tell me more about what happened at this party on Friday night."

"It's just like I said, I explained to Holly how I was going to be independent from now on and she was really nasty about it.

But Tom wanted to talk to her about some property thing, so I couldn't even have a proper discussion with her. It would have been different if Michelle was there to back me up. That's why I went back the next night, so that I could have it out with her in private."

"Why would Michelle back you up?"

"Because she was talking about getting out too. Moving more into the investment side of things. It was Michelle that encouraged me to go out on my own. She told me how she had made this amazing property sale happen and that her cut was going to be six figures."

"Is this Michelle that you and Andi are talking about the one that works in the hippy shop?"

"That's the one. She started selling Solaverse like the rest of us and now she's going to pay off her mortgage."

Bernie was getting tired too, but she wanted to wrap this case up. "I'm going to go and talk to this Michelle woman. You didn't nick any money from her did you?"

"Of course not."

"Okay, then there's just one thing left to do. Transfer that money back to Andi while I watch to make sure you do it."

"Are you kidding?"

"Does it look like it?"

"No, but then you always did have a sour face."

Bernie gripped the table until her knuckles went white. "Transfer back that woman's money and I won't delete your number from Ewan's phone."

Deborah's face brightened. "And I can phone him any time?"

"Until he gets sick of you, sure." Bernie knew that wouldn't be too long. In the end, it only took a couple of minutes for Deborah to open up her banking app and ping the money over to Andi's account.

"Aren't you going to say thank you?" Deborah said, her mouth twisted into a grimace.

"Nope. But I am going to say goodbye."

Chapter 42: Walker

Walker had just got out of the shower at Mary's place after his run when he heard a banging on the door. He pulled on his jeans and a t-shirt and hurried down the stairs.

"Oh, it's you."

"Nice to see you too Bernie. I'm afraid that Mary's not here. She's taken the kids shopping."

"She's not answering my calls," Bernie said.

Why did the woman always give him an instant headache? "Maybe she's busy. With the kids and the shopping, you see?"

"Why aren't you with her? You should be using those gym muscles to carry the shopping bags."

"Because I... Was there something you wanted?" Walker said, counting to ten inside his head.

"I wanted to ask her about her undercover stuff. You look tired. Have you been taking those supplements I gave you?"

"I had a rough day yesterday," Walker told her. "Macleod was taken to hospital. He collapsed at the station."

Bernie tossed her head back. "Ha! I told him to watch what he ate. All that refined sugar and no exercise."

"He's doing fine thank you very much."

"Don't be banal," Bernie replied. Walker wondered if he would get in trouble with Mary for shutting the door in her face.

"I wanted to talk to Mary about this party that was held at Holly Moore's house on the Friday night."

"What party?"

"Ah, they didn't tell you about it either, that makes me feel a little better. You know, you could invite me in."

"Fine," Walker said with bad grace. "Come in."

Bernie walked into the hall and then turned around so that they were in a confined space together. Walker had to stop himself from backing up against the door.

"There was a party at Holly Moore's house two nights before she died. My mother was there, along with Tom Field, Michelle Rallie and Bella Terrance. And I guess a whole bunch of other suckers."

"We definitely weren't aware of that," Walker thought, picturing the crime scene. "If anything it could cause us a whole lot of trouble. It means that the fingerprint evidence that we collected is pretty useless if someone at the party was the killer. There would be no way to tell whether the fingerprints were left Friday night or late on Saturday."

"True. I'm hoping that someone at the party might have threatened Holly or said something useful. I'm going to speak to the hippy woman that recruited Mary. According to Deborah she was thinking of leaving the company so she might be willing to dish the dirt."

"Mary is all right doing this undercover thing, isn't she?" Walker asked. "I mean, you're not putting her in any danger are you?"

"Nothing she can't handle," Bernie said curtly. "Now if you see your missus you tell her that I want a word. If she has to throw herself at Field to get some evidence, then tell her I said it was okay."

"Throw herself at who now?" Walker asked.

"Never mind. I'm off to fit in a round of handball before I do some more interrogating."

With that she strode out of the door, stretching her calf muscles as she walked back to her car. It probably wouldn't even be fun to fight her, Walker thought to himself, she'd just bounce right back up again, like rubber.

When he went back inside he heard a buzzing sound from the living room. In a couple of steps he grabbed his phone and was pleased to see Dianna's number. After his chat with Bernie he needed a conversation that didn't feel like fencing with a sabre-toothed tiger.

Dianna had called with some interesting news.

"One of the names connected with your murder case has just set some alarm bells ringing down here."

"Is it James Moore again?"

"No, this is a person of interest further down the list, but something about it smells dodgy. Are you aware of a Tom Field?"

Was that the name that Bernie had mentioned? Walker pulled up the files on his phone. "Oh yes, that's a director of one of the businesses connected with Holly Moore. And he might have been at her house just before her death too.

"Ah, you'll be interested in this then. Tom Field changed his name around eight years ago. Nothing dodgy about it, all legal and above board. But it did mean that we only just connected the dots on his previous identity."

"Which was?"

"Tom Field was formerly Benjamin Morningside. And he has a record for benefit fraud."

"Benefit fraud? What, claiming something he wasn't entitled to?"

Dianna laughed. "If that was all he would probably have got a slap on the wrist. But no, this was a lot more sophisticated. It was an orchestrated fraud scheme where they made up hundreds of fake identities using real addresses to con the system. There were three of them involved, I'll send you over the details. This was twenty years ago and Field or Morningside as he was then was the junior partner so he only got a year inside."

"Thanks for letting me know," Walker said. He thought about telling her that he'd been bumped off the case, but he didn't want another pep talk. Instead, he sent Suzie an email with the full details and a link to the documents that Dianna had sent him.

Walker stood at the window in Mary's house and stared out at the broken trampoline and the muddy patch that used to be a lawn. The thing was, he knew that he would be able to help with this case. And it was his day off, so it wasn't like he was neglecting the damn burglary reports. But MacKinnon had made it perfectly clear that he would be on thin ice if he kept forcing himself into this case.

But at the end of the day, there was a murderer still at large somewhere. In his town, living their life quite happily with no consequences for their actions. And that just pissed him off.

Coming to a decision, he picked up his phone and dialled Liz Okoro's number.

"Are you looking for Mary?" Liz asked.

"No, you." Walker swallowed, then talked quickly before he could change his mind. "My friend Dianna in London just got back to me this morning with something interesting. You know how you've been looking into this Tom Field guy?"

"The one that Mary thinks is handsome?"

"Yes that's the... wait what?"

"Never mind, you were telling me something important."

"Right." Walker tried to find the thread of his thoughts once more. "Well Tom Field used to be known as Benjamin

Morningside and he had a record for fraud."

"I knew it! What sort of fraud?"

"Some sort of benefits scam. It was a bunch of them running false identities to claim benefits. I don't know the full details, but that was the jist of it. He spent a year inside."

"Brilliant." There was a pause at the other end. "Should you be passing all this on to us?"

"Probably not," Walker admitted. "But I'm off the case and I reckon you guys might be close to solving it."

"And you reckon that if we solve the case then the guys at the station will be thinking 'geez, if only we'd had that Walker on the case, we should get him back immediately'."

"That was a Bernie Paterson-type comment."

"Sorry, you're right. She kind of rubs off on you. The good and the bad."

Chapter 43: Liz

Two emergency WWC meetings in one week meant that Liz's gin supply was running low. Along with her biscuit supply as Mary had brought her children with her this time.

"Sorry to be a pain," Mary had said as the children ran out into Liz's garden with all the sounds of a mid-size warzone. "I didn't want to ask my mum to babysit again and all of Bernie's nieces are at a Taylor Swift concert."

"It's fine, Sean likes entertaining them. Or bossing them around, more likely."

"Good luck to him," Mary said, leaning her elbows on the counter. "Make mine a large one will you? I've got another 'Change your Life by Investing in You!' seminar later and I need to be tipsy to get through it.

"Right you are," Liz said, topping up the glass. She was glad that some of the shine had come off Mary's MLM experience. Especially with what they'd learned about the company in the last few days.

"Sorry I'm late," Bernie said, coming into the kitchen and positioning herself in front of the radiator. "I've not even had a chance to dry my hair. There was a bit of an incident at handball. Honestly, if you can't keep up with the level of everyone else you shouldn't be there."

"What did you do," Liz asked.

"Nothing. But anyway, that's what pacemakers are for, right?"

Liz shared a look with Mary and they mutually decided not to ask any questions.

"Anyway, I was hoping to get to see Michelle Rallie after handball but it didn't happen."

"Michelle? Why?" Mary asked.

"Because Deborah only just told me that there was a party at Holly's house on the Friday before she was killed. My mother was there along with all the head honchos from dare2dream and that other company with the stupid name."

"Better Life Now," Liz reminded her.

"That's it. Sounds like a slogan for Valium. Anyway, Deborah told me that Michelle was thinking of getting out of the company. Apparently she had made loads of money and was going to strike out on her own."

"Really?" Liz frowned. "That's news to me. I thought she was dare2dream's number one fan?"

"Me too," Mary said. "She's still going to most of the meetings."

"Well, that's what Deborah said, but as you know she's full of crap. So I was going to go and see her earlier only the whole ambulance situation slowed me down. I'll head over this evening."

"She should be in around eight," Mary said. "On the zoom call earlier Michelle said she would miss the investment talk because her dog needed some medicine or something."

"Perfect," Bernie said, "and then I'll –"

She broke off as a small child tottering in through the back door and headed over to Mary, hand outstretched.

"Present for mum!" Lauren said, opening her hand to something wriggling.

"I'm sorry sweetie," Mary said without missing a beat, "could you take your little centipede out of here, we're trying to solve a murder."

"Okay," Lauren said, taking her prize back out to the garden.

"Nothing about those kids sends you into a flap, does it?" Liz asked.

"Well it's like that old saying, a bug in the hand is better than the time that they put an earthworm under my pillow."

"Did they really –"

"Can we get on please," Bernie said severely.

"Yes Bernie," the other two chorused.

"Now we're running out of time here. Detective Inspector Macleod is in hospital and I don't trust any of those other wallies at the station to make any progress on our case. Which means that Deborah is going to be hanging around like a bad smell. And I can't put up with that anymore. So I want to go through every single possible suspect and see if there's something we've missed."

"Sure," said Liz. "Where do you want to start?"

"I think we need to consider our client, Bella Terrance. In her favour, she seemed to be genuine in her grief for her sister. Against: she inherits the business."

"I'm not sure that's such a great thing after all," Liz pointed out. "I've been going through all that paperwork and despite all the signup fees, dare2dream was barely scraping a profit. If they started actually paying out all those 'thirty day refund guarantees' then they would probably go under."

"Noted. We'll put her in the long-shot category. Who else?"

"What about Michelle?" Liz asked. "Mary said she looked upset with Tom Field the other day. And Deborah said she was thinking about getting out."

"I know what Deborah said," Mary replied, "but Michelle really loves dare2dream. Even if she had wanted to branch out, I can't see her wanting Holly dead. I mean, today she was still going on about the make-up and everything. She's a proper paid up cult member."

"True," Liz said. "She goes to the bottom. What about Tom Field?"

Bernie was already nodding her head. "He seems just the type to kill someone who got in his way. A ruthless sort."

"And Walker came good with his background check," Liz said. She filled the others in about Field's alter ego and previous conviction.

"Benefit fraud?" Mary looked stunned. "Jeez, I thought he had more class than that."

"I'm still waiting for the court records on that one," Liz said. "I'm going to see if I can dig around a bit and find out exactly how much of it was his idea."

"I wonder if Holly knew about his past," Mary said.

"Maybe she found out and that's why he killed her. He's top of my list."

"I agree," Liz said. "Who else do we have?"

"Have we definitely ruled out James Moore?"

"I reckon so," Bernie said. "There's still a chance that he could have contracted out the killing, but the man's broke so how would he have paid for it? Plus it just seems a bit more Chicago gangsters than Invergryffe ex-husband."

"Okay, is there anyone else we're missing?"

"I suppose Deborah has to be on the list," Bernie said. "Although as I've said before, the fact that she came to see me for help rather than doing a dramatic confession makes it rather out-of-character."

"I can't see Andi or any of the others further down the chain attacking Holly," Mary said. "I mean, yes they lost money, but not enough to murder someone."

"So Tom Field is our best bet, with Bella as an outside chance.

I'm going to ask Michelle if either of them was behaving oddly at this party they were at. If we're in luck she might have seen something."

"Deborah didn't notice anything?" Mary asked.

"Are you kidding? It was a party, she'd have been thinking about herself. Right, I better get going. I'll phone a taxi. Mary, do you want dropped off?"

Mary shook her head. "No thanks. Walker's going to give me a lift. He's at a bit of a loose end since they took him off the case."

"You can tell him that if he ever decides to leave the force he's got a job with us," Bernie said.

Mary's mouth dropped open. "What? Bernie, you don't even like him."

"I don't hate him," Bernie replied. "And he's a half-decent investigator. And I bet his cake expenses aren't as high as yours."

Chapter 44: Mary

Mary would be glad when it was time to hang up Maria Johnstone's shiny suit. It was starting to make her itch and it was definitely too small around the hip area. Still, the case was moving forward and she was determined to find out exactly what was going on with this company and if there was any connection to the death of Holly Moore.

Walker drove her over to the seminar. This time for some unexplained reason it was taking place in the function room of a pub. Mary thought Liz might be right about the money trouble; the venues were certainly becoming less fancy. A banner outside proclaimed 'Change your Life one Giant Leap at a Time' which made her and Walker giggle.

Mary checked her watch. "I'm sorry, but I've got to go inside."

"Oh, that's okay," Walker said, with his sad-puppy eyes.

"Why don't you come with me?"

She wasn't too surprised when he jumped at the chance. Mary hoped that he would get back on the official murder investigation soon. Walker was one of those guys that needed a challenge to keep him out of trouble. She couldn't believe that the police wouldn't acknowledge how brilliant he was. Perhaps Bernie's offer of employment wasn't completely out of the question.

"You have to remember that I'm in charge when we're

undercover," Mary said before they got out of the car. "And that you're just my assistant in the investigation."

"You're loving this a bit too much, aren't you?" Walker's mouth curled up at one corner.

"Maybe. Now shut your pretty mouth and let me work."

Mary led them up the stairs to the function room. She placed her hand on the door and then paused as something struck her.

"Damn, we forgot to work out our cover story."

"Are you kidding?" Walker asked.

"Certainly not. Look, I'm Maria Johnstone, okay, and I guess you can still be my boyfriend."

"Gee thanks," Walker said, not looking too impressed.

"You can choose your own fake identity if you like. It's kind of fun."

"All right," Walker said, "just say I work in a shop or something. I guess they might not react well to having a cop here."

Mary was disappointed that Walker hadn't gone for a more exciting alter-ego, but then he wasn't experienced in the art of espionage like she was.

"What about your name?"

"John."

She rolled her eyes but said nothing. Who ever heard of a spy called John?

Mary led the way into the function room where a dozen people were milling around a mismatched collection of chairs.

"Oh, Tom is coming over. Just, you know, be cool."

Walker looked like he was about to say something else, but Mary ignored him. Tom Field gave over and gave her a kiss on the cheek.

"Maria? I didn't realise you had a significant other," Tom said, holding out his hand to Walker.

Walker grinned with only his teeth and shook the other man's hand. Mary noticed that both men's sets of knuckles went white with the force of the grip. She felt an almost overwhelming urge to giggle. Male posturing always made her laugh.

"This is Tom from Better Life Now," Mary explained. "Tom has been running the show for dare2dream since Holly died."

She didn't miss the fact that the man flinched.

"I've been helping out. Such a terrible tragedy."

"Had you worked with Holly for long?" Walker asked.

"A while. She was an inspiration to so many people. And her legacy will live on. Excuse me, I have to set up." Tom hurried away to the other end of the room where a sad-looking banner and table had been set up.

"He made her sound like Princess Diana," Walker whispered.

Mary laughed, then put her hand over her mouth. He was going to get her in trouble at this rate. They went to take their seats while the last stragglers entered the room.

"Crap, there's Bella," Mary whispered, spotting Holly's sister. "I should have realised that she'll recognise you. Scoot down."

Walker slumped as much as possible in the seat beside her and luckily Bella took up a position on the other side of the room. Mary knew they were in trouble though. There was no way they would be able to leave without her recognising the cop in the room.

No time to worry about that now, however, as Tom had started another one of his inspirational pep talks from the table at the front. Mary had to kick Walker on the ankle a few times as he kept snorting with laughter whenever Tom mentioned his favourite inspirational buzzwords, but other than that the talk went without a hitch. Mary noticed that there were half a dozen new people in the room, all women, all looking just as nervous as she was on her first day.

A squeaking noise from the door told her that someone had arrived late. When Mary swivelled around in her seat she was surprised to see Liz, standing at the back and waiting for Tom to finish. Not sure if she was meant to acknowledge her friend or not, Mary turned back around. The ten minutes that Tom continued to blather on about investment potential and property deals seemed to drag on forever.

As soon as the talk finished, Mary hurried over to see Liz,

dragging Walker along with her.

"What are you doing here?" Mary asked.

"Is this a friend of yours?" Tom Field appeared beside her, looking Liz up and down. Mary thought he might start salivating when he clocked her friend's expensive clothes and bag.

"A very good friend, but that's not why I'm here," Liz said. "I would like to have a word with you, Mr Field."

At that moment another figure appeared next to Tom.

"What is that cop doing here?" Bella asked.

"Cop?" Now Tom really did look nervous. "What cop?"

"Um… this is Walker. I mean, John. Um…" Mary looked to Liz for help.

"It's my day off," Walker said, giving her hand a squeeze.

"I'm a private investigator," Liz explained. "And I'm a specialist in corporate fraud."

Tom's eyes flicked towards the door, but Bella just crossed her arms.

"And you're meant to be working for me," the woman said. "How exactly does it help me to interrupt this meeting?"

"This has nothing to do with your sister's murder. Well, not directly, at any rate. Although you might want to ask yourself if Holly would still be alive if you had chosen a less dodgy means of making money."

"How dare you!"

They were drawing a bit of a crowd now, which was why Tom put his hand on Bella's shoulder in an attempt to calm her down.

"I think we should take this outside," he said.

"I think not," Liz replied. "The people here deserve to hear this. They deserve to hear that your real name is not Tom Field. It's Benjamin Morningside, isn't it?"

There was a pleasing gasp from the other people in the room. Tom Field wisely stayed silent, giving Liz a glare that would have silenced a less confident person.

"I mean I get why you might want a new start," Liz continued. "Take control of your life. Inspire your future, isn't that what you said? But I do feel it's a bit deceptive not to tell the people investing their money with you that you have a history of fraud."

Liz had a grin on her face that reminded Mary of Emperor Palpatine when he was about to destroy a planet. It was funny, everyone thought that Bernie was the tough one, but Liz could be just as scary when she wanted to be.

"I really don't think this is the time or place…"

"I'm afraid it is. A woman is dead, Mr Field. A woman that you knew very well. Because that's what I discovered today. It took a bit of digging around but I found out the names of the other people who were convicted alongside you at the time. Two sisters named Holly and Bella."

Another gasp, this time from Mary who hadn't seen this one coming. Tom and Holly knew each other? It made sense in a way and explained why the companies were so interlinked. She shook her head. People were so sneaky.

Next to her, Liz was still talking. "And part of the court judgement in the case was that none of you were to be Directors of a company again. Which all three of you were. You'll be pleased to know that I've passed this on to the proper authorities."

In a nice sense of dramatic timing, the doors at the back of the hall opened and two police officers walked in. Mary recognised Walker's friend Neil and a younger constable who also looked familiar. Mary gave them a little wave before Walker stepped on her toes.

"Oops, sorry," she whispered, putting her professional face back on.

"People don't go to prison for that sort of thing," Tom Field said, all of his charms now slipping away.

"No they don't," Liz said. "But it was enough ground for warrants to search your properties. I suggested to the officers that it might be worth detaining you while they searched. I mean, I wouldn't want any important documents to disappear. I know Bella has a habit of leaving the back window open."

Mary grinned at this one, but Bella didn't seem too impressed.

"Cocky bitch," she said.

Liz put her hand to her chest in mock-injury. "Ouch. I might not have found all the evidence to put you away yet but I'm sure once they start rooting around in your computer systems they will find everything they need."

The police officers walked over to Bella and Tom and all of a sudden Liz wasn't in charge anymore. She stepped to one side while the cops did their thing. Soon enough, Walker's friend and the other police officer walked Tom Field and Bella Terrance out of the room. The hush that had fallen descended into the frantic chatter of everyone around them.

"What was that about, Maria?" One of the other women asked.

"Um, I can't really say, sorry." Mary hurried over to join Walker and Liz as they were walking out of the door.

Outside, Walker was chatting to Neil while the police constable put the two suspects into the car. Like Liz, Mary knew it wasn't going to be a life sentence for Bella and Tom, but she was sure that the tech wizards at the station would find enough evidence of dodgy financial practices to shut down the two companies.

As if reading her mind, Liz said: "I've passed on all my files on their financial dealings. I reckon there's enough there for a conviction. They'll never run a company again, that's for sure."

Mary was pleased. Part of her had enjoyed the community and the self-esteem boost of being a part of dare2dream. Tom

Field's charm alone had been a reason to join. But when she looked at the other women filtering out, she realised that they had all had a lucky escape.

Walker came back to join them as the police car drove away. "Can I speak to you both for a minute?"

"Sure," Liz said.

"I just heard something interesting from Neil. There's been a development on the Holly Moore case. A new report has just come in from the pathologist. They took another look at the wound and found some sort of particles inside. And it turns out to be salt."

"Salt?" Mary frowned. "What does that mean?"

"I don't know," Walker said. "But I was hoping you guys might."

"Maybe she was attacked in her kitchen," Liz said. "The weapon could have been contaminated or –"

"Oh my god, I've got it!" Mary felt her heart race. "Bloody hell, I think I know who did it. And I think we've just sent Bernie over there."

Chapter 45: Bernie

"You have a lot of those orange things," Bernie said as Michelle Rallie handed her an herbal tea. "What do they do exactly?"

"They're Himalayan salt lamps, carved from rock salt. It's an ancient practice."

"Using ancient lightbulbs?"

"I can see you have a difficult aura," Michelle said firmly.

Bernie was about to retort with her exact opinion on auras, before she remembered she was meant to be keeping the woman on side. She had only been in the flat for five minutes, but all the incense was making her sneeze and the herbal tea had bits floating in it. Bernie searched for something to get the woman to open up to her, but unfortunately, small talk wasn't her strong point.

"It's a nice flat," Bernie lied, looking around the cluttered living room which was full of hippy paraphernalia and one fluffy and dense-looking dog.

"It's smaller than most bathrooms," Michelle said, passing over the glass of water. "But it suits me for now."

There was a cloying scent in the room that the incense couldn't hide. Bernie looked over at the curly-haired dog in the corner who let out another loud round of flatulence.

"He's lactose intolerant," Michelle said, which Bernie wasn't sure was an explanation, but she just nodded along.

"Could we hurry this along, please? I'm working on a new dress," Michelle said, holding up the blotchy coloured thing. "I like to make my own."

"Tie-dye gives me a headache. It's all the swirls."

Michelle looked at her for a second, then pretended she hadn't spoken.

"I suppose I should get to the point. I'm a private investigator and we've been looking into dare2dream."

"Really? Why?"

"Well, you must see that dare2dream is not a great business to be a part of. My friend Liz calls it a Multi-level marketing company. I don't understand what that is apart from that it seems designed to part people from their money without much in return."

"Dare2dream has been good to me," Michelle said. "And I do love Solaverse makeup. Just because it hasn't been run properly, doesn't mean that the idea isn't sound in the first place."

"Is that why you wanted to start your own company?"

"I don't know what you're talking about."

Bernie decided to go in a different direction. There was something quite skittish about Michelle, she kept fidgeting and glancing around her. Bernie didn't want to scare her off altogether.

"I wanted to ask you about this party at Holly's house on Friday night," Bernie told her.

"I wouldn't call it a party," Michelle said. "Holly had them quite regularly. She called them her 'little gatherings'. It was a chance to talk strategy, that sort of thing. And drink wine."

"Lots of wine?"

"Sometimes. I don't drink though, I'm allergic to sulphates."

Bernie rolled her eyes. "Well, I wanted to know if you remembered anything about the party. Was Holly upset? Did Bella or Tom Field say anything unusual? That sort of thing."

Michelle picked at a thread on the dress. "There was lots of arguing. I think Tom might have even threatened her."

"Really? You didn't mention this before?"

"I didn't want to get anyone in trouble. But now I come to think about it, maybe they were fighting over something."

Bernie was suspicious of how quickly the woman had latched onto this idea. Could Bella be climbing up the suspect list herself?

"I heard that you had your own issues with Holly," Bernie said.

"Who have you been talking to?"

"Deborah O'Flannery, mainly," Bernie said, not bothered

about dropping her mother in it.

"She likes to shoot her mouth off, doesn't she?"

"Yep. This time she was shooting her mouth off about you leaving dare2dream."

Michelle bent down to stroke her dog who had padded over to them. "Why would I do that?"

"That's the weird thing," Bernie said, knowing it was time to play her ace card. Liz had emailed her over some extra information just a few minutes before she got to Michelle's house. Now it was time to see what the woman thought.

"My friend Liz is a genius with a computer," Bernie explained. "She found out that there was a property transaction six months ago that went through for over three million quid. This wouldn't be the one that you had arranged would it?"

Michelle had gone quiet.

"I wondered if it was, because it turns out that it's the same strip of shops where you work. So it seems to me that you would have been the perfect person to spot the opportunity. And so you would be in line for the finder's fee according to their policy, wouldn't you?"

"Ten per cent," Michelle said, her body rigid with tension. "Ten per cent of three million, that's what I should have got."

"But they never gave you it, right?"

Michelle sniffed. "They said that because I had mentioned it to

Holly before, that she was the one who should get the commission. But I don't think that was why. I reckon they'd already spent it and that's why they couldn't pass it on. Holly and Bella. Spent it all. Pink Range Rovers and fancy holidays abroad... that's where my money had gone."

"Wow, you must have been pretty mad about it."

Michelle glared at her. "I was at first. But Holly said she would sort it all out. And she would have, if she hadn't died."

"Uh huh." Bernie was not convinced. Michelle had definitely moved to the top of the suspect list and Bernie was mentally underlining her name.

"Would you like another tea?" Michelle said.

"All right," Bernie replied, thinking she would use the time when Michelle was in the kitchen to message the others. Michelle Rallie might just be the person they were looking for.

"I'll make you a peppermint one this time," Michelle said as she disappeared into the other room. Bernie reckoned she would have to pour the tea into one of the plant pots, just like she had the last one. Only idiots ate or drank anything offered by potential murderers.

Michelle had been in the kitchen for a few minutes when the dog got up and jogged over to the door. Then it started barking.

Bernie was on her feet in seconds, rushing towards the kitchen. She pulled the door open to see Michelle's arse as she was trying to wriggle through the window.

"Oh no you don't!" Bernie grabbed her leg.

"Let me go! I'm just going to get out of here, I won't cause any more trouble. It was all an accident you see, I never meant to –"

If Liz or Mary had been there the talking would have probably gone on for hours, Bernie thought. They would be sympathetic to this woman who was a stone cold murderer. Probably thought about how awful her childhood was or something.

Bernie's method was a sharp elbow to the woman's kidneys. That stopped the talking straight away. Michelle fell back from the window and Bernie dragged her over to the living room where she promptly sat on her.

"You bitch," Michelle puffed, trying to catch her breath. "What the hell was that for?"

"That was on behalf of Holly Moore."

"Exactly!" Michelle tried to sit up, but she hadn't reckoned on the fact that Bernie could plank for more than three minutes. No bolshy lady with false eyelashes and a bad attitude was going to out-fight Bernie Paterson's abs.

"Will you get your arse off me," Bella groaned.

"Not until the police arrive. They are on their way, if you were wondering. I've already sent them a message. Pretty soon you are going to be locked away for the rest of your life."

Just at that moment, the door to the flat burst open, the lock shattering as Walker came through in a cloud of splinters.

"That was bloody quick!" Bernie said.

Michelle Rallie's dog, riled up by the exploding door, started running around the room barking at Walker and snapping his teeth.

"You're scaring him," Michelle wailed.

"Quite right," Bernie agreed. "Sensible dog."

"Could I possibly get some help here," Walker said to her.

"If I must." Bernie took her knee off Michelle's back. "Now I know it's going to be tempting for you to set your dog on the copper and do a runner, but how far do you think you'll get? If I have to chase after you then don't get me wrong, my thighs will enjoy the workout, but when I catch up to you I will thump you into next Tuesday."

"That would be police brutality," Michelle said with a sniff.

"Not a police officer, I'm afraid. So if I feel like giving you a beating then I jolly well will. Now grab that dog, will you?"

Michelle put her hand on the dog's collar and he calmed down enough that Walker could get into the room. Mary and Liz followed behind.

"You're a bit late," Bernie said, brushing dust off her knees. "Michelle here was just confessing."

"No I wasn't," the woman said, trying to smooth down her hair. "I don't know what this idiot is talking about."

"Well that's very nice –" Bernie began, but she was interrupted.

"I know that dog," Walker said.

"What, it didn't murder anyone did it?" Mary seemed a bit confused.

"The doorcam from Holly Moore's street. I'm sure there was a picture of that dog. Does his collar flash?"

Bernie hauled the creature toward her and poked around his collar. A strobing red light pulsed out into the room.

"Been taking him out walking anywhere recently? Say around Holly Moore's street?"

Michelle had her jaw clamped shut.

"I think I can just about put it together," Walker said. "You went to see Holly late on Saturday night to try and convince her that she should give you the money you were owed. Things got heated. I'm sure you didn't mean to kill her but there was an argument and you hit her with the lamp. Where is it by the way?"

Michelle said nothing.

Bernie stepped forward. "What's sad is how wrong you were, Michelle. Because I think you killed your friend for nothing."

Michelle didn't quite manage to hold her tongue this time. "What the hell do you mean?"

"My friend Liz is about the cleverest person I've ever met," Bernie said and noticed that Liz gave her a thumbs up, "and she's been over the dare2dream accounts with a fine-toothed-comb. There's no money there and there never was. It wasn't Holly or Bella that pocketed your fee. It was Tom Field."

"Bastard!" Michelle said, then snapped her jaw shut again. "I can't believe I made you tea," she said, turning to Bernie with her hand raised.

"Wanna try it?" Bernie said, moving into a boxing stance. "Be my guest. It wasn't bad enough that you murdered someone. But you did something much worse. You made me talk to my mother!"

"All right ladies," Walker said in his most patronising cop voice, "let's take Michelle down to the station. Will the rest of you find someone to take in that dog?"

"Get in touch with my mum," Michelle said, "she'll look after him."

"Sure," Mary said.

"Thanks Maria."

The women of the WWC looked at each other for a second then burst out laughing.

"I'm so glad I can get rid of this suit," Mary said, once the laughter had subsided and Walker had taken Michelle downstairs to wait for the police backup.

"I won't say I'm sad that this one's over," Bernie said. "But on the bright side, this case has really improved the investigating stats in my favour."

"What stats?" Mary asked.

"Never you mind."

Epilogue

Everyone had their heads down in the office when Walker turned up for his meeting with the Superintendent. News of a bollocking travelled fast and no one wanted to meet his eyes lest they be tainted by association.

"Good luck," Suzie O'Connor whispered as he walked past. She was packing away all the Major Incident equipment from the conference room.

"Thanks," Walker said. He just had to hope that the fact that the Holly Moore case had been successfully concluded would count in his favour.

Not for the first time, he wondered if he was in the right job. After all, would he have done anything different to save himself from getting in trouble? Probably not. The rigidity of the police force wasn't something that suited him. He had pushed back against it when he had been in the army and now the same thing was happening here. Depending on what the Superintendent said, it might be time to move on. He certainly wouldn't stick around to suffer the indignity of a demotion, if that was what the boss was thinking.

"Take a seat," MacKinnon said, not looking up from his computer. Walker knew this was a power-play designed to intimidate him, but there wasn't much else he could do. He took a seat.

"I have been made aware of some irregularities in your

behaviour recently. Particularly in regard to the Holly Moore case."

"Sir?"

"I believe that you were the one to arrest the suspect, Michelle Rallie, who has since been charged. It was a lucky break that she had kept the murder weapon hidden under the kitchen sink. In fact, the whole arrest seems like it was mainly luck."

"Yes sir." Like all junior officers, Walker knew that his only reply to anything in this conversation was going to be 'yes sir'.

"You will remember that I explicitly instructed you not to be a part of this case?"

Damn, was he going to actually get fired? Walker swallowed, horrified at the thought. It was almost funny. It wasn't until the prospect of losing his job had reared its ugly head that he realised how much he would miss being a cop.

"Normal procedure might be to mark this down as a disciplinary issue," MacKinnon said, raising his head to stare evenly at Walker.

"Yes sir."

"But I have decided you can be someone else's problem."

"You're… I'm getting transferred?" Walker's heart sank.

"In a manner of speaking. I have recommended you for the Specialist Crime Division. I see that you have already completed the requisite courses so I hope they'll take you on their next intake. If you're so desperate to be a detective that you're going to go against direct orders from a superior officer, then you might as well do it."

Had he heard that right? Walker stuttered, his brain struggling to catch up with his ears.

"I... um, thanks?"

"Thanks sir," MacKinnon said.

"Thanks sir," Walker said, unable to keep the smile from his face.

"HR will be in touch no doubt to sort out the logistics. In the meantime, I expect you to finish those burglary reports, understand?"

Walker nodded.

"All right, get out of my sight then."

He was walking on air as he passed back through the office to his desk. His colleagues were clearly curious, but none of them would ask him what had happened while MacKinnon was lurking in the background. Walker could feel that his face was hot and if the others took that for shame rather than excitement he wasn't quite ready to explain just yet.

He texted Mary the news and received a picture of Peter Capaldi announcing he was going to play Doctor Who which he assumed meant 'congratulations'. He had just put his phone away when there was a commotion at the other end of the office. When he looked around he broke into a grin.

"All right everyone," Macleod said, fending off well-wishers with a wave of his hand. "I'm doing fine. Just my blood sugars in the end and a bit of bother with the old liver."

"It's good to see you back," Walker said, making his way over to him.

Macleod led him over towards the window so that they were away from the others. "I hear that you and Neil did me a turn, not that I remember anything about it."

"We just put in the call," Walker said. "The paramedics did the real work."

"Aye, sure they did. Anyway, thanks mate," Macleod said, giving him an awkward one shouldered hug. It was the male equivalent of bursting into tears. Walker felt his own eyes were getting a little dusty.

"It's good to see you," Walker said. "How are you feeling?"

"Like I've gone ten rounds with Ali, even in his Cassius Clay days. But I'm on the mend now, so the Doctors say. I'm off to Shetland for two weeks of recovery."

"You'll be bored stiff," Walker laughed.

"Not only that I'm going to be bloody starving. You can imagine what the wife's going to feed me after this. Anyway, I just popped in because I heard your big news."

"Bloody hell, even for station gossip that's quick."

"Who do think told MacKinnon that he'd be mad not to

transfer you over to plain clothes? You're lucky I nearly died because I had a bit of goodwill there. Just think, if I'd eaten more salad you'd be in uniform for the rest of your life."

"Thanks again."

"You're welcome. Now don't screw it up."

"I won't."

Afterword

Hello lovely readers! I've been thinking a lot about predatory business practices recently, particularly given what you see on social media. There's something so sinister about posts full of false claims and toxic positivity, would it be surprising if they led to murder? That's where the inspiration for this book came from. And I do hope if anyone tries to sell you coaching that you don't need, or suspect products that you don't want, you have the strength to say no, no matter how nice the sellers appear to be. Channel your inner Bernie and let them know exactly what you think of them!

That's my little public announcement for today. I love writing these books and one of the reasons is that I get to talk about things that are really important to me, along with some jokes and a little murder to keep you interested. If you would like to join my newsletter where I witter on about crime novels, talk about my own writing and recommend new authors, you can do that at this link: www.subscribepage.io/tescottmystery

The next Wronged Women's Co-operative book, *Body of Water*, is available to order now from Amazon.

Love ya huns! #blessed #livelovelaugh

Printed in Dunstable, United Kingdom